STOLEN
DARLINGS

BOOKS BY HELEN PHIFER

DETECTIVE MORGAN BROOKES SERIES

One Left Alive

The Killer's Girl

The Hiding Place

First Girl to Die

Find the Girl

Sleeping Dolls

Silent Angel

Their Burning Graves

BETH ADAMS SERIES

The Girl in the Grave

The Girls in the Lake

DETECTIVE LUCY HARWIN SERIES

Dark House

Dying Breath

Last Light

STANDALONES

Lakeview House

STOLEN
DARLINGS

HELEN PHIFER

bookouture

Published by Bookouture in 2023

An imprint of Storyfire Ltd.
Carmelite House
50 Victoria Embankment
London EC4Y 0DZ

www.bookouture.com

ISBN: 978-1-83790-348-1
eBook ISBN: 978-1-83790-347-4

For the brilliant Claire Benni Benson, thank you xx

ONE

The six women parked behind one another on Castle Lane. It was almost six thirty, and dawn was just breaking across the snow-tipped peaks of Helvellyn and High Seat, the dramatic backdrop that looked down onto the ancient stone circle on Castlerigg. There was a nip in the air, and a slight touch of dampness that would fizzle out when the sun rose at seven. Freya, the yoga teacher who was leading the Ostara celebration, counted the women as she passed each one a yoga mat, eye mask and blanket from the boot of her car.

'I think we may be in for a real treat, the sky's much clearer than I thought and we should get a fabulous view of the sun rising at seven. Just in time for our sun salutations; then we'll finish with a quick seated meditation if the ground isn't too sodden. If it is then we'll each grab a stone and lean against it to soak up all that fabulous energy.'

Izzy laughed; she was the youngest of the group. 'We might get transported to a different time if we're not careful.'

Sadie turned to her and smiled. 'As long as it's not the 1600s, because we'd all get burned for being witches.'

The whole group laughed, and Freya couldn't help thinking

that Sadie wasn't wrong; if they had even got together as a group of women back in those days, they would have been locked up and taken to Lancaster Castle to be tried. Thank goodness they didn't still persecute women for their love of collecting crystals and rocks, drinking herbal teas and trying to read tarot cards, or they'd all be doomed.

'We're just missing Cora, but she'll catch up. Let's get started and warmed up because it's a bit too cool to be hanging around waiting for her, and we don't want to miss the sunrise on this wonderful, most special of days. I don't know about you but I'm more than ready to welcome in the light and banish the dark.'

Sadie nodded. 'Bring on summer, I'm ready to burn.'

The women laughed.

Sadie had the most vibrant head of ginger hair Freya had ever seen, and she was covered from head to toe in the most beautiful freckles, but her skin was so pale it turned pink in the blink of an eye.

Izzy, who was already walking ahead, turned and grinned at them.

'I'm getting the best stone to sit on and meditate, see you at the top.'

The top wasn't that far away. It was a moderate climb up a not too steep hill to reach the stone circle; and Freya smiled, thinking how they were going to have to shoo the sheep away, because she could see a flock clustered around the stones. She chatted to Sadie as the rest of the women chattered amongst themselves.

No one was paying attention to Izzy, who was jogging towards the stones, until she let out a high-pitched scream.

It pierced the air around them so loud that it echoed through the hills.

Freya dropped the yoga mat, blanket and eye mask she was carrying under one arm and ran towards Izzy, thinking she'd hurt herself somehow, although she was still standing upright. As Freya reached Izzy, she saw what she was pointing at. Izzy was making a low keening noise from the back of her throat that sounded animalistic. Freya turned around and held up her hands to the other women, and yelled, 'Stay there, and someone phone the police.'

They stopped, a look of confusion spreading across their faces.

'Tell them there's a dead body here and they need to come now.'

Freya turned back to stare at the body. She knew who it was instantly. Her dear friend Cora.

Cora was draped across the flattest of the three lowest stones. Her beautiful friend's eyes were staring up at the sky; her throat was a gory, open, gaping wound, and a river of blood was flowing from it onto the volcanic stone and seeping into a puddle on the hillside. Cora had a flower crown of striking, deep pink roses on her head, and a garland of evergreen leaves around her neck were coated in dark red blood.

Freya felt her legs begin to wobble as a sheep wandered close to the body and began to lap at the blood on the grass. Izzy let out another loud scream. Freya ran towards the sheep, chasing it away. She could hear someone on the phone asking for the police as a ringing sound began to fill her ears. She was going to faint: her vision narrowed, and she stumbled backwards not wanting to fall onto Cora's body. Her knees buckled and she felt arms grab hers and then everything went still as she collapsed.

TWO

Detective Constable Morgan Brookes was up far earlier than she needed to be. She had tried so many times to complete the Couch to 5K and failed every time, but even though she hated exercise – and wasn't afraid to admit it – she needed to increase her fitness, or at least that's what she kept telling herself as her feet pounded against the uneven stony ground, her breathing a lot heavier than when she'd set off, and she was too hot despite the cool chill in the air.

The truth was that Morgan hated running, but she had begrudgingly agreed to take part in the Keswick half marathon because Cain was on some fitness quest and had said she would never beat him in a race. She'd laughed it off at first and had told him she didn't care whether or not she could beat him, but then he'd got all serious about it. Her secret-cake-eating buddy was now going running almost every day, and he was no longer eating cake, which really upset her. Then Amy had riled her so much about how Cain was a reformed character, saying that she should take it up so she could run away from all the killers she kept having confrontations with, that two days ago she'd finally turned around and told Amy she could beat Cain any day in a race. Which was obviously the biggest lie that had ever left her mouth, and she was now seriously regretting it. Ben, whom she'd left in bed this morning, had thought it was hilarious at the time and had told Amy to get an office sweepstake running on who was going to win. Amy had found an old whiteboard and had it propped against the office wall, and now the entire Rydal Falls police station was talking about it and had placed bets. So here she was.

She was sweating profusely as she tried to navigate the path up to Rydal Caves without breaking her ankle again. She hated her life, was out of breath and was contemplating if a second broken ankle would be worth the pain just so she could get out of the mess she'd got herself in to, when her brand new Apple watch began to ring. It was a present from Ben to help with her running, he'd told her yesterday when he'd presented it to her. She had no idea it could take phone calls as well or she'd have told him to take it back. She stopped, feeling stupid, and looked around to see if anyone was in hearing distance then pressed the green button.

'Hello.'

'Good morning, Morgan, it's Sean from control, have I disturbed you?'

She realised she was breathing hard. 'God, no. I'm out trying to jog and failing miserably at it.'

'Close call, that's a relief. I have bad news for you. A group of women found a body at Castlerigg Stone Circle and you're down as duty DC along with Ben.'

She sighed, had she just manifested this as a way to get out of jogging?

'I need to go home and change, but I'll be there as soon as I can. I'll bring the DS with me.'

'Thank you, I'll let the officers on scene know you're aware and travelling.'

She turned around, heading downhill, grateful to not have

to continue up the steep rocky path, but at the same time wishing she didn't have to deal with another body.

It had been a long time since she'd visited Castlerigg. No idea why, because she had always loved the ancient stones. She supposed it was the same with everything: too busy with work to get out and enjoy the Lake District like a tourist, when she lived smack, bang in the middle of it. She dealt with nothing but the serious crimes and murder investigations.

The ankle she'd broken previously was giving her a bit of trouble and she hadn't even made it up the path to the top. Had she also wished that on herself? she wondered. Sometimes, she had to be careful because things would have a way of doing exactly what she wished in the most random of ways.

By the time she reached the car park and was inside her car she realised that she should have started off on the flat anyway. What was she thinking? That she would be able to start walking, fast jogging up the side of the fells without any consequences?

The drive home took just over six minutes, and she felt glad to be back to doing what she did best: working cases and solving murders were much more her thing than trying to get fit.

THREE

By the time Ben had driven them to Keswick and up Eleventrees, it was crazy. An ice-cream van was set up in the lay-by before the entrance to the stone circle, just in front of the crime-scene tape at the start of the cordon. He leaned forward in the seat, his fingers gripping the steering wheel so tight the skin was taut and white.

'You've got to be kidding me. Who the hell said he could park up at a crime scene?' Ben said. 'What is this, some kind of joke? Morgan is there a body or is this some wind up, because I don't think we should be queuing for a Mr Whippy if it is.'

Morgan, who was a little shocked herself, shook her head.

'Not a joke. The question is, who told him he could park there?'

Ben slammed on the brakes. There were groups of walkers with huge backpacks coming out of the field opposite, and there was no one to grab them before they tried to enter through the gate for the stone circle. Morgan was out of the car before he could say a word and jogging towards them.

'Whoa, stop there,' she said loudly.

The walkers stopped and turned to stare at her. She was

dressed from head to toe in black. Her red hair in a topknot and black winged eyeliner did not give the impression of a police detective, which was another reason she purposely chose to dress this way; she liked to surprise people. A grey-haired man who looked as if he was leading the way looked at her.

'And you are?'

'Detective Constable Morgan Brookes. I'm afraid you can't go any further, this area is a crime scene and I'm going to need you to turn around.'

'This area is a public footpath.'

She saw a flash of fluorescent yellow out of the corner of her eye as whoever it was jogged up to stand with her.

'That may be, but there has been a serious crime and I can't let you access it.'

Amber was standing next to her, the police constable that Morgan least liked, but for once she was glad she was here. Amber stepped in front of her; for some reason people took orders far better from a person in uniform.

'I'm afraid my colleague is right. I'm going to need you to turn around and leave the area.'

The man looked exasperated. 'What if I don't? What if I refuse?'

Morgan smiled at him. 'Then I will have to arrest you for obstruction, refusing to comply with an officer of the law and probably a few more things while we're at it.'

A woman stepped forward and pulled his arm, tugging him back towards her.

'We're very sorry, of course we will turn around. Won't we, Seamus?'

Seamus didn't look as if he agreed with her, but he nodded and turned away just as a now suited and booted Ben arrived.

'Is there a problem?'

Seamus shook his head, looking as if he was suddenly realising that there must indeed be a serious incident going on. 'I'm sorry, we're leaving.'

Ben nodded. 'Good, because I don't have enough staff to be wasting time arresting you for being stubborn when there are far more important things to deal with.'

Ben grabbed hold of Morgan's arm and pulled her away. He whispered, 'Let Amber deal with them, and go get yourself some coveralls on.'

She whispered, 'Arsehole,' under her breath, and Ben looked at her.

'Steady on, I'm not that bad.'

'Not you, him.'

Ben nodded. 'Oh, yes. Seamus was enjoying being the leader of his pack, wasn't he? I don't think he wanted to do what you women were telling him to. Yes, he is an arsehole of the highest degree.'

He walked towards the small wooden latched gate that led onto the field where the stone circle was and yelled at Amber, 'Scene guard this gate, please, no one in or out except for us; and who is on the other gate?'

She shrugged, and Morgan thought, *bad idea, Amber, don't shrug at the investigating officer. Show some respect.*

Ben was still staring at Amber. 'What? You don't know or you don't care?'

Morgan headed back towards his car. He hadn't eaten breakfast and was not a morning person without it.

Amber, probably realising her mistake, began to back-pedal. 'Scotty should be up there. Mads sent him to guard it. Do you want me to run the scene log?'

Ben paused for a split second. 'Yes, I do. I wanted you to run the log the moment you got up here. Who has gone into that field already?'

'Mads; CSI were putting down footplates, but the area is

too big, and Wendy said she didn't have enough so she's put them halfway.'

'I can see that, thank you. Just get everyone logged down and no members of the public. Did you say the ice-cream van could park up?'

Morgan ripped open a packet and shook the paper suit then began to navigate her way into it with as much speed as was possible, waiting to hear Amber's reply and hoping for her sake that she hadn't.

'Mads said he could, said he always parks further along and if we're closing off the entire area, the least we could do was let him park in front of the cordon so he doesn't lose a day's business, and the tourists can still get an ice cream even if they can't get to see the stones.'

Morgan tugged the zipper up, slid her feet into the shoe covers and double gloved her hands, walking back towards Amber. Ben was already trudging up the grassy slope. Morgan stopped. There was a group of women all huddled around a car inside of the cordon, sipping coffee from flasks and whispering. She reached Amber and took the pale green logbook from her.

'I'll sign myself in, don't worry. Who are they and why are they inside the cordon?'

'Witnesses, the one who looks deathly pale was the deceased's best friend. She fainted on the spot and doesn't feel up to driving yet. The younger one with the blonde high ponytail found the body.'

'What were they doing here?' Although she didn't really need a degree to figure it out: they were all wearing yoga pants and crop tops underneath their jackets.

'Spring equinox yoga session by the stones, apparently.' Amber rolled her eyes dramatically.

Morgan walked away; she thought that sounded a lot more fun than trying to run up Loughrigg Fell on your own, feeling sorry for yourself. Amber was clearly not a fan of anything remotely witchy, unlike Morgan, who took after her aunt Ettie, a fully-fledged kitchen witch with her own pet raven and house in the woods. Ettie was living the dream, and Morgan envied her for it.

She tried to catch up to Ben, but he was almost at the stones, along with a flock of sheep. By the time she reached him, he was flapping his arms about trying to get the animals to move away, but they weren't remotely bothered by this and totally ignored him.

'Someone call the farmer to come get them. Jesus Christ, this is like some bad sketch off a TV cop show: ice-cream van, flock of sheep running loose through my crime scene, and walkers coming from every direction.'

Mads nodded. 'He's on his way; this is a farce and sorry about the ice-cream van, that was a bad judgement call. The body is over there.'

Ben was already staring at the body, and Morgan wondered how much he would take before he exploded. Her eyes fell onto the stone which the woman was draped across, as the pair of them stepped onto the metal plates Wendy had put down for them to get a closer look.

'Mind you don't slip; the grass is wet. Those things are lethal with those plastic boots on.' Wendy was busy photographing the scene and surrounding area.

Morgan walked as close as she could get and felt her breath catch in the back of her throat.

The woman was wearing a simple, long white cotton night-gown or dress, but it was the gaping wound across her throat that drew Morgan's eyes in. It was so brutal. It was likely she had bled out here. How had someone got her to lie still while they slit her throat? she wondered, because it didn't look as if she'd put up a struggle at all. Her hands were crossed on her front. They had taken on the waxy yellowy pallor of the dead. The flower crown of roses on her head was so out of place, along with a necklace of oak leaves that had been strung together on garden twine. Her eyes were staring up at the sky.

Ben asked Wendy, 'How long has she been here?'

'Not that long. I think those yoga women probably missed the killer by minutes. She was still warm when Amber and Scotty got here. She's Cora Dalton, was supposed to be joining her friends for the yoga session.'

'Looks like she beat them to it. What are the chances of prints on the crown and garland?'

Wendy stared at him. 'I'm good, but I don't think that's going to be possible. I'd say there is more of a chance on the garland than the flower crown. I'll try my best.'

He smiled at her. 'That's all I could ever ask for.'

Then he turned and looked around the area. Morgan crouched down to examine Cora more closely.

'She's not dressed for yoga like the others. We should ask them about the flower crowns and the garlands – were these things they made or used in any of their meetings? Perhaps they wore them to feel better connected to nature? She looks posed, and there's no signs of a struggle... Perhaps she was modelling, having a photoshoot. Maybe he's a photographer, lured her up here under false pretences and the minute he had her in the perfect pose, he slit her throat so deep she bled out in minutes. Perhaps she was showing off to someone – posing for them. Did he know her? Did he leave her knowing that her friends would find her?'

Ben was nodding. 'I like all of that, sounds plausible, unless she wanted someone to cut her throat? It could be some form of suicide pact.'

Morgan shook her head. She thought for a moment. 'Where's the other body if it is? I think she's a sacrifice.'

The look on his face was priceless, and under different circumstances she would have found it highly amusing.

Ben stuttered. 'A sacrifice? To whom, for what?'

'To whoever the killer is trying to impress, the Gods, the devil, himself.'

'A sacrifice?' Ben repeated it as he stared at the body and scrubbed a hand across the stubble on his face.

'It's Ostara.'

'And what is that supposed to mean?'

'It's the celebration of the day when the hours of sunlight match those of moonlight exactly; it's a celebration of rebirth and life. Samhain celebrates the dead, this is the opposite, and it's becoming more and more popular amongst the modern day witches, pagans, and anyone else who has taken to celebrating it. On Instagram there's a whole movement on there around reclaiming your power and birthright of being a witch.'

Ben was staring at her. 'Am I even supposed to know what any of that means?'

She shrugged, took out her phone and tapped the Instagram app, then did a quick search for Witches of Insta, as the feed loaded she turned the phone to Ben who stared at the pictures. 'Ask Ettie, she can give you a more in-depth explanation. Back in the days of the druids, who would have used this as a meeting place, they may have used human sacrifices. I can't remember if they did or not here, but maybe whoever did this has taken their ways and made his or her own interpretation of it.'

She could see Ben was processing what she was telling him and having a hard time. Standing next to her, Wendy shrugged.

'She's certainly been posed to give whoever found her a shock; it shocked the hell out of me this early on a Wednesday morning before my coffee.'

Ben turned back to the woman. 'Cora, Cora. I think I know that name. There aren't that many of them around. Where did she work, do we know?'

'Do you want me to go and speak to the women who found her?'

Morgan was a little distracted, trying to remember what

Ettie had once told her about the stones when she'd asked her what they were for. She smiled fondly thinking about her aunt. They had been talking about her herbal teas, and when Morgan told her she had been struggling with insomnia that woke her at 4.25 every morning, Ettie had suggested that Morgan make her bedtime cup into a little ritual, where she sipped it in silence, holding on to her large chunk of smoky quartz to soothe and ground her soul ready for bed. She was sure Ettie had mentioned how far society had come now they didn't use human sacrifices like the druids had at the stone circles. She would need to check with her if they used to do anything of the sort here.

'Please, and take a few of those bloody sheep with you.'

The sheep were edging their way back towards the stones.

Morgan's radio blared into life, breaking the silence.

'Farmer's here, can you ask Ben if he's allowed up on his quad bike?' Amber's voice filled the still air.

'No, he's bloody not, he can walk up.'

Morgan had the talk button pressed in, and said, 'Did you get that?'

'Loud and clear, so did the farmer.'

All three of them turned to watch a guy in a checked shirt and wellies begin to walk up the hill, with a black and white border collie by his feet.

Ben was shaking his head. 'Somebody pinch me and wake me up from this nightmare, please.'

Wendy leaned across and nipped his arm.

'Ouch.'

'Sorry, it's not a nightmare, it's the beginning of your working day. It can only improve, Ben, because it sure as hell isn't going to get any worse. If that bloody dog comes near here, I might have to chase it away, and I won't be happy if I have to run because I don't run.'

Morgan grinned at her. 'Me either until yesterday.'

Wendy nodded. 'Ah, the rumours are true then. Who'd have thought it, you and Cain running a half marathon for fun. The pair of you are even crazier than I thought.'

Morgan shook her head as she began walking back down the hill, passing the farmer. He whistled and the dog took off in the direction of the sheep to begin rounding them up. Morgan was truly impressed; if only the dog could round up killers as quickly, her life would be so much easier.

FOUR

Morgan reached the group of six women who were now huddled into two cars with the engines running. She felt bad for them. Keswick was a stunning, thriving market town and an area of outstanding natural beauty, with the backdrop of the mountains, hills and fells surrounding it. The stone circle was minutes away from the houses that skirted the outside of it, and yet it felt so isolated up here, because you couldn't see the cottages, and it felt so wrong not to mention surreal to find a body so brutally desecrated in such a place. The shock these women must have felt at seeing their friend that way would stay with them forever. Morgan knew this all too well. She still remembered every single victim and the horror she felt when she first saw them at their time of death, before she got to see a smiling picture of them alive and happy, living their lives to the full.

A woman got out of one of the cars, and Morgan nodded at her.

'I'm Freya Walker, Cora's friend.'

Morgan instinctively reached out a hand.

'Detective Morgan Brookes, I'm so sorry for your loss,

Freya. I can't imagine the shock it must have been finding Cora like that.'

She sniffed and wiped her eyes along the sleeve of her fleece jacket. 'Can't believe it, she is, was, the kindest soul you could ever meet. Who would do that to her?'

Morgan wished she knew. 'Can you tell me where she lived, if she's married or has a partner, does she have kids?' She prayed the woman had no kids.

'She's not married but lives with her partner, Jay Keegan. He's a history teacher. Oh, God who is going to tell him? I don't think I can.'

'It's okay, we will do that,' Morgan replied softly. 'Can you confirm her address and what school he works at?'

'He works at Keswick Senior School; and they live in the flat above Cora's shop – Black Moon, on Main Street.'

Morgan nodded. 'Can you talk me through what happened today, from as early as possible this morning? Understanding all your movements will really help us figure out the day and get justice for Cora.'

Freya smiled but it didn't reach her eyes, which were full of tears ready to leak from them.

'I always do an Ostara yoga session outdoors, weather permitting. My friends love it. Cora messaged me last night to say she would meet me here if she was running late – we normally, always, drive up together. I didn't think anything of it, then Izzy, bless her, ran on ahead and found her lying there like that.'

'I noticed Cora wasn't dressed for a yoga session. Have you seen the dress before, and do you wear flower crowns and garlands as part of the class with it being Ostara?'

'No, as beautiful as that dress Cora is wearing, it wouldn't be practical for the session, the same with the crowns and garland. They would just get in the way. I can't imagine Cora was coming to the session dressed like that.'

Morgan was taking note. *Where were Cora's yoga clothes if she had agreed to join in with Freya's class? Had she intended to get changed, and if so where? Or was she never supposed to be up here in the first place?*

'Was there anyone around when you arrived? Did you notice any walkers or tourists leaving the area?'

Freya shook her head. 'Just us and the sheep...' She sighed and Morgan knew what that meant. Who knew they would be such an integral part of a murder investigation? They were the key witnesses, but there was no way to get a statement from them.

'I'm going to need to speak to you all at some point, but for now I think you should go home or back to the studio, wherever you can make yourselves a hot drink. I'm going to see Cora's partner, Jay, very soon and pass on—' She stopped; the words *death message* were not the nicest way to describe it, although that's what it was, but *death notification* sounded just as cold and uncaring. 'I'll tell him the tragic news; I would appreciate it if you could all keep this to yourselves until we've spoken to Jay, and to Cora's family. We don't want them to hear about it on social media, that would be horrendous for them.'

'Of course, we won't say a thing until they know.'

'Thank you. I'd appreciate that. Can you get everyone to write their names and addresses on a piece of paper for me, please.'

'I don't know what to do.'

'Pardon?' Morgan turned to look at Freya; her whole body was now trembling, and the tears were flowing freely down her cheeks.

'I've never lost anyone like this, I can't even.' She began to sob, loud, hitching breaths, and Morgan felt terrible.

She went to Ben's car and retrieved her notebook and pen, which she then passed to Freya, who opened her car, the book trembling in her hands. She passed it to another woman to take over.

Morgan asked kindly, 'Please could I have all of your names and addresses?'

Izzy began to write down the details of the women all sitting silently staring at Morgan. Freya got back into the car; the tears were still falling from her eyes and another woman was patting her shoulders. Izzy finally passed the notebook back to Morgan and she slipped it into her pocket.

'Thank you and once again, I'm so sorry for your loss.'

Then she closed the door, feeling as if she'd intruded enough into their grief, and walked to where there was a PCSO she didn't recognise standing in front of the blue and white police tape.

'Those two cars are leaving now. Can you just take their number plates down for me to add to the log, if it hasn't already been done, and lift the tape so they can get away?'

'Yes, ma'am.'

Morgan did a double take. 'Oh, it's just Morgan, that's fine.' She smiled at her and realised she was new or at least new to her. 'Sorry, I don't know your name?'

'Gracie.'

'Welcome to the team, Gracie. Unfortunately, guarding a scene will be a regular part of your duties. The only good thing about this one is you have nice views to stare at for hours.'

Gracie smiled at her, and Morgan left her holding up the tape as high as she could for someone who was 5'4" so the two cars could drive under it.

The farmer was on his way back to his quad bike which was parked in front of the ice cream van. Morgan had never come across a crime scene anything like this. He nodded at her, and she realised he was a lot younger than she'd first thought.

'Bit of a mess this, isn't it?' he said, and she nodded. 'That's certainly one way to put it.'

'Poor lass.' He was shaking his head, and she realised he'd probably seen Cora's body up close while he rounded up his now bloodthirsty sheep.

'Have you been up and about early today?'

'Every day I'm up at the crack of dawn, but I haven't been over here until now. Was busy sorting out the cows, until I got a phone call from you lot to ask me to move the sheep. I thought I'd seen everything there was to see at these stones. People having sex, doing rituals, you name it, but I was wrong, I've never seen something like that.'

He was staring at her, right at her, and she nodded, wanting to be able to say neither had she, but that would be a lie because she had seen some terrible things and it never got any easier.

'Well, thanks anyway.'

'Just a thought, can anyone confirm that you were at the farm?'

'The cows could, so can my wife. She helped me. I had nothing to do with this, if that's what you're implying.'

Morgan smiled at him, trying to ease the tension, because he was clearly offended by that question. 'It's just a routine question, and good, that's great. Thanks.'

He ducked under the tape and made his way to the window of the ice-cream van. She watched, realising that she wouldn't be in the least bit surprised if he ordered an ice-cream cone with a chocolate flake and strawberry sauce, because things were so surreal this morning. He didn't, though. He leaned across the counter and was talking to the older guy with a head full of white hair, wearing a white cotton pinny. She should probably warn the pair of them not to say anything, but Mads could do that. He was the one who'd given him permission to park up as if it was just another day, after all. She wondered if anyone had actually asked the guy in the ice-cream van about his whereabouts, knowing that some killers liked to go back to the scene of the crime to watch everything, and realising there wasn't a more perfect opportunity than this one.

She headed towards him. The farmer realised she was coming their way and walked off, back to his quad bike and his waiting dog. As she reached the window to the van, the man smiled at her, his blue eyes crinkling at the edges.

'What can I do for you, officer? I'm so sorry to hear about that poor woman. I'm Ray.' He held out his hand and she took it.

'I'm Morgan, I was wondering if you saw anything or have noticed anyone hanging around the last couple of days.'

'It's been pretty quiet to be fair. I've only just started parking up again last week. It hasn't really been ice cream season. So, I can't say that I have. I wish that I could because I know that's not any help to you.'

Morgan smiled at him. 'No, unfortunately it isn't. Do you ever go up to the stones?'

'In my younger days quite a lot, not now. Well, not since I lost my left leg below the knee. I haven't really done anything too strenuous. I have a prosthetic leg, which is a game changer when I need to stand up and serve ice cream, but it's not that good for walking uphill with. I could get a better one I suppose, but I don't see the point. I don't enjoy going for hikes any more, I'm far too lazy. I'm more of a read a book and chill kind of old guy.'

'Me too, I love reading, it's my favourite.'

He nodded. 'My wife is more of a Netflix and chill, but not me. Nope, you can't beat a good book.'

'You didn't notice anything this morning?'

'I got here after you lot, so no. I don't usually come so early, but with it being Ostara I reckoned there might be a few early birds around visiting the stones. I never expected in a million years that something like this could happen, not here.'

'I know what you mean. Thanks, Ray. Would you mind

keeping this quiet for now until we've notified the victim's next of kin?'

He motioned pulling a zip across his mouth. 'I wouldn't tell a soul, love, it's not for me to gossip about. That poor girl, God rest her soul, deserves more than that.'

'She certainly does, thank you.'

Morgan turned away. She didn't get the feeling Ray was their man.

As she walked back up the hill, despite the chill in the air she could feel a thin film or perspiration on her forearms and brow. It was the second paper suit that she'd put on so far, changing out of the old and into a new one after speaking to the witnesses. It wasn't made for walking up hills in. At least she was getting some walking practice in, having no idea what the Keswick half marathon entailed.

Ben was on the phone when she got back, and Wendy had erected a pop-up tent over the body, which was better than having her on show for the world to see. It made quite a sight, the white tent pitched over the circle of stones high up on the hill. It really did look like something out of a movie.

When Ben ended his call, she said, 'It's dramatic, it's all very theatrical, isn't it?'

'What is?'

'This whole scene, the setting for the murder, the dress, flower crown, it's like some stage setup for a West End play. He's all about the drama. I wouldn't be surprised if he's not watching all of this somehow and admiring his handiwork.'

Ben began to look around the area. 'There's nobody around except us.'

'How would we know if he was hiding out somewhere? He could be watching through a pair of binoculars some distance away.'

As she spoke the skin began to crawl on the back of her neck and she got the feeling deep inside of her gut that she was right;

he was watching them. She didn't know how or where he was, but there was no way he was going to miss all of this. She bent her head close to Ben's ear. 'We need to watch what we're saying, because I think he can see or hear us.'

Ben straightened up and began to do a three-hundred-and-sixty-degree turn.

Morgan tutted. 'I mean don't make it obvious or anything.'

He came full circle and then whispered, 'Ask for a dog handler and see if there's a drone operator on duty.'

She nodded, turned away from him, and walked towards the tent, stepping inside of it out of sight, where she took out her radio handset and requested both a search dog and a drone.

Ben stepped inside. 'You could be right; this is like some circus sideshow. Is there a dog available?'

'Cassie is on her way with Brock, Al is on his way with the drone.'

'Perfect. That's pretty ballsy though, isn't it? To have the guts to spy on us when there are not many people around.'

'I might be totally wrong, but it feels like he could be.'

The tent flapped open and in stepped the DI wearing his protective clothing.

'Wrong about what, Morgan?' he said. 'And holy crap...'

He was staring at Cora's body. 'That's...' He didn't finish his sentence; he just looked at Morgan, and for the first time in a long time she realised that he had nothing to say.

FIVE

It felt like hours before the Home Office Forensic Pathologist – and Morgan's friend – Declan arrived at the scene. He'd set off as soon as he'd got the call. They were lucky he always prioritised their calls for assistance. She didn't know if it had something to do with being Ben's long-time friend or whether that was just the kind of person he was.

Al had arrived with the drone and was setting it up ready to scour the area for anyone hiding and watching. The DI was standing next to him. Cassie and Brock had taken off in the opposite direction to the entrance to the site.

Cassie turned to them and yelled, 'He's picking up a fresh trail leading from the body, could be the suspect's.'

Ben nodded at Morgan, giving her a respectful thumbs up that she might be right. It looked like their killer had gone off on foot, most likely across the fields.

Declan's voice broke the silence. 'Well good morning to you two. I have to say I've been meaning to come and visit this place for years, and now here I am on the most unexpected of days and here you are. Yet I have a feeling I'm never going to see this place as I would have liked to, am I?'

Morgan shrugged. 'Sorry, you're absolutely not.'

'I thought as much. Don't tell me anything, I'd prefer to look for myself.'

Ben led the way to the tent and Morgan followed. She was feeling creeped out thinking about the killer hiding and watching them, and was glad to get inside of the tent out of sight.

'Holy Mary.' Declan was staring at Cora's body, his eyes wide in disbelief. 'What is this? Is she purposely on display?'

Ben muttered, 'Morgan thinks so too. Why do you say that?'

'The setting, the stones, the flower crown, the dress, the blood, everything screams *look at what I did.*'

'Christ, this is a mess. It could be a photoshoot gone wrong.' Ben was staring at Cora's body.

Declan put his heavy metal case down and opened it to take out some paper bags to secure around Cora's hands.

'Yes, it could be, but honestly it looks like what it is and that's just my observation, obviously you know what's what.'

Declan crouched down beside Cora, careful not to step in the pool of dark, thickened, congealing blood. 'Well, I'm sorry that we have to meet this way.' He looked to Ben, and Morgan realised they hadn't told him her name.

Ben whispered, 'Cora Dalton.'

'Cora, such a pretty name. This is just terrible, Cora, but I'm here to take care of you and I will make sure you are looked after on this part of your journey. I'd really like to know what happened to you, Cora. How did you end up here, like this?'

He began to do his initial observations. 'She's not in full rigour; she hasn't been dead long at all.'

Morgan nodded. 'She was still warm to the touch when the first officers on scene arrived.'

'Wow, that's unusual for a homicide, or it is in my experience of them. Well, Cora, you are a first for me in more ways than one, and I'm so sorry that nobody found you soon enough to help or save your life.'

Ben asked, 'It's definitely homicide then, she didn't do this herself?'

'Well, no – it would have been very difficult for her to get the angle right. The big giveaway for me is the wound: it's a deep, single cut, although it needs cleaning up to tell for sure. I can't see any hesitation marks or drag marks, plus her hands are clean, and there doesn't look to be any blood spatter on them. Which brings me to the question: how on earth did someone get her to lie still while they cut her throat?'

'It doesn't look like she fought back. It would be interesting to know if the toxicology reports show that she was drugged or incapacitated in some way.'

Morgan said, 'There's no knife, Ben. She didn't do this herself. Do you think she wandered off to hide the knife, cleaned her hands and then lay down to die? Maybe he tied her hands together or held on to them while she bled out.'

Declan lifted one of Cora's hands again. 'If he did, he didn't tie them tight. He used something soft to do it with, as there are no marks to suggest he did. The garland and flower crown should be bagged up and sent for forensic examination. I'm not sure if you'll get much back from them, but definitely worth a try. Has she got shoes on? Did she walk up here barefoot?'

Ben pointed to the long dress covering Cora's feet. 'Be my guest.'

Declan lifted the hem and revealed a pair of scuffed white Converse.

Morgan had the exact same pair at home. 'She walked up here willingly. There are no drag marks that we've come across, and the soles look a bit dirty from the damp grass.'

Ben's head was tilted as he stared at Cora's ivory legs. 'Photoshoot, had to have been. Why would she agree to dress this way and walk up here without a struggle if she wasn't convinced that it was safe to do so? Perhaps she knew her killer, or at least was comfortable enough to trust him.'

Morgan tore her gaze away from the Converse. 'You're right, she definitely had to know him. I mean it's freezing, and she's got no coat on. Where is her coat, and how did they get here if there is no vehicle? Do you think they got dropped off, or she got dropped off and he was already here waiting for her? If so, why didn't she get suspicious? Plus, she was supposed to be meeting the yoga women, so where is her change of clothes? Is there any chance she could have been killed elsewhere and carried here, Declan?'

'I'm not convinced, but I can't rule that out. It would explain a lot if she was already dead when she was brought here and had her throat cut, and that would also explain the lack of arterial spray and the fact that her hands aren't covered in blood. I'm afraid there's only one way to be sure, guys. We're speculating and I really don't like to do that, it leads you down the wrong path. I prefer to work with the evidence in front of me and figure it out that way.'

'Yeah, that's right, I know you do but we have to speculate so we don't waste too many hours. For once we might be able to beat the clock.'

Ben left them both staring after him as he exited the tent.

Declan whispered, 'What's up with him?'

'Upset by how pointless this is. Poor Cora, why would someone do this to her? Although he's hangry, probably.'

'Throw him a Snickers, Morgan. He's not a morning person, is he?'

She wanted to disagree, it was usually her that hated mornings, but she'd been up since the ridiculous hour of five trying to make her way up Loughrigg with a head torch, all to win a ridiculous bet.

'Do you want me to wait to supervise the body removal or are you happy to sort that out when you're ready?'

'I don't think we're going to be ready for some time yet, Declan. There's a lot going on with this one.'

He snapped his case shut. 'You can say that again. I almost crashed into that ice-cream van. I can't believe Ben has let him park up.'

'It wasn't Ben, it was Mads. His regular spot is right outside the gate to the site, and he felt sorry for him.'

Declan shook his head, then leaned over and kissed her cheek. 'Tell the big guy I'm ready for Cora when he sends her. I'll clear the decks and make room.'

He left her alone in the tent with Cora, and she couldn't tear her gaze away from the awful, gaping wound in her neck. She didn't look quite as serene with the brown evidence bags secured around her hands.

Morgan whispered, 'I hope you scratched the shit out of whoever did this and there is lots of nice DNA under your fingernails. We need something to work on, Cora, if we're going to find this animal soon.'

Then she slipped through the opening and let out a long, drawn-out sigh. Ben was standing with Al and Marc, and she could see Cassie and Brock in the distance, but it looked as if they were coming back. Wendy was pacing up and down after photographing and filming the entire area. She stopped beside Morgan.

'He's not daft, is he? It's not like there are houses that over-look this area or people walking past at this time in the morning. I feel like we're missing something. I keep expecting that poor woman to stand up and say *just kidding*.'

Morgan knew what she meant. It was all so surreal, and she couldn't get her head around it.

SIX

Keswick Main Street was beginning to come to life. He slipped into the shop yard through the back door so no one would see him. He needed to get cleaned up, not that there was as much mess as he had anticipated, which was a good thing. He knew now what it was like: all the years of living in a fantasy world had ended at 6.14 this morning. He had slipped from the world of the normal into one of the sick and depraved. He thought he'd feel guilt, so much guilt about what he'd done, but he had felt nothing of the sort; the excitement and thrill had been far too exquisite to waste, and he'd savoured every second. The power was unlike anything he'd ever felt, and it had all happened so fast. It had gone to plan with not one mistake or deviation. Cora had been a willing subject, her only stipulation was that she must make it in time to meet her friends for their yoga session at the stone circle. He had made sure she had got to the stone circle in time to meet her friends; in fact, there had been minutes in it.

He went into the small bathroom. He needed to make sure it was clean should he get any unwelcome visitors. He knew the police would probably call at some point; they would speak to everyone on this part of the street. House-to-house enquiries are an integral part of every cop show he'd ever watched.

The place didn't smell of death much to his relief. He had expected her to lose control of her bowels and bladder. Had been dreading that part, but obviously Cora had been to the bathroom before she came here, thank the Lord for small mercies. She had been here minutes before he'd taken her out, so it was never going to smell of decomposition. He knew better than that. He wasn't going to keep her body here so the customers would smell it as it began to rot away. He wasn't that kind of sick person.

He had watched the documentaries on Nilsen and Dahmer – just how they thought they could do what they did and not get caught by the smell alone puzzled him greatly. He liked his shop clean; he liked it to smell of his favourite scent of fresh pine and had diffusers, candles and plug-in air fresheners all keeping the air smelling like a walk in the forest. He loved Whinlatter Forest, it was his happy place. When things got too much for him, he'd walk through the glades of Norway spruce, Scots pine, Douglas fir and inhale the scent of fresh pine. He'd spent hours wandering the trails, and mountain biking through it on the days he couldn't be bothered to walk. Now, he went into each room armed with his cleaning kit, and began to spray Zoflora from the bottle of Sparkling Spruce that he'd diluted onto every surface, ready to wipe them all down and remove every trace that Cora Dalton had ever stepped foot inside of here.

By the time he'd finished he was sweating and could smell his own body odour. He looked around the storeroom that sparkled it was so clean. He opened the window to let the damp surfaces dry out, and then went into the bathroom where he turned the shower on to hot. He removed all his clothes and put them into a black plastic sack ready to dispose of in the huge bin at the rear of The Old Bank pub that got emptied every Thursday. If he shoved it underneath some other bin bags it should be okay. He knew the police were good, but he didn't think they would be that good that they would trace her last movements to here, and besides, she lived in the area anyway. By the time they even got close to trying to work out what had happened, the bin would have been emptied along with his clothes and cleaning rags. They'd be at the landfill site, and he doubted they'd bother to go search that in a hurry.

He got dressed, combed his hair and sprayed some after-shave on. He liked to smell as good as he could, not too over-powering but enough to make someone appreciate the time he took over his appearance. He strapped on his watch and looked at the time. It was time to go to work. Today was going to be interesting, he could guarantee it, and he could barely contain his excitement at the thought of being the cause of such a fuss that was about to break loose and cause complete and utter chaos in the picturesque market town.

SEVEN

They left Cora Dalton's body in situ at the scene, still draped across the stone she'd been laid upon and covered by the white tent. Amber had been moved up the scene to guard the tent, and the PCSOs had taken over the entrances to the site. The ice-cream van, much to Ben's relief and after a heated discussion between himself, the driver and the DI, had now been sent on its way. The last thing they needed while they were back at the station for the briefing was hordes of tourists turning up and trampling all over the narrow road that led up to the stone circle. It had now been taped off partway down, and it was no longer possible for anyone to walk or drive up that far.

Ben, Morgan and Marc all arrived back at the station within minutes of each other. The mood in the station was sombre; usually there was laughter filtering through from different offices, but today it was painfully quiet which matched the heaviness Morgan felt pressing down on her shoulders perfectly.

Cain and Amy were in the office waiting for the briefing. Ben went straight to the briefing room; Morgan went to get them.

'Have you heard?'

They both nodded.

'It's bad, it's weird too. Wait until you see the photos, you won't believe it.'

Amy shrugged. 'Weirder than what they usually are?'

Morgan smiled. 'I think so, it's the way it's been staged, everything about it is dramatic, the poor woman. It looks like something out of a Shakespearean play. Ben was having a meltdown because there were sheep all over the place and an ice-cream van parked up.'

Cain looked up from the message he was reading on his phone. 'An ice-cream van?'

'Uhuh, briefing in five minutes in the blue room.'

Amy stood up, grabbing the mug of coffee off her desk. 'Blue room it is.'

Morgan realised that neither she nor Ben had eaten breakfast or had a warm drink, so she left them to go up to the canteen. It was early, hopefully there would be something warm left.

She smiled at the woman who was standing looking bored.

'Two sausage and egg buns, please.'

'Brown or white?'

'White.'

She knew she should have got them both brown, that it was better for them, but they needed stodge to keep them going. She began to feed coins into the coffee machine and pressed the button for a latte, repeating it so she had two drinks. The woman passed her the warm buns wrapped in aluminium foil and smelling so good that her mouth was watering.

She took them straight to the blue room and passed one to Ben, who looked as though he might cry with relief.

'You have to eat, my orders.'

She also passed him a takeaway coffee cup.

He looked her straight in the eye and asked, 'Will you marry me?'

Morgan rolled her eyes at him, sat down and began to unwrap her breakfast roll. Opening a sachet of tomato sauce she squirted it all over the fried egg and took a huge bite. 'Absolutely not,' she said through a mouthful of mashed-up egg, sausage and bread.

'What, you don't want to marry me?'

'Not because you're hangry I don't. Ask me again when you have something romantic planned, because I sure as hell would not accept a proposal in this shithole, even though it's like our second home. You know most people have little cottages, lodges by the lake or caravans near to the seaside as second homes. We have a bloody police station that smells of sweaty feet, stale curry and body odour.'

Ben began to choke on the mouthful of food he'd been chewing, and she had to get up and slam the palm of her hand into his back a couple of times. He swallowed the food down.

'So, you'd think about it though?'

She shrugged. 'Not sure I want to be tied down to a miserable sod to be honest.'

A look of pain flashed across his eyes, and she felt bad. 'Obviously I mean a grouchy boss who isn't much fun. I'd think about it if my handsome partner asked me somewhere nice. It could be a possibility, just saying.'

They heard the three steps that led down to the room give an almighty creak before Cain walked through the door.

'If that was you proposing, boss, you need to work on that a little more, if you want my advice.'

Ben's cheeks burned a deep shade of red. 'It was a joke, Cain.'

Morgan shrugged. 'See, he's just being nice because I fed him. I bet he'd ask you to marry him if you fed him too.'

Cain roared with laughter. 'He's definitely not my type.'

Ben gave them both the middle finger, but Morgan made eye contact with him and smiled, giving him a little wink, and he smiled back making her feel better; she was forgiven for now.

The room began to fill with task force officers who would be making up the search team of the area surrounding the crime scene. Cassie walked in, followed by Wendy, and last of all Marc.

Ben had finished his breakfast and was washing it down with as much caffeine as he could swallow. He wiped his mouth with a small serviette that Morgan passed to him and looked around.

'Ready?'

All heads nodded at him as he enlarged a picture of Cora Dalton's body draped across the stone, and a low murmur went around the room as he clicked on the close-up of her cut throat and pooling blood on the grassy ground.

Amy looked from the photos to Ben.

'What's with the flower crown and long white dress? Why was she wearing that at six in the morning with no coat on?'

Before Ben could answer, Morgan did. 'I think she was either dressed once she was dead and then her throat was cut, or as Ben thinks, it was a photoshoot, it's staged. I'm not sure who he was wanting to shock: her friends that found her or us. Most likely for Cora to get her into the position she was found in. I asked her friends if they wore flower crowns for their outdoor yoga session and it's a no regarding them, the necklace and the cotton dress she is wearing.'

Ben continued. 'I'm not going to lie; I feel as if I'm living in some kind of murder bubble and that's all we get to deal with. But, that being said we are well equipped to deal with it so I suppose we should get on with it. This opportunity doesn't come along very often, but we are literally in the golden hours people.' He looked at his watch. 'Cora Dalton has been dead approximately three hours give or take a few minutes when she was found. She was still warm to the touch when the first patrols arrived. The pathologist has been to view the body, so once I'm satisfied we've done everything we can forensically around it, she can be moved to the mortuary. Morgan and I are going to inform her partner, who is probably at school now.'

Cain's head lifted. 'Her partner is at school, how old is he?'

Amy punched him softly in the arm, and Ben shook his head. 'A teacher, sorry that wasn't very clear. I sent a patrol to the flat above the shop they shared, but there was no answer, so I'm guessing he went to work early.'

'Or he didn't want to answer,' replied Morgan. 'If he's responsible he might have been getting himself cleaned up.'

Ben nodded. 'Or that, yes, I'm not ruling it out. As we're all aware, stranger homicides are rare, and the chance is most victims know their killers or know of them. I think we're working on the premise that Cora Dalton knew her killer, maybe not intimately but because there are no defence wounds or signs of a struggle, she felt comfortable enough in his company to let her guard down.

'As you know it might be some time for the toxicology reports to come back, although I've asked for them to be fast-tracked, because if she was drugged that would make sense as to why she didn't put up a struggle.

'The drone footage as far as I know hasn't picked anyone up hiding out there, which we had considered a possibility.

'Cassie said Brock found a scent that led from the crime scene across the fields that then doubled back and ended up back on the road through a different gate quite some distance away from the entrance to the stone circle. Whoever it was must have got into a vehicle, narrowly missing the victim's group of friends who were on their way up there.

'So, here's the plan: task force are going to do a fingertip search of the area; Cassie has already had Brock go through it and he interestingly followed a trail through a gate that leads onto a huge open field. I need a search of that vicinity; Morgan and I will inform her partner. Amy and Cain, I want you to go and interview the women who discovered the body. Morgan has a list of their names and addresses.'

Morgan held up her hand. 'What about looking for anywhere he could have hidden and been watching everything?'

'Morgan thinks that somehow he may have been watching us, maybe look out for a hiding place, something like that too.'

Cain asked Morgan, 'What about a trail camera or one of those wildlife ones you can buy off Amazon? He could have one of those set up to keep an eye on the area.'

She smiled at him, and he winked at her. Marc was looking at his phone and finally lifted his head.

'Actually, he could have, they're really good if you get a half-decent one. Although I don't know if you have to retrieve the memory card or can view it live. Definitely worth keeping an eye out for something like that, because if he does have access to one, he also has access to the investigation at the stone circle, and I don't like the thought of that one little bit.'

Ben continued. 'Post-mortem will be later on this afternoon, once the body has been moved. Myself and Morgan will do the honours, unless anyone has a burning desire to attend.'

He looked around the room, and no one made eye contact with him, and Morgan knew they wouldn't; no one wanted to go to a post-mortem unless they had to. She didn't want to go, but it seemed that her and Ben nearly always caught the short straw.

There was a pile of scrap paper on the windowsill, and she leaned back to take a piece, then began to write down the names and addresses of Cora's friends from earlier. She passed it to Amy. 'Freya is the yoga teacher and Cora's best friend; Izzy found the body, although the others weren't far behind her.'

'Not the nicest of ways to start your day, finding your friend like that. They have promised to all keep quiet until the family have been told. Morgan, what about her parents, did they mention them or siblings?'

She shook her head. 'Freya got really upset so I just got all their names.'

'I suppose her partner can tell us more. I'm going to draft in some PCSOs from Barrow and Ulverston to help canvas Main Street. We'll check CCTV, in case we have her on camera this morning or going into another property. Are there any photographers in Main Street?'

Nobody could answer that question except for an internet search, which Morgan could do once they left the briefing.

'Are we clear on what we're all doing?'

Heads nodded.

'Good, thank you. Let's go find this bastard before he can do it again.'

He shut his laptop, grabbed his coffee and walked out of the room, leaving everyone else to file out after him.

Cain hung back waiting for Morgan; Amy had already left to go get her stuff.

'Are you okay, Morgan?'

'Yes, thank you. Why are you asking?'

'You look a little tired.'

She wondered if he was being sarcastic, then realised this was Cain: he was kind and caring more than he was anything.

'I'm good thanks, just a bit of an early start. Are you okay?'

'Great, that's okay then, because you know I don't want you making yourself ill just to prove a point that you can beat me in a race. We all know that you'd beat me hands down any day if I hadn't stopped eating so much cake.'

She smiled at him. 'Yeah, well I miss my cake-eating buddy a lot. I'd rather have him than some running obsessed fitness guy.'

Cain looked sad. 'You would?'

'Of course, I would, I have no one to sneak off and eat cake with now when I'm feeling crap, and it was far more fun when the two of us could do it together, but I get that you wanted to feel better, so I'm very proud of you for doing that. I'm also very proud of you as a person in general because you rock, Cain, and always have done. I'm not sure who you think you need to impress, but you don't unless it's yourself.'

He leaned over and hugged her tight. She closed her eyes and savoured the moment.

'Thanks, Morgan, I needed that, and I think we should both sneak off and eat cake at some point this afternoon. I miss it too and our chats when we put the world to rights while catching crumbs and licking our lips.'

She laughed. 'You better keep that promise, Cain, or else I'm not going to forgive you for a long time if you don't.'

He turned and left her sitting alone at the huge oval table, and she smiled after him, hoping he was okay. She would ask him later to make sure he was, and she was holding him to the eating cake too; she was going to need something to look forward to this afternoon because it was going to be one long day.

EIGHT

The office was empty. Amy and Cain had left already, which meant they were keen to get away before they got a worse job than interviewing witnesses and taking statements from them. She could hear Ben on his phone, though his office door was closed. She sat down at her desk, the coffee she'd bought was cold, but she drank the last of it and tossed the cup into the bin before logging on to the computer.

She vaguely knew Keswick Main Street, had been a few times, and an image of Wendy's gran lying battered and dead on the cobbled street behind it popped into her mind. The poor woman had stood up to a violent killer eighteen months ago, and paid the price with her life yet it felt like yesterday. How Wendy had continued to do this job after that she would never know, then again her own father, Stan, had been brutally murdered and it only made her more determined to catch these violent abominations who walked around masquerading as human. Morgan hadn't been back to Keswick since then, so she had no idea what shops there were.

She was amazed to find there were seven photographers but none of them on Main Street, unfortunately, so they weren't going to capture images of Cora going inside any of them. She sent the list to the printer so she could go and visit them all; from Google Maps she could see that one of them had pictures of the stone circle, but they were all landscapes without a single person in them. Next, she searched for florists, as someone had to have made that flower crown, unless their guy was incredibly artistic, which might be true: who was she to say they hadn't made the crown themselves at home? But they needed some kind of break so a connection to a local florist would give them something to work with. That search gave her three florists and three gift shops.

When Ben came out of his office, she smiled at him and asked, 'Can you send me a photo of the flower crown, please? I want to print it off to show to the local florists and see if they recognise it.'

'I will, but if it wasn't hers, do you think he'd be so reckless as to buy it locally?'

Morgan felt her momentary hopefulness fade away, as she realised that he probably hadn't bought it locally. There was a very good chance he could have ordered it from any florist in the north west and driven to pick it up.

'Damn it.'

'It's still a very good idea though, because maybe just once we might be one step ahead of them and they didn't think it through; and we have to check every possible lead, so it's definitely a good idea, Morgan.'

She smiled but had a feeling it was going to be like hunting for a needle in a haystack. He might even have bought it online, which meant it would be impossible to use it as a lead to find him. If they suspected someone, they could use the purchase as evidence, but they didn't even have a suspect yet...

'Are we going to talk to Cora's partner?'

Ben nodded. 'Did we get his surname?'

'Jay Keegan. Apparently he's a history teacher.'

She grabbed her jacket off the back of her chair and tugged it on, then followed Ben out to the car park.

Keswick Senior School looked deserted from the outside, the white building reminding Morgan of an old church, with a few portacabins thrown up around the back. The place was quiet for a school. They pressed the buzzer at the front door and waited for someone to let them inside. The door clicked, and she pushed it open. There was a strange little cubicle where the secretary was watching the pair of them intently over the top of the latest issue of *Good Housekeeping*.

'Can I help you?' she said.

Morgan smiled at her. 'Detectives Brookes and Matthews, we'd like to speak to Jay Keegan if that's possible?'

The woman dropped the magazine, and it landed with a loud thwack on the desk. She leaned forward. 'Is he in some kind of trouble?'

Ben shook his head. 'Not at all, is he here?'

She turned her attention towards Ben and gave him a big smile. 'Of course he's here. This is his place of work and lessons began fifteen minutes ago.'

Ben nodded at her, but she didn't move. 'Well could you please go find him then? This is urgent.'

She stood up. 'You need to sign in, then I'll go find him. Have you got ID?'

They both flashed their warrant cards at her through the glass screen, and she nodded and then began to type their details into the computer.

'Need you to stand in front of the camera, please.'

Morgan didn't look at Ben because she knew he'd be about to lose his cool any moment now. She stepped in front of the small camera mounted on the wall and waited for it to snap her photo. Ben did the same and within a couple of minutes they both had stickers with their names and faces stuck onto the front of their jackets. The woman finally came out from her little closet and let them through the double glass doors, pointing to a row of wooden chairs that looked uncomfortable.

'Be right back, take a seat.'

She scurried off down the corridor, and Ben leaned forward, resting his elbows on his knees and cupping his face in his hands.

'Headache?'

'Yeah, and stress ache, what a farce. Why weren't our ID badges good enough? They're warrant cards, for Christ's sake, they should have made her quiver in her boots and open the doors.'

Morgan smiled and shrugged at the same time. 'I have ibuprofen in my bag, I'll get you some when we get out of here.'

A woman stepped out of an office further down the corridor and walked towards them.

'Good morning, I'm Mrs Brown, head teacher, can I help you?'

'We need to speak to Jay Keegan.'

Mrs Brown nodded. 'You can use my office. I take it by the look on your faces this is serious and unpleasant.'

Ben nodded. 'Yes, it is.'

'Follow me, did Samara offer you a drink?'

Morgan stood up. 'There's no need, thank you.'

They followed her to an office which was covered in drawings and paintings of all manner of sunflowers, of every shape, size and colour, in homage to Vincent Van Gogh; there were also photos of the students who must have painted them below each one, standing in front of huge images of the sunflowers at the Van Gogh Experience. Morgan liked it a lot, reminded her of when she'd bring pictures home from school and Sylvia would stick them on the front of the fridge.

'Nice pictures.'

'Thank you, I think so. I like to keep all the artwork that a student makes for me, reminds me of my days teaching and why I do this thankless job at times.'

There was a knock on the door and Samara stood there with an ashen-faced Jay Keegan standing behind her.

Mrs Brown said, 'Thank you, Samara, that's all for now.'

Samara looked annoyed that she'd just been dismissed, but nodded her head and closed the door behind her.

'I'm not sure if you want me here, Jay, or if I should leave? It's up to you.'

Mrs Brown smiled at Jay, who looked as if he was about to throw up. His face had gone a greenish shade of white. He looked so young. He had collar-length, dark brown hair and the bluest eyes; his white shirt was undone at the collar, and he had a pair of faded jeans on that gave him the look of anything but a history teacher. Morgan thought that he must be quite popular with the teenage girls. She had expected someone much older, wearing a tweed jacket with patches on the elbows. Her teachers had never looked this good.

Jay didn't answer her, and Ben put him out of his misery.

'Jay, you aren't in any trouble if you're worried about that, and I'm sorry we've had to come and speak to you at your place of work, but it can't wait.'

Jay glanced at Mrs Brown. 'Would you stay?'

'Of course.' She pointed to the chairs behind the desk, letting Jay take hers as she stood against the wall behind Morgan and Ben. Jay sat down and looked at them both.

'What's wrong?'

Ben talked in a calm, quiet voice. 'I'm afraid we have some tragic news for you and there is no easy way to say this. Earlier this morning a body was found at Castlerigg Stone Circle.'

'And what has this got to do with me?' Jay was looking frantically to Morgan and Mrs Brown.

'The body has already been identified as Cora Dalton.'

Jay stared at Ben, his eyes narrowed. 'What? Don't be ridiculous, that's impossible.'

Morgan took over. 'Cora was found by her friends, Freya and Izzy, this morning on their way to an outdoor yoga session. Jay, we have reason to believe she was murdered.'

Jay jumped out of his chair; he began to feel in his pockets for his phone then he patted his shirt. He was shaking his head and repeating the word, 'no,' over and over. He turned and ran from the room, then came rushing back in with his phone clamped to his ear. They all heard a happy, sing-song voice say, '*Hi, it's Cora, I'll ring back.*'

'Cora, ring me now, please.'

Mrs Brown was blotting her eyes with the corner of her sleeve.

Jay turned and stared at Morgan. 'She's not dead, she can't be.'

Ben stood up and softly placed an arm on his. 'I'm sorry, Jay, but she is.'

'What if you have the wrong person?'

'We haven't, Freya and the rest of the yoga group confirmed it was Cora.'

Mrs Brown let out a loud sob and began to cry so loud that Jay turned and glared at her. It didn't make a difference, as she continued.

Morgan took her by the arm and led her outside. She closed the door behind them, and Samara appeared, a look of puzzlement on her face.

'Is there somewhere we can go, Mrs Brown?'

Samara pointed to a door a little further down, then hurried to push it open.

'Is everything okay, Mrs Brown?' Samara asked her.

She shook her head as Morgan ushered her inside the small room that contained a single desk and chair. Mrs Brown sat down on the chair, and Morgan perched herself on the desk, while Samara hung back by the door unsure whether to stay or leave them, until the phone in her office began to ring and she made the decision to go answer it.

Morgan looked around and spotted a roll of toilet paper. She tore some off and passed it to the sobbing woman.

'I'm sorry, poor Jay. What a mess I am and there he is acting as if he's not just had the worst news of his life. I'm a disgrace, I'm no good with stuff like this.'

Morgan was surprised that Jay hadn't been the one to break down, but she'd been doing this job long enough to know that people dealt with terrible news in all manner of ways; everyone had their own coping strategies and denial was often the first.

'What happens now?'

'How did Jay seem to you this morning when he got to work? Did you see him arrive?'

She shook her head. 'I'm always first in, last out, the curse of running a school. He was late this morning though, which isn't like him at all. He's usually one of the first staff members to arrive.'

'Did he seem flustered at all?'

'Not that I noticed. He said something about sleeping through his alarm. You don't think he did this, surely not?'

'I didn't say that, I'm just trying to figure out what happened, Mrs Brown, no one is pointing fingers, they're just standard questions.'

She nodded. 'Sorry, yes, of course and call me Beth.'

'Did you know Cora?'

'Yes, everyone knows Cora. There is a group of teachers who love to visit her shop for card readings, she's very good. We don't talk about it in front of Jay, because he thinks it's a load of rubbish.'

'Did you go there? What kind of card readings?' Morgan knew she would say tarot, but there were so many other card decks available; it could be an oracle card deck.

'Yes, once a month, and they were tarot cards; she was so good at it. I got the death card once and almost died of shock on the spot, but Cora was fabulous and explained it all to me in great detail, putting my mind at rest.'

Morgan smiled at her. She knew that the death card didn't actually mean you were going to die; it signalled new beginnings, the ending of a major phase in your life and the start of a new one.

'Did Cora ever mention if she was having relationship troubles with Jay? It can't have been easy if he didn't agree with her line of work.'

'No, they are or were as in love as any young couple should be. Just because he doesn't agree with tarot cards and stuff doesn't mean he didn't love her. I should imagine his talking about history to her bored her stupid. He can get a bit overzealous at times, and a teacher's wages aren't really wonderful, especially living around here. The cost of living is tough on everyone. Cora's shop is a little goldmine, and I know he was proud of her for having the guts to open it in the first place in a town like this.'

'What do you mean when you say a town like this?'

'Oh, you know old-fashioned and stuck in its ways. The people who live here prefer gift shops and tea shops to magical shops.'

Morgan was scribbling everything down. She looked up at Beth, who had composed herself a little. 'Did Jay have any problems with his students or colleagues? Has he mentioned anyone who might be upset with him?'

'Upset enough to kill his partner? The oldest pupils are sixteen; I would like to think none of them are harbouring murderous personalities. And his colleagues are not killers, that I know of.' She shook her head. 'There's the usual run-in with mouthy year eights who think they know it all, but the older kids like him and enjoy his lessons. I would say he is one of my most popular teachers. I should go and tell him to go home, he shouldn't be here. Is that okay?'

Morgan nodded. 'Yes, of course.'

She followed Beth back to her office, where Ben was sitting with Jay.

Ben stood up when they arrived.

'Jay doesn't want an FLO. He's going to go and see Cora's parents now and break the news to them.'

Jay's face looked an almost deathly shade of white, and he had a shocked expression that seemed to have fixed itself to his features.

Morgan narrowed her eyes at Ben.

'Should we drive you there, Jay? Come in with you and help?'

He shook his head. 'No, I want them to hear it from me, it's the least I can do for Cora. She adored her mum and her stepdad.'

'Wouldn't you like someone to be there to answer questions they may have?'

He glared at her. 'What, like you both have for me? You haven't told me anything of use, except that Cora has been murdered and her body found at the stone circle. Come see me when you can tell me you've caught the sick bastard that has done this. Until then I don't want to see either of you.'

Ben reached out and patted his shoulder. 'I'm sorry for your loss, Jay. We're unable to guarantee that, I'm afraid. We are going to have to inform Cora's parents and offer them a family liaison officer to help get them through this. It's what we do, and we would be failing at our job if we didn't. Can you give me their address? And we will need to search the flat, maybe you could stay with Cora's parents for a couple of days while we do that.'

Jay blinked away the tears pooling in the corner of his eyes, and he stood up.

'Don't take anything away that belongs to her.'

'I can't say that we won't, but I will tell you what we take if we find anything that might help with the investigation.'

'She's really dead?'

Morgan nodded.

'When can I see her?'

'If you ring me, I will arrange for you to go and view her body once it's at the mortuary. Her parents might want to come with you.' She took a small contact card with her details on out of the back of her notebook and passed it to him. He didn't look at it, just pushed it inside of his pocket.

Beth reached for his hand. 'Let me come with you, Jay. You don't have to do this alone.'

He shook his head. 'I need time to think. I don't want to have to be considerate of your feelings, Beth, when my own are so fucked up. I'm sorry and thank you for the offer, but I'd rather do this alone.'

He walked towards the door and pushed it open. He didn't look back, and all three of them watched him until it slammed shut.

NINE

There was no sign of Jay as they exited the school car park. Morgan was looking at all the cars to see if he was sitting inside of one, but he wasn't. Her eyes looked up to the snow-tipped peaks of the Skiddaw mountain range which overlooked the school and the rest of the flat vale that was Keswick. It was breathtakingly beautiful, yet she hadn't the slightest desire to ever climb those mountains, because she knew that the ascent up Loughrigg Fell was the most she could ever handle or even want to. She was happy to leave the mountain climbing to the experts. She finally turned her gaze towards Ben.

'That was hard. Do you think he's okay?'

Ben shrugged. 'I doubt it, but there's only so much we can do. He didn't want us to help him. He has your number, if he needs anything he'll call.'

She tasted copper in her mouth and realised she'd bit the inside of her lip, something she'd started to do when her stress levels were rising. Something felt different about this case. She remembered the horror of when they'd gone to visit the lovely dad of her old school friend to pass on her death message – he had been so shocked his heart had stopped beating instantly and he'd died of shock on the spot. Something was wrong here, though she couldn't put her finger on what exactly it was. Until they searched their flat there was nothing to suggest that Jay Keegan was involved in Cora's murder. It was however also their job to prove that he wasn't and that meant searching the flat for evidence. She took out her phone.

'Are you ringing Wendy?'

She nodded. 'Not to search the flat – we don't want to risk cross-contamination – but she can request another duty CSI to attend. What are we going to do now? The body needs moving, and the flat needs securing until a search team can attend. Do you want to drop me off at the flat and I'll wait there until CSI get there and you go back to the scene?'

'Would you mind?'

'No, once they've arrived, and I've searched the flat myself, I'll go interview the shop owners either side and see if they saw anything or have anything, CCTV or otherwise, to help with the investigation.'

'I would really appreciate that, Morgan, thank you.'

'It's what I'm supposed to do.'

He smiled at her. 'I know, but you make my life a lot easier than it should be. It means a lot to me that you do.' He lifted his hand to touch her lip. 'Your lip is bleeding. Are you okay?'

She folded the sun visor down and looked at her lip. There was a thin line of blood across her bottom lip. Embarrassed, she dabbed at it.

'Fine, I accidentally bit it.'

He glanced at her, but she didn't tell him the truth. He'd make her go to the doctor if he thought she was letting the job affect her and make her nervous. She was usually fine, nothing she couldn't handle, so why had talking to Jay Keegan made her feel that way? She didn't know, unless her inbuilt alarm system was going off and trying to warn her he was involved in Cora's murder.

'Hey, did you notice he didn't ask how she died?'

'I did.'

'What do you think about that?'

'Shock is a funny thing; it affects everyone in different ways. We have the privilege of seeing first-hand how victims have met their untimely deaths, but not everyone wants to know that part of it.'

'Are you defending him, Ben?'

He shrugged. 'I don't know, I'd like to say it was him let's lock him up and case closed, but at this moment we have nothing to go on. Maybe after you've taken a look around their flat and found me some evidence to prove it, I'll think differently, but for now I don't think he's involved.'

Ben drove down Main Street and stopped as near to Black Moon as he could. Morgan leaned towards him, kissing his cheek, and got out of the car, waving at him as he pulled away.

She hurried along to the shop which was tucked in between a bookshop and a florists. She wondered if maybe they had it all wrong: could Cora have bought her own flower crown if it was a photoshoot? Why exactly had they thought it was the killer who had put it on her head? She felt her heartbeat do a little double beat at the thought of being able to tick that off the list so easily.

Maybe this wasn't going to be as complicated as they originally thought. Were they giving whoever killed her more credit than they deserved? She'd spoken with a former prison guard once who had told her that most criminals weren't that clever. Some of them were just lucky that they didn't get caught sooner. Although a lack of resources didn't help. The police were always short staffed. Her own team was small, but staffing should be appropriate. Headquarters just didn't seem to factor in the unusually high number of murders in their area.

Morgan stopped outside of the entrance to Black Moon and tugged on a pair of gloves before she tried the door handle, which didn't move – it was locked. Morgan pressed her face against the glass door to look inside. It was dark and quite hard to make anything out, but it didn't look as if there had been a disturbance in there. She would take a look; damn it they should have asked Jay for a key to the shop and flat. She continued walking up the street until she reached a narrow alley which gave access to the rear of the shops, and she slipped through it into the back road.

She took out her phone, and Ben answered immediately.

'*What's up?*'

'We didn't ask him for keys to the shop or the flat.'

'*Christ, what were we thinking? Is he there?*'

'No idea, the shop is locked up tight. I'm about to go check the flat.'

'*Okay, let me know if it's locked, and I'll try and get hold of him. If not we'll have to put the door through.*'

'I'm sure he's going to love that on top of finding out his partner has been murdered.'

'*We need access to the flat, Morgan.*'

She hung up, deciding there was no point in arguing with him until she knew if they could get in. She reached a sunny yellow painted back gate and realised it must belong to the florists, because the front of the shop had been painted the same colour. At least she was almost there. She heard the rumble of a bin being moved around in the yard next door. She tried the back gate to Black Moon, which was a deep mauve colour with a black crescent moon painted on it. Even if she hadn't guessed the florists, it wasn't hard to figure out which belonged to Cora. She smiled; it was a nice touch.

Ettie would love this door. She would probably love the shop too, which brought her to the question: did her aunt know Cora? It looked as if they were into the same things. Morgan carried the small piece of smoky quartz Ettie had given her, to keep her grounded and protected, everywhere with her in her pocket. She had found a piece of black tourmaline after it fell out of Ben's trouser pocket a while ago. She'd picked his trousers up off the floor and it had rolled along the bedroom. She had smiled to herself, realising Ettie had also given him his own little piece of protection, which was good because God knows they needed it.

'Good morning, are you looking for Cora?'

The voice startled her out of her own mind, and she jumped, looking around to see who had spoken. A man wearing a black T-shirt and joggers was smiling up at her from the yard next door as he let go of the wheelie bin lid.

'Oh, yes, I suppose I am, sort of.'

He arched an eyebrow at her. 'Really, that's a strange answer, if you don't mind me saying so.'

She smiled, realising she'd sounded weird. 'I'm from the police and actually looking for Jay. Have you seen him?' It didn't seem right announcing Cora's murder across the entire back alley for everyone to hear.

'Not today, but he'll be at school. Have you been there?'

'Yes, I have.'

He shrugged as if he didn't really know what to say to her.

'Have a nice morning. Cora should be opening the shop soon. She's late this morning, but I don't know if she had something planned with it being Ostara.'

Morgan nodded. 'Thank you, you too.'

He looked at her, smiled, then walked back towards the rear of the bookshop, and she felt like an idiot, but she wasn't about to yell down the stairs that Cora would never open the shop again. A wave of sadness washed over her. It was so sad and so utterly pointless. She did call out to ask, 'When was the last time you saw Cora?'

He looked up at her, a strange expression on his face. 'Yesterday afternoon.'

'You haven't seen her this morning before she left the flat?'

'Definitely not.'

'Okay, thanks.'

He stared at her for a few moments more and she turned away to knock on the door to the flat. She tried the door handle: it was locked up tight.

She rolled a glove off and phoned Ben again.

'Going to need someone to locate Jay or bring me a whammer to get the door put in because this is locked tight. It doesn't look as if there's anything of note at the rear of the shop either.'

'Leave it with me.'

She couldn't get into the flat or the shop, nor could anyone else unless Jay was already in there. She bent down and lifted the letter box, then sniffed. It didn't smell bad, or of anything other than a hint of an air freshener.

'Jay, are you in there?'

She hammered on the door again; the likelihood was that he was at Cora's parents' house, where he'd told them he was going and breaking the awful news to them. She couldn't hear any movement from inside, so she decided to interview the shop owners on either side until Ben got back in touch with her.

The florist was on the phone and had a customer waiting, so she went into the bookshop that had rows of both new and second-hand books on shelves outside. The shop was crammed with books, and she felt her shoulders drop slightly as she breathed in the scent of ink and paper that was like some kind of sedative to her. There was a small counter at the back where a grey-haired man was sitting reading a magazine. He looked at her as she approached him and smiled.

'Morning, do you need any help?'

'I'm investigating a serious incident and wondered if you'd heard anything from Jay or Cora this morning?'

He put his magazine down and shook his head. 'I can't say that I have. Are they okay?'

She knew it was pointless not telling him, as it would be all over the local newspaper and social media soon. The younger man from the backyard stepped into the shop. He smiled at her.

'Hello again, did you get hold of them?'

Morgan looked around to see if anyone else was in the shop, but it was just them.

'I didn't, and I'm sorry to have to tell you this but Cora was found deceased this morning. This is between us for the time being.'

Both men looked at each other, eyes wide, mouths opened slightly. It was the older guy who asked, 'How?'

'I'm sorry, I'm not at liberty to say just yet, but I need to know if either of you saw her this morning or heard anything suspicious from the flat?'

The younger of the two was shaking his head. 'Not a peep. I'm Lewis Heywood and I live in the flat upstairs; and Jim Edwards, who owns the shop, lives in a bungalow on The Headlands. The stairs are a little too steep for him now with his bad knees. I can't believe Cora is dead. Does Jay know? Is that why you're looking for him?'

It was always a tough judgement call knowing how much information to share with people, but they seemed nice enough and genuinely upset over the fact that their neighbour was dead.

'Can I ask where you both were this morning?'

The men looked at each other. Lewis looked offended by the question, but he still answered.

'In bed until my alarm went off at eight, then I ate breakfast, made myself a coffee and came down to open the bookshop.'

Morgan turned to Jim.

'At home in bed. I was up a lot earlier than young Lewis here. My knees ache all night long and it's painful lying down for too long. I got up around six thirty and made myself some tea and toast so I could take some painkillers. I didn't get here until about ten minutes ago.'

'I'm sorry to have to ask you this, but did either of you have company?'

Jim laughed. 'Lord, I wish that I did, but it's been some time since I've had company. I can't talk for Lewis, of course, he's a lot more active than I am.'

Lewis was shaking his head. 'No, I didn't, I was alone. Look, why are you asking us these questions? We didn't see anything, and we certainly didn't do anything to hurt Cora. We both adore her, she's wonderful and I'm absolutely heartbroken to hear that she's died.'

'I'm sorry, they're routine questions but thank you for answering so honestly.'

Lewis was blotting the corner of his eye. 'This is terrible, she's so lovely and always in and out of here buying books. I can't believe it.'

Tears filled the old man's eyes. 'Poor Jay, he'll be devastated, and her parents, I know them; they live a few doors down from me.'

'What number?'

'Thirty-two. I'm at 26.'

'Excuse me?'

She rushed outside, leaving Lewis and Jim staring after her open-mouthed, and phoned Ben.

'Jay should be at 32 The Headlands.'

'*I know, Control did a quick address search, and there's a patrol on the way to get the keys from him. They'll be with you shortly. Everything okay, Morgan?*'

'Yeah, I'm just talking to the neighbours.'

She was about to hang up when she heard Ben shout, '*Stop him*'. And then she heard heavy footsteps as he began to run. Her heart in her mouth, she wondered who he was chasing after. The line went dead, and she pulled the radio out of her pocket and twisted the volume button.

'*Control, we have the deceased's partner at the scene, he's managed to get access to the area.*' Ben's voice was breathless.

'Oh crap,' she muttered as she listened, horrified, hoping Jay hadn't made it to the white tent with Cora's body inside.

'*One coming in for breach of the peace.*'

Amber's voice also sounded out of breath.

'*He's cuffed and putting up a bit of a struggle, but we're going to have to bring him in for his own safety.*'

Morgan knew that they wouldn't be charging Jay with anything; they just needed an excuse to get him away from the crime scene as quickly as possible.

She breathed a sigh of relief to see Claire pull up in the CSI van alongside her.

'Where to?'

'The entrance to the flat is around the back. But you won't get the van down the alley; it's too narrow.'

Claire rolled her eyes. 'I can walk. Have we got access?'

Morgan shook her head. 'Waiting on a key. Have you been listening to the radio?'

'No, I have a headache and can't be doing with all that noise this morning.'

She leaned into the van window and began to fill her in on the last five minutes. Claire's face was a picture as she listened in shock.

'Poor guy, I kind of get how he feels though. I wouldn't believe it either unless I saw it for myself if it was my partner.'

Morgan thought about how she'd feel if it was Ben. 'Me either, I don't think I'd be able to accept it.' The thought of losing Ben like that sent a chill over her entire body and her eyes began to water a little. She blinked the tears away before Claire noticed. She continued. 'But we're assuming that's why he was at the scene...'

Claire parked the van a little further along, where it wasn't as narrow, and Morgan followed behind, and then the pair of them got suited and booted. Main Street was starting to get busy now and they were stared at by almost everyone walking past. A lot of people began to loiter in the chocolate shop nearby just to watch them.

Claire whispered, 'Do you ever just want to tell them to take a picture it will last longer?'

This made her laugh a little too loudly. 'All the time, I guess it's only natural that they're nosey, this is probably the most exciting thing they've seen in a while, although it would be nice to tell them to bugger off and stop staring.'

An unmarked car parked behind the van, and Sam and Tina, the Rydal Falls PCSOs, got out. Tina had a key ring dangling from her finger that she was swinging around.

'Present from Ben.'

Morgan smiled at her, removing them from her finger. 'Thank you, is everything okay at the scene?'

Sam gave Tina a side glance then they both shook their heads, before she replied, 'Well, it is now, but it was mental before all hell broke loose. Ben had to rugby tackle the boyfriend to the ground before he reached the tent and saw the body. I never knew he could run like that; he was slick like a pro and took him down. I think Amber caught it all on bodycam because she followed the pair of them, never realised she could run too. Especially uphill, she's always moaning about how she hates the gym.'

Morgan gasped. 'Ben ran after him and took him down? My boss, Ben.'

They both nodded. 'Your boyfriend, Ben, you know the one you live with? It was him, how many Bens are there at the scene?'

'Blimey.' She was at a loss for words. Ben had lost weight since they got together – not that he'd needed to – she loved him no matter what his waist size was; but she didn't know he could run, especially up a hill chasing someone. She smiled at the thought of it; she was impressed.

She led Claire to the alley and around to the rear of the flat. Sam followed behind to guard the entrance to the scene, and they left Tina out the front of the shop to make sure that was secure too. They walked up the metal staircase that led to the front door, while Sam waited at the bottom. Morgan passed the key to Claire who opened the door into a narrow hallway that smelled fresh, nothing untoward to note.

Claire nodded. 'So far, so good. Let's hope it stays that way.'

'I'll wait here for you to have a look around before I come inside.'

Claire disappeared into a room. 'Living room looks fine.'

There were another five doors to open, and Morgan watched as she ticked each one off.

'Master bedroom, bed made, no mess, looks tidy. Bathroom, bit messy but it's clean; there's an open make-up bag with a bottle of foundation with no lid – it looks as if she got ready in a hurry and left. Kitchen, pots in the sink but only from breakfast, empty wine bottle and two glasses on the table, remnants of a Chinese takeaway. Nothing broken, no signs of a struggle. Small office, very messy with papers and stuff, books everywhere, no sign of anything criminal; second bedroom is tiny with a single bed, not a thing out of place.'

She snapped photos of the entire flat then walked back to where Morgan was leaning against the doorframe.

'Looks clean to me, no signs of a struggle, no blood. Do you want to take a look and tell me what you think?'

Claire squeezed past her, and Morgan stepped inside. She began where Claire had finished, with the small bedroom, which was so tiny if you sat up in the bed too fast in the middle of the night there was a good chance you'd hit your head on the low oak beams.

Morgan wasn't feeling it, nothing suggested that Cora had

been killed or taken from her home. She went into the master bedroom, which wasn't huge either. She looked around. There was an iPad which she would seize and submit for evidence, but apart from that... She opened the drawers, feeling like a sneak thief as she rifled through them looking for a diary or journal, anything that could be classed as evidential. There was nothing, a few discarded condoms still in the silver packets at the bottom of Jay's underwear drawer, but nothing else. Cora's were devoid of anything except underwear; the bathroom still had dried toothpaste on the side of the sink from whoever had brushed their teeth last and spat out in a hurry, not bothering to rinse it off.

If something had taken place here, she'd expect the sink to be sparkling, along with the taps that had sudsy soap stains around them. Cora's make-up looked exactly like hers did when she was in a rush to get to work or somewhere: an uncapped bottle of foundation, no lid on the loose powder, brushes all over the small shelf above the sink. Morgan let out a sigh. She was convinced nothing had happened here. It didn't mean that Jay was completely innocent, but if he had killed Cora then he hadn't done it here. The walk down the steep, slippery metal staircase carrying a body would be enough to deter someone from doing something so awful, and the fact that Cora had got up and got herself ready before leaving the house proved she had been alive when she was last here. 'So, where did you go and who did this to you?'

'Pardon?' Claire yelled, and Morgan squirmed, she hadn't realised she'd spoken aloud.

'Talking to myself. I don't think there's anything here. Should we check the shop?'

'Lead the way.'

Morgan shuffled past Claire. She hated the white paper crime-scene suits with a passion; they made her sweat like she'd been in a sauna and played havoc with her hair and eyeliner.

They trudged down the stairs and Morgan stopped at the rear door to the shop, realising there must be a key for it on the bunch that Tina had passed her, because she didn't think Cora would spend half of her life running around the block every time she opened up. She tried a couple and then the next one turned in the lock, sending a sigh of relief out of Morgan's mouth.

'Bingo, well done, Brookes.'

Morgan snorted. 'It wasn't exactly rocket science, Claire.'

Claire shrugged and Morgan pushed open the door. She was immediately hit by the scent of incense; it made her eyes water it was so pungent and sweet. She disliked it. Scented candles, diffusers and essential oils she loved, but incense was always too overpowering for her. She let Claire go in first with her camera while she stood back and surveyed the shop.

It was very similar to the flat, nothing unusual, no signs of a struggle. There was a black velvet curtain covering an area not too far from where she was standing, and she leaned across and drew it back to see a small table, a couple of chairs and a deck of tarot cards spread across it. In the centre of the table was a large crystal ball. Morgan wondered if it was a real one and was tempted to reach out to touch it and see if she could peer inside of it to see her future. Or was that a load of old mumbo jumbo? She didn't realise people still used them to be honest. She thought they'd died a death years ago, it just showed how much she didn't know. Her feet took a couple more steps inside then stopped. She dare not go any further or Claire would tell her off. The shop reminded her of her aunt Ettie's kitchen with its jars of herbs and spices stacked on the shelves, and there were baskets of crystals on a large table. Lots of crescent moon shaped things too, crystals, bowls, ornaments, pictures of the moon. A brilliant flash of white light broke her out of her trance, and Claire grinned at her.

'You looked so demure then, lost in thought. Sorry to be

the bearer of bad news, but I don't think there's anything here either. The search team will go through everything, but I don't think this is the primary scene or a crime scene full stop.'

Morgan nodded in agreement.

'Thanks, me either. Is there a laptop or iPad anywhere?'

Claire pointed to an evidence bag on the counter containing a laptop.

'You're good.'

'So, I've been told.'

She rang Ben.

'Hey, Claire has a laptop from the shop but there are no indications anything happened at either the flat or here.'

'*Great about the laptop, was kind of hoping there would be a great messy scene with lots of forensics and we could link it all to Jay.*'

'If only. Are you okay? I got told you took him out like a pro rugby player.'

Ben laughed so loud she had to hold the phone away from her ear.

'*Sam and Tina?*' he questioned.

'Of course, said you impressed them.'

'*Really, well then it's a shame I've got grass stains all over my knees and I've grazed my shins.*'

'Bless you, Ben. I'll bathe them for you after. Did you stop him going inside the tent?'

'*I did, just, but it was close and for a few minutes I wondered if we should let him see her that way if that's what he needed, but then I thought about how I still see images of Cindy lying dead in the bathroom late at night when I can't sleep and that's what made me take him out. He's going to struggle with this for a long time. Why make it any worse than it already is by imprinting that image on his mind?*'

'We try our best to protect people from the awful truth but

maybe sometimes they need to know it so they can accept it, but that's very thoughtful of you. What should I do now?'

'*Did you look for a diary?*'

'I did and couldn't find one.'

'*Never mind, I'm going to see if Marc is happy for the body to be moved. There isn't much else to be done here.*'

'Are you keeping the area closed off?'

'*Yes, at least until the searches have been carried out.*'

TEN

Claire had left the shop and both it and the flat were secure with a PCSO guarding them in case Ben decided that there may be something of forensic value, and he was going to send a full search team inside. Morgan was waiting for Ben to come pick her up, so she went into the pretty little flower shop and inhaled the sweet smell that lingered in the air. It was tinged with the scent of greenery. Not sure if that was how she could describe it, but underneath that initial fragrance hit, there always seemed to be an underlying, not as pleasant, scent that lingered. She smiled at the man making up the bouquet on the workbench when he looked up at her, but he didn't smile back, and she knew that he knew she was police. Some people could pick out a copper from a mile away even in plain clothes.

'Can I help?' he said as she approached him.

'I hope so, do you sell flower crowns?'

A slight look of confusion crossed his face, and she felt a tiny surge of joy that she'd thrown him off track. He put the secateurs down on the counter and wiped his hand on the yellow apron he was wearing. Turning to look at her this time he did smile.

'That I do, lots of them to be exact. What type are you after, fresh flowers, dried, silk, have you got a preference?'

'Actually, it's not for me. I'm trying to find out where this one came from.'

She turned her phone towards him, and he stepped closer to look.

'It's not one of mine, sorry. I haven't made any fresh ones this week. I have three to make up for a wedding at the weekend; and I haven't had those roses in for quite some time now, they're more of a specialist variety and a little too expensive for my customers.'

'Oh, thank you.' The disappointment on her face was obvious.

'It's pretty, I might be wrong, but it looks like the style a florist in Ulverston makes, if that's any help.'

'It is, thank you, do you know the name of the shop?'

'Rustic Rose, they specialise in roses and have many more varieties in stock, far more than I do. Can I ask why you want to know?'

'Yes, sorry, I'm Detective Morgan Brookes, I'm investigating a murder and the victim was wearing it.'

His face paled considerably, and he crossed his arms.

'Would it be anyone I know?'

'Yes, maybe, I'm sorry to tell you this but it's Cora from next door.'

This time his mouth dropped open, and he let out a gasp. 'No way, I mean no.'

She nodded, realising he must be friendly with her – after all they had shops next to each other.

'But I was only speaking to her last night, and she was looking forward to her outside yoga session this morning.'

Morgan felt a little bad that she hadn't thought they could be friends. 'Did she tell you anything else? Sorry, I didn't catch your name.'

'Elliot Boothe. Not really, we were gossiping about the guy a few doors up who's been having an affair with an older woman. I feel sick, I knew you were a copper the minute you walked in. I should have known something was wrong.'

Morgan gave him her most sympathetic smile. 'How did you know? I'm not in uniform.'

'I saw you out the back in a white suit going into Cora's flat, and I thought maybe her and Jay had a domestic or they'd been broken into. Oh my God, did Jay do it? I knew he would lose his temper and go too far one of these days.'

'Was he violent towards Cora?'

Elliot shrugged. 'She said not, but I'd hear him crashing around and shouting a lot.'

Morgan was hoping that this was the lead they needed. 'Did you ever see Cora with any injuries?'

'No, to be fair I didn't, and we spoke almost every day.' He paused, and Morgan studied him. He seemed an honest person. 'I can't believe it.'

'It's hard to take in. I'm sorry to have broken the news to you. When was the last time you saw her?'

'Last night, when I was bringing the buckets of flowers inside before I went home. She was coming out of her shop in a hurry.'

'Did she say where she was going? If she was meeting anyone?'

'I only said hiya and have a fun time this morning.'

He looked as if he was going to faint, as all the colour drained from his face and he sat down heavily onto a chair.

'Are you okay, can I get you something?'

He leaned forward and put his head between his knees. 'Sorry, I'm not good with this kind of thing.'

She looked around but couldn't see any cameras. 'Do you have CCTV?'

He shook his head.

Morgan felt awkward and wished she was better at consoling people, but she didn't reach out and touch his arm or his shoulder. Instead she asked another question to distract him. 'Who is the guy having an affair you mentioned?'

'Ray, from the chocolate shop. He's been seeing one of the customers who is at least twenty years older than him. It's a bit bizarre really, she goes there every Tuesday and Thursday evening just as the shop shuts, and he ushers her inside then draws the blinds. I'll tell you I don't know what they're getting up to exactly, but it's enough to put me off buying my boiled sweets from there.'

Morgan smiled at him. 'I'll leave you to it. Are you going to be okay?'

He didn't speak, just lifted his hand and waved her away. She turned and was almost at the door when he asked. 'Do Jim and Lewis know? She was in the book club and well, I think Jim thought of her as a daughter.'

'They do.'

'Oh, I'm sure they're devastated. I think I'll go check on them when I've got myself together.'

She walked outside, but there was no sign of Ben yet, so she decided to go back into the bookshop before Elliot did. They hadn't mentioned a book club or how close they were to Cora, but then again, she had just dropped a bombshell onto them that might have left them feeling as shocked as Elliot.

The bookshop was still empty, and she wondered how it survived. Jim wasn't sitting behind the counter and there was no sign of Lewis, so she began to browse the books, searching for the shelf containing true crime, her favourite. She had recently discovered a brilliant new podcast called *Fifty States of Madness* and had been getting her fix from listening to Gina and Shannon discussing true crime and going on eerie adventures in the US that left her longing to go on a three-week vacation and visit all the places they'd talked about.

'You're back.'

She turned around, still clutching a book in her hand, to see Lewis standing there.

'Yes, sorry I'm waiting to get picked up and well, I love books, so I thought I'd have a browse.'

He smiled at her, his cheeks turning pink.

'What kind of books do you like, true crime?'

'How did you guess?'

He laughed. 'You're holding an old copy of *Mindhunter*, the last one which is on the shelf with the true crime books.'

She looked down at her hands then at him. 'Ah, I thought you were some kind of super psychic book guy.'

'Sorry to disappoint you. It's funny, we don't sell a lot of true crime; it's mainly romance, crime fiction and books about the Lake District which pay the bills. So, if you see any you like help yourself, they're taking up space that we should really fill with stuff that does sell.'

'I couldn't do that, but I will buy one.' She carried it over to the counter and put it down. 'Is Jim okay? I'm sorry to have broken such bad news to you both.'

'He's gone home to have a lie down. He really loved Cora. He had a soft spot for her. She came to book club every month, always bought the book but never read it which tickled him.'

'How about you, are you okay?'

He shrugged. 'I'm sad beyond belief and, to be honest, a little shocked. It doesn't seem real. I can't take it in that she's not here any more, that we won't see her soft smile again.'

'It's very sad to lose someone so young in such an awful way. She still came and bought the book? Why didn't she read them?'

'I think she was too busy and preferred reading stuff that we didn't at book club. She sells witchcraft books in her shop. We don't sell them, so they were never chosen as the book of the month.' His eyes filled with tears. 'She is a lovely woman;

everyone likes her. Jim will never get over this. She told him she reads the blurb and the reviews online, so she knows what they're talking about, and sounds interested. She was very funny and it's such a loss.'

Morgan laughed. 'She sounds like my kind of person.'

Lewis brushed his sleeve across his eyes and nodded. 'It's so sad.' He slid the book into a paper bag and handed it to her.

'How much is it, please?'

He shook his head. 'No charge, like I said it's been there for years and taking up space. I'd rather you take it than it get thrown out.'

'Thank you, that's really kind of you. Do you mind if I ask you a few questions about Cora?' He nodded, and she continued. 'Did you ever hear Jay and Cora arguing? I imagine the walls weren't too good at keeping loud noise out.'

He sighed. 'Sometimes, he likes the sound of his own voice, if you know what I mean. He'd bang around and yell, but Cora didn't yell back. She was always so calm. I think it made him worse because she didn't argue back.'

'Did you ever have to intervene or were you worried about her?'

'It's awkward, isn't it? I mean we all argue, no one has a perfect relationship, but I never got worried enough that I thought I should go round there and thump him or call the police. Not that I'm the thumping sort, but I could if I had to.'

'It is difficult, isn't it? If you think of anything that might be important can you let me know? If you ring 101 and speak to the control room, tell them to send me a message. Morgan Brookes in CID. I'd give you a card with my details on, but I've run out of them.'

She liked Lewis, but for some reason she hadn't wanted to give him her personal mobile number. She thanked him and walked towards the door.

'Hey, you should come to book club. We're always looking

for new members and if you enjoy reading it might be fun for you.'

Morgan turned and smiled. 'Thank you, I might do. When do you meet?'

'Every fourth Thursday at seven, the next one is tomorrow. We used to meet in here, but it got a bit too busy. Now we meet at The Oddfellows Arms, in a room upstairs where dogs aren't allowed because I have an allergy to dog hair. It starts at seven, but don't worry if you're late; I know you're really busy.'

'Thank you, that's very kind of you. I might do that if I can.'

She grinned at him and left the shop to see Ben's BMW parked a little further up the street. She could get to know the members and see if there was anyone who could be worth checking out. It was a good way to inject herself into the small community. As she got inside his car, he eyed the book but didn't say anything to her.

'Before you ask, I wasn't shopping, it's a gift.'

He arched an eyebrow at her. 'For what, it's not your birthday, is it?'

'No, a gift off the guy who runs the bookshop. He said they don't sell many true crime books. Anyway, here's something: apparently Jay has a bad temper and would shout and bang around a lot, arguing with Cora. The florist on the other side said the same; he confirmed that he didn't make the flower crown unfortunately, but he did say there was a shop in Ulverston that could have. Apparently the roses are a rare type.'

'Ulverston?' She nodded. 'Why is nothing ever simple and easy? I was hoping you were going to give me something that would lead us straight to the killer's door. But I'll let you off, you did get some useful information and a free book. If there's a chance there was domestic violence in the relationship, we need to look much closer at Jay. I'll ask Amy to do the background checks and see if she can delve a little deeper. I can request someone from South go interview the florists for us and save a bit of time.'

'You could, but it won't take that long for me to drive to Ulverston, and I'd rather go speak to them myself.'

'I knew you were going to say that.'

'Maybe you have a bit of a sixth sense going on there.'

He arched one eyebrow at her. 'And maybe you're being sarcastic, Brookes.'

She shrugged. 'I heard you took him down to stop him getting into the tent, well done.'

'Sam?'

'Can't divulge my source, sorry.'

'Yeah, well I managed to stop him, but I hurt my knees and now I have damp patches on them.'

Morgan let out a giggle, despite trying her best not to because it wasn't funny at all.

'I'll have to watch the replay later.'

'No, you bloody won't. You can go to Ulverston instead, if you promise not to watch it.'

'Thank you.'

'Will you be calling at any more bookshops on the way?'

'Only if it's part of the investigation. Are you jealous I got a freebie? I'll let you read it first.'

He tilted his head to read the title. '*Mindhunter*, isn't that a Netflix series? I'll watch it instead.'

'Your loss, at least you could have told Susie something interesting this time instead of fibbing about what book you didn't read.'

'Are you deliberately trying to annoy me?'

'Not at all, boss, just stating the facts.'

He drove them back to the station so she could grab a plain car to continue her enquiries. As she got out, he asked, 'Will you be okay going to Ulverston on your own?'

'Yes, thank you. I'm all grown up and know the way there without getting lost. Can you manage without me?'

'I suppose I'll have to.'

Before he could change his mind, she crossed the car park and swiped her card against the fob to get inside and grab a set of car keys.

ELEVEN

Ulverston was fairly quiet, and Morgan managed to get parked on the main street right outside a small Tesco store. The cobbled streets were quaint, as were the shops, the only problem was most of them were in darkness because she discovered it was half-day closing, meaning a lot of the shops had shut at lunchtime. She hoped that the florists were open and was relieved to see the buckets of flowers and planters outside. There was a woman inside who was making the most beautiful flower crown from delicate pink roses with gypsophila laced through it, and Morgan thought if she ever got married, she would want one of those. Then she caught herself and realised that the probability of her getting married wasn't very high. She smiled at the woman and pulled out her phone, and after introducing herself, she showed her the photo.

'Yep, that's one of mine. I made quite a few for Ostara, but that was the only made from Darling roses; the customer was quite specific they wanted that type of rose.'

Morgan would have high fived her if she could, but she didn't want to look unprofessional.

'Could you give me the details of the customer, please, it's urgent.'

'I'll have a look.'

She went through her order book until she found a page with only a couple of lines of writing on it.

'Here you go, oh damn it, I'm sorry.'

Her heart sank. 'What's the matter?'

'It was a cash sale; I remember now he was quite specific: he wanted three identical flower crowns all from Darling roses. He said it was a surprise for his girls; he didn't give me an address or contact number. He paid in cash and came back for them the next day.'

'Do you have CCTV?'

'No, I'm a florist, I don't carry much cash, most orders are paid with contactless or Apple Pay; I don't sell alcohol and there isn't much to steal.'

'Do you think you could give a description to a forensic artist, to see if they could match his likeness?'

The woman grimaced. 'I could try if it will help, but what's it for?'

'I'm investigating a murder in Keswick, so it's vitally important we try and identify the man who bought them.'

She stared at Morgan. 'I don't know what they have to do with a murder, I mean that's awful and I'm sorry to hear that.'

'The victim was found wearing that crown on her head.'

'Oh.'

The woman was shaking her head. 'That's awful, oh God, I'm so sorry.'

'It's not your fault, you weren't to know. I don't think he will come back, but if he did would you be able to ring 999 and get officers here as soon as possible?'

'Do you think he will come back?' A look of fear crossed her face.

'I can't say, probably not, but I want you to be aware of how dangerous he is. Can you give me a description for now?'

'Taller than you, but not really tall, about five nine, maybe; he was wearing a black North Face beanie; I didn't see any hair, I assumed he had a shaved head.' She closed her eyes trying to recall a description. 'Medium build, not big but he looked like he maybe was fit. Blue jeans, black waterproof coat, one of those snood things pulled up over his mouth. He seemed nice; he was friendly, and he didn't say anything that made me think he was up to no good. Probably in his thirties or forties maybe, but I'm rubbish with age, brown eyes. Sorry, that's not much help, is it?'

Morgan was scribbling it all down, and she looked up at her. 'It is, thank you. Did it not make you wonder why his lower face was covered?'

She shrugged. 'Not really, well not since Covid; there are still a fair few people who wear face masks, scarves that kind of thing. I just thought he was being cautious.'

Morgan nodded. 'I suppose there is that; Covid has a lot to answer for. I can get officers to do CCTV enquiries along the street, to see if he's captured on it. When did he come in?'

'Yesterday morning: as soon as I opened at 9.30, he was here to collect.'

'Did you see a car? Was he with anyone?'

'I didn't look, I was busy. I had no reason to see what he was doing. He paid for his order and left, saying thank you. He was pretty much the perfect customer.'

'Did he say anything else?'

'Just that they were beautiful, and he thought they would look perfect.'

This time Morgan did scribble her phone number down and passed it to her.

'I'm sorry I didn't catch your name.'

'It's Joanne Gaffney.'

Morgan looked around at the bouquets and flower boxes, there were roses of every colour and it smelled divine.

'Thank you, Joanne, I'll be in touch about the forensic artist. If you think of anything at all that might be relevant, can you ring me on that number?'

She nodded. 'Of course, I will.'

Morgan walked out and stood looking up and down the street for CCTV cameras; the Tesco had a camera outside and so did a pub a bit further down. She went into the supermarket to speak to the manager, who told her the camera wasn't working. She tried not to get so despondent in front of him, but the disappointment had never hurt so much. She thanked him for his help. Then walked down to the pub and hammered on the door, but there was no reply, so she went back to the car.

It was only as she started the engine and was replaying what Joanne had told her once more when she felt a cold finger of fear run down her spine as she whispered to herself, *he bought three flower crowns for his girls, oh God.*

She phoned Ben.

'Anything?'

'He bought three of those flower crowns and told the florist they were for his girls.'

There was silence on the other end of the phone as she let that sink in.

'Dear God, he's planning more. Get back here, Morgan. Did she give you anything we can work with, name, address, big colour photo of his face?'

She read out the description to him, and he repeated it word for word to whoever was sitting next to him in the office.

'I've told her we'll arrange for a forensic artist to see her, but he paid cash, gave no details and did a pretty good job of disguising his face and hair.'

'Get back, we'll sort out officers to go back for CCTV and

statements. I want you here, with me, Morgan, not driving around the county on your own.'

'On my way.'

For once she didn't feel like arguing with him. She could feel the coffee she'd drunk earlier churning in her stomach and felt as if she was going to throw up. They had to stop him before he killed again.

A sudden thought had her getting got out of the car and running back into the florists.

'How long do those crowns keep?'

'If they're kept in the fridge or in a cool place and spritzed with water, they could last up to a week, but I'd say three to five days before they start to dry out.'

She nodded. 'Thank you.'

Getting back in the car, Morgan gripped the steering wheel and stared onto the busy cobbled street through blurred eyes.

Three to five days to find his next two victims, or to identify and stop him: it wasn't an awful lot of time. She just wanted to cry at the helplessness of the situation. Instead, she sucked in a deep breath, used her sleeve to blot at her eyes and whispered, 'You can do this, Morgan, go find that bastard and end it now.'

TWELVE

Morgan walked into an office full of people: Al from task force was there with a huge map of Keswick spread across the spare desk; Marc was on the phone talking animatedly to whoever was on the other end; Ben leaned over his desk staring at his computer. Amy was the only one not caught up with anything, and she smiled at Morgan.

'We have a lead.'

'We do?'

She nodded. 'A good one too. There's a photographer who was offering Ostara photo sessions in Keswick. I went in to speak to him and he said I could book a session with him; he would provide me with a flower crown, a white dress and had some props I could use. I told him I wasn't interested in that, but he was a bit of a creep and offered me a discount because his client that had booked for this morning didn't turn up. I asked him who it was, and he said it was a woman called Cora, and when I told him I was from the police, he got all arsy and wouldn't tell me anything else.'

The smile was so wide across Amy's face her cheeks were stretched tight, and Morgan worried her skin might crack.

'Wow, that's amazing, well done, Amy.'

Morgan realised her stomach had stopped churning at the thought of having a suspect so soon; it had to happen occasionally, didn't it? The laws of averages said that.

'Thank you but it was just blind luck really, not exactly detective of the year stuff. Cain is parked outside the shop, watching it to make sure he doesn't disappear. He radioed in ten minutes ago to say the guy turned the sign on the door to closed, but he hasn't come out, he's still inside.'

'Interesting.'

Morgan glanced over at Ben and Marc, who were also now leaning over the map. 'Are we having a briefing? What if it was someone who knows him and pretended to be him to lure Cora to her death?'

Ben looked up and shook his head. 'No time, we need to move quickly on Amy's lead, or he could be getting rid of evidence while we're deciding what to do. We'll consider if this is a possibility once we've got him in custody and access to the shop and flat. We found no hiding spots at the crime scene, the house to house hasn't brought us anything, and as far as I'm aware Cora's friends and family have alibis. Al has got an armed entry team ready to deploy; you and Amy will go in and do a quick search once he's been arrested and removed from the property. Claire will be there with you on standby, ready to document anything and recover the flower crown or anything pertinent to the investigation.'

Marc straightened up. 'Morgan, Amy, you heard Ben. Wait in the car until you are given the all clear. I don't want either of you anywhere near until he's been cuffed.'

Morgan felt a little... she wasn't sure what the right words were, perturbed, or pissed that he was telling them both to stay out of the way. Her arms were folded across her chest as she glared at him.

'Where will you and Ben be?' She realised by the tone of her own voice she was ready to pick a fight with him.

'In the other car waiting for the all clear.'

The fight left her as soon as it had come. 'Oh, okay.'

She turned to Amy; she hadn't expected that and had thought there was some masochistic male stuff playing out, when really, he was just warning them both to keep out of the way. Amy had cupped a hand over her mouth to hide the smile and winked at Morgan. Al, Ben and Marc left the room, and Amy laughed.

'You were about to give him hell then, weren't you?'

Morgan shrugged. 'I thought he was being a dick and trying to say we had to keep away because we're women.'

This made Amy laugh harder. 'To be fair, he was probably thinking of the possibility that you'd get yourself in trouble.'

'I don't always, and in my defence it's not my fault, well it isn't most of the time.'

'Yeah, right. Come on let's get there while they're still stroking their guns.'

This time it was Morgan who snorted with laughter.

They went down to the car park and were driving out of the gates before the armed officers were even inside their armed response vehicle.

Amy parked at the opposite end of the small street to where Cain was.

'Should we go sit with him so we can see the action? We can't see anything from here.'

Morgan was out of the car before Amy could answer her and striding towards Cain's car. She got in the back seat letting Amy have the front. This was her job; she wasn't taking that away from her. She stared down the tree-lined street at the houses with their perfectly maintained small front gardens, evergreen shrubs giving them year-round greenery. The shop was the only one without a garden. It had a parking space out the front, and it looked out of place in the residential street. She wondered what the residents thought of it, what they would think once the armed police turned up and disrupted the area, bringing the owner of the shop out in cuffs.

She asked Cain, 'What's up?'

'The big boys are on their way, we have to keep a low profile.'

Amy opened the door and got inside. 'Much happening?'

'Not really, I can see him moving around inside on his phone through the curtains, but that's it.'

Morgan could see the bottom of the street in the rear-view mirror and saw Ben stop his car further down, moments later the ARV turned into the street.

Cain was still watching the shop but whispered, 'Well, if this isn't exciting, we have front row seats for the matinee.'

Just as the officers got out of their vehicle, a steady stream of school kids came heading into the street. Ben's voice broke the radio silence that they'd all been keeping.

'Someone stop those kids from coming down here.'

Cain was out of the car, Morgan too, and they both jogged up to meet them with their hands out. The teenagers were staring at the pair of them.

'Stop, you need to go a different way, this street is closed.'

Two girls who were in front stopped and dead-eyed him. 'Yeah, said who?'

He pulled the lanyard out of his shirt that had his warrant card tucked into it.

'I do, police.'

The teenagers were joined by a large group, swarming around Cain and Morgan.

'Sorry, guys, you need to turn around and go the other way,' said Morgan.

'Why can't we wait here and watch? Have they got guns? Oh my God, those coppers have guns.'

The group of teenagers began to murmur and try to get past Cain, who bellowed, 'Get back now, turn around and find a different route home or you'll get shot.' He stood there, his shoulders wide along with his feet, making himself look as imposing as possible.

'God, you can't say that,' said one girl who had her phone out.

He reached down and plucked the phone from her hands. 'Yes, I can, now move and if you want your phone back get your parents to come pick it up from Rydal Falls police station. Open your mouth again and you'll be accompanying it there.'

The teenagers all sighed but turned around and began to walk off back the way they'd come. Morgan turned to Ben and waved, and the next thing she knew the armed officers had put the door of the shop through and had charged inside, their shouts filling the air.

'Can't believe you took that kid's phone off her.'

'Why not? They are so full of themselves. When we were kids, we wouldn't have dared give cheek to a copper and especially not when there were cops with guns not too far away.'

'Kids, eh. Times have changed, Cain, no one respects anyone these days. Same as that guy early this morning, he was arguing back when there was a murder victim not that far away from him.'

They turned around to see a man with a shaved head, wearing an Adidas track suit. His jacket was zipped up, but so tight it had ridden up his midriff, and there was an expanse of white flesh below it, peeking out at everyone. He was being led from the front of the shop in cuffs, an officer either side of him and one standing guard out the front.

'Guess we're on if the coast is clear.'

Cain smiled at her. 'Enjoy.'

She headed back down towards the car and then turned back. 'Is there a search kit in the boot?'

He nodded slowly. 'You're welcome.'

Amy was already out of the car and opening the boot. When Morgan reached her, she passed her some gloves.

'Are we suiting and booting?'

'Should we have a quick look around and see what we find first?'

Marc's voice spoke behind them. 'You are suiting and booting, I don't want anything compromised.'

'Yes, boss.' They both spoke at once.

He strode back to the car, where Ben was talking to Al.

'Rude.'

Morgan laughed; they got dressed and she turned to Amy. 'I really hope we open his fridge and find two more fresh flower crowns that match the one Cora Dalton was wearing.'

'Me too.'

Morgan didn't know whether she believed they would, she wanted to but there was this niggling feeling inside that this had all been far too easy, too much of a coincidence. The guy she'd watched being put into the police van didn't match the description of the one Joanne the florist had given; this guy had a bit of a beer belly and looked as if he enjoyed a lager or two.

She let Amy go first and followed her inside. The cop with the gun wasn't familiar but she smiled at Morgan and whispered, 'Good luck.'

'Thanks, we're going to need it.'

'We all do, isn't that what this whole job runs on? A wing and a prayer, being in the right place at the right time to catch a break.'

Morgan smiled back. 'I'm Morgan, are you new?'

'Daisy, and new to this area but I've been a response cop in Barrow for four years.'

'Welcome to the most beautiful, violent part of Cumbria you could ever visit.'

She walked into the shop to see Amy in the small kitchen area at the rear with the under-counter fridge door wide open. Morgan's breath caught in the back of her throat, and she held her breath and crossed her fingers.

'Nothing except his lunch, can of cola and a pint of milk.'

She exhaled sharply. 'There's his house to check yet, where does he live?'

Amy pointed to the ceiling. 'Apparently, he lives upstairs. This used to be his living room; he converted it into a studio two years ago he told me earlier.'

Morgan saw the door and crossed towards it. Pushing it open, it was dark inside. She felt along the wall for a switch. Her gloved fingers finding one she pressed it in, and bright, white light flooded the small room that had a backdrop of Castlerigg Stone Circle against one wall and a bench in front of it with a flower crown on it; but it wasn't made from fresh flowers: it was silk and a burnt orange colour. Morgan picked it up and turned it around in her hand to study it.

Amy stood in the doorway, watching her, and whispered, 'Crap.'

She turned to face her. 'It doesn't mean that he isn't our guy; he's obviously up to something the way he acted.'

Morgan put the crown back on the bench. 'Just because he has a silk flower crown it doesn't mean he hasn't got the real ones stored in a fridge somewhere. Let's search the rest of the place before we give up hope.' Morgan knew she sounded a lot more confident than she felt.

'Yeah, but for all we know it's something not even related to the murder.'

'We won't know until we've searched everywhere, and he's been interviewed.'

She walked outside and phoned Ben. 'There's a flower crown, but it doesn't match the one found on Cora.'

'Damn it, are you sure he bought three the same?'

'Yes, I'm sure.'

'Get Claire to photograph it and bag it up, keep looking until the search team get there, they'll take over.'

He hung up.

Daisy was watching her. 'How's it going?'

'Not as good as we'd hoped.'

She sighed. 'It never does, but you'll find him if this one isn't the guy.'

Morgan let out a short laugh. 'I wish I had your confidence.'

'You're Morgan Brookes, aren't you?'

She looked at the woman in front of her. 'I am.'

'Look I know this sounds weird, but you're the main reason I transferred here.'

Morgan was taken aback. 'Why?' she asked quietly.

She shrugged and lowered her gun a little. 'You're amazing, you've caught more killers than any other detective on the force and you're what twenty-two? You're an enigma, they all talk about you down South. I wanted to work up here with you or as close to you as I could, and I know it sounds like I'm a right weirdo, I'm not. I just admire you and want to be a part of the same team. So, this is like day one of this investigation and there's already someone in custody, two if you count the boyfriend. What I'm trying to say in the worst way possible is that you should cut yourselves some slack.'

'Twenty-three, and I don't know what to say, thank you.'

Daisy shrugged. 'No need to thank me, I'm just stating the facts in case you were feeling a little bogged down by it all. I don't think any of us get enough credit for all the hard work we put in.'

'Al's a great boss, you'll be fine with him and you're certainly going to be busy.'

'That's cool with me.'

Morgan smiled at her and went back inside, where Amy was on her hands and knees looking under the desk with a torch.

'What did the boss say?'

'To keep looking, there's a search team on their way.'

'Oh, good. Means we can go back to the station as soon as they arrive.'

She left Amy on her hands and knees and went upstairs to the flat above the shop.

It smelled of stale lager and sweaty socks, which turned her stomach. Morgan headed straight to the kitchen area which was much tidier than she'd expected. She looked at the fridge and crossed her fingers behind her back. Squeezing her eyes shut, she whispered, 'Please let there be two flower crowns inside.' Then she had crossed the floor and was tugging open the door. Her shoulders drooped: it was emptier than her and Ben's fridge after working a full set of shifts. There were six cans of lager, some cheese and a packet of honey roast ham that was curled up at the edges. She opened the bottom door of the freezer in case he'd stored the crowns in there, but that wasn't much better. Some fish fingers, sausages and a half bag of hash browns. She slammed the door shut and thought about what Amy had said. She wasn't sure about them being able to go back to the station, as there was a lot to do. She'd like to speak to Jay about the arguments that Elliott had mentioned and Lewis had confirmed. It would be good to hear his point of view. Did he think they were over the top? Did he know about Cora meeting someone? And what about the photographer they'd just taken in for questioning? If he wasn't their guy, who knew he was meeting Cora this morning? She wondered if he had a pub he used as a local; did he have friends he discussed his clients with? It was worth asking these questions to see if he could give them a lead that might help them figure this out.

THIRTEEN

The search team arrived and a few moments later PCSOs turned up to take over from Daisy. Morgan and Amy left them to it; they were almost at the car when Daisy caught up to them.

'Can I get a lift back with you guys, please, I'm not needed now.'

Amy looked at the gun. 'Is that thing loaded?'

'Of course, not much point carrying it around if it isn't. The safety's on, it's perfectly okay.'

Amy didn't seem convinced but pointed to the front passenger seat.

'You're not sitting behind me with that thing in case you accidentally shoot me in the back when I'm driving.'

Daisy laughed. 'I've never accidentally shot anyone yet but thank you.'

'No, well there's always a first time.'

Morgan got in the back seat, happy to not have to make eye contact with Daisy, who was lovely if not a little overfriendly. She had a headache and was trying to make a mental list of all the leads that needed following up on. This case felt different to all the others she'd worked on; it had been a full day of action, but they hadn't actually got anywhere, which was frustrating beyond belief. Daisy chatted all the way back to the station, and Morgan was glad of the distraction.

Ben and Marc were nowhere to be found and she assumed they were in custody with the photographer, and she realised she didn't even know his name.

'Hey, what's the guy called in custody?'

'Oliver Parker.'

'Has he got previous?'

Amy nodded. 'He has, he served two years for distributing indecent images a few years ago.'

'And he's a photographer, people take their kids to him for photographs?'

'Sick bastard, talk about being brazen about it.'

'Is he not on licence?'

'Not any more, that was ten years ago, and he seems to have kept his nose clean since.'

Morgan typed his name into the intel system on her computer and stared at the picture of him that filled the screen. She began to read through his file and stopped.

'He likes teenage girls according to what they found on his computer when he was arrested. It doesn't make sense.'

'Maybe he realised it was too risky with the teenagers and changed his preferences?'

Morgan didn't answer, she didn't think so. He might mask it and pretend that he wasn't interested in them, but if that was the case wouldn't he, after spending years dreaming about carrying out his most sadistic sexual fantasy, choose a teenage girl as his first victim? Why would someone whose sexual preference was teenage girls pick a twenty-eight-year-old woman?.

She went to find Ben, hoping that he hadn't gone into interview yet.

The custody area was dead, the only detainee was Oliver Parker. Jo, the custody sergeant, and Michelle, the detention officer, were eating sandwiches and Morgan realised she was hungry when her stomach let out a growl a Rottweiler would have been proud of.

'Are they in interview?'

Jo shook her head. 'Not yet, Mr Parker is with his brief, who I reckon has told him to go no comment.'

'Where are they?'

'Coming up with a clever and cunning plan somewhere, most likely in the canteen because they were both eyeing up our sandwiches, and I love Ben, but I don't love him enough to share me tea with him. Are you not feeding him, Morgan? No wonder he's lost weight.'

'He's a forty-four-year-old man who can feed himself. Thanks, I'll go see if I can find them.'

'Why are you looking all worried?'

'Am I?'

Jo and Michelle both nodded at the same time, and she shrugged.

'Just trying to figure things out, there's so much to do and we seem to be going backwards instead of forward.'

'Don't you think he's the guy?'

'I don't know what I think. Have they let Cora's partner, Jay, out of custody yet?'

'About fifteen minutes after he arrived. He got picked up by his friend called David Salt, works with him at the school, who was told to keep an eye on him. Poor guy, he looked devastated.'

'Yeah, what a shock. I can understand why he wanted to see her though.'

Jo nodded in agreement.

Morgan left them to their sandwiches and began to climb the stairs up to the first floor to the canteen, where she saw both Ben and Marc tucking into something in the corner. Ben raised a hand at her as she got closer and she dragged a chair to sit opposite the pair of them.

'You didn't find anything concrete then?' he asked, and she shook her head.

'His previous is indecent images of teenage girls.'

Marc's eyes narrowed as he looked at her. 'And?'

'Am I the only person who doesn't think a pervert with a fetish for teenage girls wouldn't kill a grown woman?'

Marc crossed his arms and pushed his chair back, and Ben stared at her, swallowed the bite of sandwich he'd just taken and muttered, 'Crap.'

'Why wouldn't he? If he's sick enough to like teenagers, why couldn't he also get off on women? There's no law saying you can't like both. He got caught with those images, maybe he thinks adult pornography isn't as shameful. People are entitled to change their minds, you know. Just because you fancy Ben here doesn't mean that in three years you wouldn't fancy me.'

Morgan stared at him. 'What?'

'I'm just saying people's tastes change and evolve. He might have progressed from girls to women.'

Ben was watching the pair of them with a genuine look of confusion on his face.

'First of all, even if Ben dumps me and I'm single I wouldn't fancy you, Marc, you're really not my type. Secondly, whoever killed Cora put effort into her murder – if this guy was going to kill someone, why wouldn't he make it worthwhile? Target someone he'd be really satisfied to dominate?'

'Ouch, tell it like it is, Morgan, don't spare my feelings.'

Ben tried to hide the smirk on his lips with a hand. 'I can see what you're saying, it does make sense.'

'So can I, but I don't think we can disregard him because of his past arrest history.'

Morgan shrugged, reaching out she took some crisps out of the packet next to Ben's sandwich and popped them in her mouth. 'It's just a point, that's all, and of course you can't dismiss him because of that, but up to now there's nothing to forensically tie him to Cora Dalton; she was supposed to meet him this morning, that's all that links them. By the way he has a background photograph in his studio of the stone circle, so he probably wasn't even going to take her up there.'

Marc threw his hands up in the air at the same time as he blew his lips out and released a long, pent-up breath. 'Morgan, did you have to come rain on my parade in such a spectacular fashion?'

'Sorry, I thought you should know and it's just my thoughts, you would want me to share any information I have with you and not hold it back or it could cost us time. Have Cora's parents been informed yet?'

Ben nodded. 'Smithy was called in as FLO, and he's gone to see them. He could have gone there now, I'm not sure.'

'Okay, what about the post-mortem?'

'Scheduled for tomorrow morning, when I told Declan we had a suspect in custody.'

'Should I go and interview the yoga group of women or has that been done?'

'No, that would be good. If you can get me some background information and statements, I'd appreciate that.'

'Last thing, the forensic artist, has that been arranged for the florist in Ulverston?'

'I've asked Cain to contact the guy who does that down in Barrow, to arrange for her to go to the station to see if they can come up with a decent Photofit.'

Morgan stood up. 'I'll leave you to it then, good luck in interview. I really do hope he's the guy.'

She walked away before either of them could say anything, with a sinking feeling in her heart that they were wasting time and the killer was out there thinking about his next girl.

FOURTEEN

Tabitha King was more than a little excited, as she had always wanted to do something like this, but had never been brave enough. With all the Instagram posts that kept flooding her timeline she realised it was now or never, and besides it would look great on her feed. It was a good way to advertise her business and get herself some pictures to be proud of. The shop was doing okay. She had her regular customers who came in for their tarot card readings and sessions to see if they could speak to their dearly departed. She'd had the gift of speaking to the dead since she was a kid. The first time she saw a ghost was when she was lying in bed and an elderly woman had shuffled into her bedroom looking lost. Tabitha had watched her both scared and amazed. Her sister was in the top bunk above her, but she didn't seem to notice her.

'Who are you?'

The woman had turned to stare at her, eyes wide; platinum hair in a messy bun she'd looked around the room then back towards Tabitha, who had sat up in her bed, then she'd pointed to herself, and Tabitha had nodded.

'Elsie Smithson, who are you?'

'Tabitha King, I'm eight, how old are you?'

'Eighty-nine, or I was. Where am I?'

Tabitha had giggled. 'You're in my bedroom, silly.'

The old woman had looked even more confused. 'But why am I in your room? Why am I not in my own bedroom?'

'I think you're dead, Elsie, you look all see-through like the ghost on *Ghostbusters*, the one in the library at the beginning.'

'I'm dead?'

Tabitha had nodded, a grave look on her face. Her sister Matilda had leaned down over the railing upside down and stared at her. 'Who are you talking to, squirt?'

She'd pointed to the woman. 'Elsie Smithson, she's lost.'

Matilda looked around the room then back at her. 'There's no one there, you nutjob, go to sleep.'

Elsie had stared at Matilda, and she hadn't even noticed her. Tabitha had shrugged at the woman and mouthed, 'Sorry.' Then she'd turned over and gone to sleep, not scared, not worried, not anything other than tired. When she'd woken up in the morning, she'd forgot all about Elsie, until she heard her mum telling her dad at breakfast that the nice old lady across the street, Elsie, died last night.

Tabitha still saw Elsie; in fact, since that night they'd become best friends, which was sometimes nice and sometimes annoying, like now. The past few years Elsie hadn't been as clear to her, but she'd been popping into her head nonstop today. All she kept seeing was an image of Elsie shaking her head and telling her *no*. She had no idea what she was telling her not to do, but she'd have to wait.

She was getting ready now and didn't want to be late. It was important to her that the photographs were taken at the precise moment the sun began to set. They would look so beautiful on her page; she might even use them as prints for her shop. She ran another coat of the sheer lip gloss across her lips and smacked them together, blew herself a kiss then pulled her full-length Dryrobe on to keep her warm. The long black cotton dress she'd chosen to wear wasn't warm or windproof, and it was always blowing a gale up on Birkrigg Common. The breeze from the Irish Sea that lapped at the coast road below made it a windy spot. Her hair was freshly waved; it had taken her an age to get the waves just perfect enough to stay in, so that it looked as if she hadn't made too much effort when, really, she'd taken an hour on the front alone.

She got into her knackered Mini. She had her favourite card deck with her, a crystal crown in case she didn't like the flower crown the photographer was bringing, and a bottle of Lucozade for some energy. She wasn't fond of the camera, but she'd been practising her poses for months now in her bedroom mirror, ready for the day she finally plucked up the courage to book a session. She was as good to go as she'd ever be, even though her hands were trembling as she gripped the steering wheel.

She parked as near as she could, on the grass verge. She had passed a couple of cars on the way up the steep single track, parked at the entrance to Sea Wood, and hoped there weren't lots of dog walkers around. She was in luck; the only car that was there was a small black car that she hoped belonged to the guy she was meeting. She parked not too far away and saw his familiar face smiling at her.

She waved, and he waved back. *This is it, you can do this, Tabby, be calm, smile and have fun.*

She got out of the car at the same time as he did. He grabbed a big holdall from the front passenger seat and a white box.

'Let me help you with that.'

She walked towards him and took the box from his hand. Lifting the lid she smiled at the blast of sweet fragrance that filled her nostrils.

'This is gorgeous, it smells divine.'

He laughed, but never spoke a word, and she wondered if he was feeling shy which made her feel better.

He led the way and she walked alongside him towards the stone circle that overlooked Morecambe Bay and the sea that was making its way in.

FIFTEEN

Morgan felt as if she had been awake for twenty-four hours straight. It was hard to believe it had only been this morning they had found Cora's body. Now, it was getting on for tea time, and the winter sun would set soon and bring with it the cold night air. She found the yoga studio, well it was more of a garage attached to a house than a studio, but she wasn't judging. She knocked on the door and waited for someone to answer. She recognised the instructor, Freya, from earlier as she opened the door, and Morgan felt bad, as her eyes were swollen and red, as if she'd been crying a lot.

'Come in.'

Morgan followed her inside what she had rudely assumed was a garage into a gorgeous light, airy space with a wall of bifold doors that looked out onto a compact, but beautiful cottage garden. The light oak floor and green walls complemented each other perfectly, and she felt a hint of envy at the assortment of healthy thriving house plants that were dotted around.

'This is wonderful.'

'Thank you, it is, isn't it,' she said, sniffing. 'I'm very lucky to have found the most perfect cottage with a garage that was bigger than the house. I converted it myself with my friend, Sasha, she's a fabulous whiz at DIY if you ever need anything doing. Do you ever do yoga or meditate?'

Morgan looked down at her Dr Marten boots and shook her head. 'I'm so sorry, should I take these off?'

Freya laughed. 'No, it's a hard wood floor, it can withstand your boots.'

'I haven't ever thought about it to be honest, the yoga, I sometimes try and meditate in bed after a stressful day.'

'That's good, I bet it helps a lot. Have you found anything out, caught anyone for what they've done to Cora?' Her voice cracked at the mention of her friend's name, and she pulled out a large floor cushion and sat down, gesturing for Morgan to do the same.

She did, hoping that her trousers wouldn't split. She wasn't used to squatting on the floor in them for an extended period of time.

'We have someone in custody, but it's routine enquiries.'

Freya was obviously good at observing people because she tilted her head.

'So, they've been arrested but it's routine? Is it Jay, please don't say it was him. I wouldn't ever forgive myself if he's done this and I didn't do anything to stop it.'

Morgan thought it was best not to divulge that Jay had been arrested but not for the murder. 'It's not him, but why do you say that? I know you and Cora were good friends and she probably told you stuff in confidence, but if you know something that might help us, now is the time to talk to me. It's just you and me, no one has to know where the information came from.'

'He, I don't think he physically hurt her, but he hurt her mentally, which was the reason she started to come to yoga and meditation. To help clear her mind. She said he wasn't always like that, but their arguments had got a little more intense and he could be very manipulative. She blamed it on the stress of work, but I think it was because he hated that her shop was getting more and more successful. She was living the dream running her own business while he was still working for an establishment.'

'He's anti-establishment?'

'Lately he's been anti a lot of things. I've known Cora for years and I always wondered how they got on so well, but they do say opposites attract and those two were the complete opposite of each other.'

Morgan was writing it all down. 'In your honest opinion, do you think Jay is capable of murder and, if so, what would have been his motive?'

She shrugged. 'That's a hard one to answer, because put in the right situation I think that every single one of us is capable of murder.'

Morgan thought about it. She'd been in some terrible, life-threatening situations and although she wouldn't kill a person in cold blood for no reason, there had been times when she'd fought tooth and nail to save herself without regarding the consequences. The only thing that had ever mattered to her at the time was her own survival.

'Yes, you're right, I think we are.'

'I think that Jay could very easily have lost his temper. He's very volatile and he could have killed her in a frenzy after an argument at the flat or in the shop. I saw Cora's body, Morgan, she was lying on that stone, her neck cut and posed as if she was sleeping. That was not the action of a man who lost his shit mid argument with his partner, that was something entirely different. It was cold, it was calculated, and I think that whoever did this to Cora enjoyed it a lot.'

Morgan agreed with Freya on every single word, and she nodded. 'Thank you for being so honest. Did Cora have any plans that she'd talked about? Had she said she was going to be at the stone circle before you arrived? Did she mention having a photoshoot? Had she been talking to anyone recently that she's only just got to know or involved with?'

'I'm sorry, but the answer to all of those questions is not that I'm aware of. Although I couldn't answer the one about her talking to anyone recently, she owned a busy little shop, and a lot of her business happens online. She never mentioned the photoshoot; I guess she either wanted to surprise us or didn't want us to know.'

'What's the relevance of Ostara? Do you think that she was killed because of it?'

Freya stood up. 'I have no idea why it would be so relevant to a killer; it's a celebration of spring. Would you like a drink, I have herbal teas, coffee, water, wine?'

Morgan thought she would quite like to drink a glass of cold wine, sitting here watching the sun set over the backdrop of the mountains and Freya's pretty little garden.

'I'm okay, thank you. I still have lots to do. Is there anyone out of the group I should talk to? Was Cora particularly close to anyone else and can you give me a little more information on Ostara?'

'We were the closest, the others all got on well with Cora and we all went out for a drink occasionally, but I don't think she would have shared anything personal with them. For me and the girls who attended my circle this morning it is a chance to be together and celebrate a way to find more balance in our lives, a time to plant the seeds for our futures, to make ourselves a priority and we do this by showing up at the crack of dawn to give our thanks to the sun for the longer days that she is going to bestow upon us.'

'Thank you, it's so much more than I thought. Whilst I'm here I'll get a statement from you, if you wouldn't mind talking me over this morning, even though I'm aware of the events.'

As the golden light from the setting sun filled the room with a warmth that made Morgan wonder if she should take up yoga, Freya began to tell her about her day up until the point that Izzy found Cora's body. There was something so wonderfully soothing about this space that Freya had made, and for the first time today Morgan felt at peace and not worried about the huge list of jobs that needed ticking off. Or finding the killer... because she knew that she would work as late into the evening as she needed to if it meant tracking him down and taking him off the streets.

SIXTEEN

Morgan left the studio feeling a lot more chilled than she had when she entered it. She'd walked the short distance to her car when her phone began to ring. The sky still had the faintest tinge of orange on the horizon towards Rydal Falls, but the rest was darkness with stars peeking through.

'Brookes.'

'*Morgan, it's Will Ashworth. Is Ben around? I can't get hold of him.*'

'If he's not answering he's in interview, Will. Can I help?'

'*I hope so, we just had an attempted murder come in.*'

Morgan sat down heavily on the driver's seat; she knew what he was about to say.

'*A woman was found on Birkrigg Common fifteen minutes ago, with her throat cut. Luckily for her a dog walker found her and managed to administer first aid until paramedics got there. Didn't you have a similar case this morning?*'

'We did, unfortunately Cora Dalton wasn't so lucky to have a passing dog walker. Did they see the guy who did it?'

'*No, but they passed a car speeding down the single track that almost ran her off the road. We're checking ANPR, because they either headed on towards Ulverston or back into Barrow. The area is flooded with cops looking for a small black car.'*

'Birkrigg Common, it has a stone circle, doesn't it?'

'Yes, not the same size as Castlerigg, but it's a neolithic stone circle, and she was draped across the lowest, flattest stone.'

'Was she wearing a flower crown of roses and a garland of leaves?'

'Yes.'

'Damn it, he bought three of those crowns, which means he has another victim in his sights.'

'Can you come here, Morgan? It might be better for you to assess the scene and Ben, too, when he gets out of interview.'

'Ben's interview is about to be stopped; he's questioning a suspect, but he couldn't have a better alibi than being in custody at the time of another murder.'

'Attempted murder, for now, she's still alive and I'm praying she'll stay that way. The air ambulance is about to lift off and take her to Preston trauma unit.'

'We'll be there as soon as possible, Will. He most likely poses as a photographer, or he might be one. Tell patrols if they stop anyone to search for photographic equipment. He must lure them there under the pretence of a photoshoot.'

'Amazing, thanks. See you soon, drive careful, Morgan.'

Morgan did not drive careful; she sped through the lanes and winding roads to get back to Rydal Falls and stop the interview, knowing fine well it was a waste of time because Oliver Parker was not their guy.

She knocked on the interview room door and stuck her head in. Oliver Parker looked like a rabbit caught in headlights. Lucy O'Gara, his solicitor, was mid sentence, and she stopped and stared at Morgan.

'Sorry to interrupt. Ben, I need a word urgently, please.'

Marc was glaring at her; she could tell he was about to implode, the anger was radiating off him in waves of heat that she could feel from where she was standing. Ben stood up and excused himself, and following Morgan outside of the room, far enough away so no one inside could hear their conversation.

'Will phoned, they had an attempted murder on Birkrigg Common at the stone circle there, around forty minutes ago.'

'What?'

'Victim was wearing a flower crown and garland of leaves; she was lucky a dog walker saw her and phoned an ambulance while doing her best to stop her bleeding out.'

'Jesus.' He ran a hand through his hair; when his head was shaved, he would scrub over it whenever he was stressed, but he was letting it grow again after proclaiming it was too cold to shave it all off.

'Right, leave this with me. Grab what you can from the office, print off some photos to compare the scenes, anything you think we might need. Where's Amy?'

Morgan shrugged.

'If she's upstairs, send her down here to bail Parker. He's too shifty, there's something going on with him. Even if he's not our guy, I want him investigated further to see what he's hiding.'

She turned to go and find Amy, and Ben called after her, 'Morgan, you were right.'

She gave him a half smile because she'd rather not have been; in fact she'd have been ecstatic if it had been Oliver Parker, because it would mean no more chasing the bogeyman and no more pointless deaths. She waved a hand at him and carried on. All that lovely zen feeling she'd had when she'd left Freya's yoga studio had disappeared into the ether. It had been nice while it lasted.

As she was walking up the stairs, she heard Brenda call her.

'Morgan, I have something for you.'

She turned to see her with a pile of books in her hands. 'Thanks, I'm a bit busy now. Can I grab them after?'

Brenda grinned at her and walked towards her. 'I'll bring them up for you. I don't want them cluttering my tidy office, it's taken me all afternoon to sort it out.'

Brenda didn't do the stairs; instead she called the lift and Morgan thought she was wise. She hadn't realised how tired she was, and her ankle still ached now and again after the time she'd hurt it jumping out of a burning building. Brenda came out of the lift at the same time she reached the top step.

'Where did those books come from?' She tilted her head to look at them; they were all true crime books.

'A very nice young man dropped them off. He said they were a gift. Lewis he was called and quite the catch too, if you ask me.'

Morgan smiled at her. 'If I was single, he probably would be, but I'm not, Brenda.'

'I know, I'm just saying if I was a few years younger I'd be chatting him up. Nice that he's chasing after you. Does he know you're happily tied down?'

'I met him this morning for ten minutes if that, on enquiries I might add, so no he'd have no reason to know anything about my personal life.' Morgan hoped that she hadn't given Lewis a rundown on her personal life, as Brenda thrust the books towards her.

'Wonder if he likes older women.'

'He runs a book club. Why don't you go along and find out?'

'He does? I might, when is it?'

'Tomorrow at seven, upstairs in The Oddfellows Arms, Keswick.'

'Keswick? Blimey I'm not trailing there on my own, never mind. If you go, can I tag along with you? You like reading, it would do you good to get some interests away from this place.'

She turned and walked back to the lift, leaving Morgan

smiling. She always talked to her the way her mum used to. She would quite like to join a book club and it might not be so bad if she took Brenda with her, so she wasn't on her own, plus she could see who the other members were and talk to them about Cora. She'd mention it to Ben.

She walked into the office, where Amy was eating a bag of cheese and onion crisps. Morgan placed the pile of books on her desk.

'Ben wants you to go to custody and bail Parker.'

'Already, that was quick.'

'There's been an attempted murder in Ulverston, same MO.'

Amy dropped the packet on the desk and wiped her hands on her jeans.

'No way, so soon?'

Morgan nodded.

Amy scurried out of the door to get down to custody, leaving Morgan to gather what she could to take to the scene with her. She looked at the ancient cracked white clock above the desk: it was almost seven thirty; she had been at work for twelve hours and had no idea when she would be calling it a day. She found herself sitting on the edge of Des's old desk, which now belonged to Cain, and closed her eyes for a moment. It felt like forever since she'd tried to run up Loughrigg Fell at five thirty this morning, and what she would do for a huge slice of cake filled with buttercream, jam and covered in sticky, sweet icing to give her a sugar rush and a boost of energy she so desperately needed. She needed something, anything, to keep her mind focused on the two cases, because things were about to get a whole lot more complicated than they already were.

SEVENTEEN

Ben sped through the lanes and roads to reach Ulverston. The girl had been airlifted to Preston or was about to be, which was an absolute miracle in itself that she had survived such a violent and vicious attack. He had told her he knew the way to Birkrigg, and he didn't at all, but he did accidentally drive past a sign for a Starbucks drive-through, and Morgan could have kissed him.

'Turn next left, please, I'm desperate for coffee and cake.'

He smiled at her. 'Your wish is my command.'

'And while you're ordering, I'll get the directions up on the satnav, because I know fine well this is the main road into Barrow and it doesn't go anywhere near Birkrigg Common.'

He snorted. 'Guess I'm busted.'

'Guess you are but get me caffeine and you're totally forgiven, Matthews.'

When he passed her a blonde roast, two shot, white chocolate mocha she sighed in delight, closed her eyes and sipped the sweet drink with a rapturous smile on her face. He also passed her a bag containing two cakes. She was eating her brownie before he'd been passed his latte. When he drove away, he looked at her.

'Next time can you get a bog-standard drink. I thought I was speaking a different language ordering that.'

Morgan laughed. 'Sorry, but sometimes a latte doesn't cut it. Do you know how many days I've been deprived of cake and sugar?'

'Why are you depriving yourself, Morgan, what's the point?'

She sipped her coffee and thought about it. Why was she doing this just to beat Cain in some stupid competition? 'I don't know really, other than to prove I can beat Cain.'

'Why do you care if he can run faster than you? It's never going to work.'

'Why not?'

'Human physiology for a start. He's so much taller than you, his strides are far longer than yours, so the odds are stacked in his favour and not because you can't beat him but because of his height. Honestly eat the cake, drink the coffee, although only if I don't have to order them for you.'

He winked at her, and she smiled. He was right, this was stupid but if she was anything it was stubborn, and she wouldn't give in that easily, just like she wouldn't stop hunting the creep who was promising beautiful women a chance to have their photos taken, then killing them in cold blood.

This time, following the direction of the satnav, Ben carried on until he reached the turnoff for Swarthmoor and followed the directions until he passed an Esso garage and a farm selling ice creams called Cumbrian Cow Ice Creams.

'Why are there so many cool places around here? There's an Aldi, Starbucks, M&S and an ice cream drive-through. Maybe we should transfer to Barrow and work this area?'

'What, and give up our sedentary lives in Rydal Falls? And you need to get out more if you think a couple of supermarket chains are cool.'

He was smiling at her, but she thought he could be right.

'What would you think if I joined a book club? They meet once a month in a pub in Keswick, plus Cora went to it; be a good way to speak to people who knew her. Brenda wants to come too, would you mind?'

'Morgan, you are your own person, you can join whatever clubs you want, you don't need to ask my permission. I think that's a great idea, and you love books, it's perfect for you.'

'Brenda thinks the guy from the bookshop, Lewis, is cute. He brought me some more books and left them with her.'

'Brenda thinks every male is cute.'

Morgan laughed. 'You're not worried I'll get caught up with the book guy and run away with him?'

'I wouldn't blame you if you did. He's more your age and likes books; he kind of sounds like your ideal man.'

She turned to look at him. 'Are you being serious? Wow, I'm glad you're ready to fight for me to stay in your life.'

'I love you more than anything, but I would never hold you back or step in the way of you being happy. What you see in me I don't know, and I can't figure it out, which proves how special you are, and I love you more than I've ever loved anyone.' He reached out and clasped hold of her hand. 'But I need you to know that if you are ever unhappy then you can walk out of the door with no guilt or regrets. I'd be devastated, but I'd survive, and it wouldn't affect our friendship, because I love you so much that to have you in my life in any way would be enough for me.'

She kept hold of his hand, turning to stare out of the window so he couldn't see the tears threatening to fall from her eyes. He was so kind and thoughtful; it broke her heart to hear him speak this way, because she knew deep down that he was wishing he'd said the same to Cindy and given her the chance to leave and get on with her life, with no bitterness or regrets, rather than her get drunk and slit her wrists. Bleeding to death on their bathroom floor when she could have asked for a divorce. She had left him with a lifetime of guilt and regret behind his eyes that he masked well most of the time, but deep down he was still hurting every day and she knew that. She squeezed his hand tight.

'There's no fool like an old fool, huh? Ben, I love you too, more than anyone, so don't you forget that. I might go to book club with Brenda, but it's only about the books and to help with the investigation, okay.'

He lifted her hand to his mouth and brushed his lips across the back of it. 'Good, that makes me very happy.'

An explosive rattling sound filled the car and she jolted. Ben laughed. 'Cattle grid, I guess we're almost there.'

And like that they were back into work mode.

He drove along the narrow single-track road up a steep hill that twisted and turned through a farm and a few houses that were lovely, with glorious views, or at least she supposed they would be in the daylight.

'This is so nice, so secluded,' she said.

'And so bloody cold when the sun isn't shining too; they're exposed to all of the elements.'

She wondered where the stone circle was, and then as he drove around another steep bend her question was answered. Brilliant blue lights pulsated into the night sky signalling they were almost at the crime scene. She took several mouthfuls of coffee; she was almost ready to start again. It felt like she was stuck in that movie with Bill Murray, *Groundhog Day*, reliving the same day over and over until she figured out who their killer was and stopped him before he killed again.

EIGHTEEN

This stone circle was a flat walk not too far away from where the police vans and cars were parked. Will was waiting for them next to the scenes of crime van. There were police cars blocking the road to stop any traffic from getting too near, although Morgan suspected it would be chaos once word got out. There would be a flurry of locals who absolutely needed to walk their dogs as near as they could get to the scene. The common was covered in brown bracken and gorse bushes on either side of the steep hill. From where they were standing with the breeze blowing, Morgan could smell the salty sea air, which totally confused her because she couldn't see the sea or hear it.

'Thanks for coming so fast, it's appreciated.'

Ben nodded, and Morgan asked, 'Any news on the victim?'

'Not yet, she was unconscious but breathing when she was loaded into the air ambulance. I've got a car travelling to Preston to give updates and secure her clothing, take forensic samples.'

Somewhere in the not-too-far distance several sheep began to baa, and it made Morgan shudder when she remembered the one from this morning, lapping at the pool of congealing blood.

'I bloody hate sheep, and why can I smell the sea?'

Will looked at her and smiled. 'These have been rounded up and put in a field by a helpful farmer, but normally they're wandering around the common, so watch where you're stepping because there's sheep shit everywhere; and you can smell the sea because at the bottom of this common and across the road is the coast road and the tide is on its way in.'

He pointed to the protective suits, gloves and bootees. 'Help yourself, I've just stripped mine off, so I'll let you guys go and take a look without me peering over your shoulders. You know what you're doing.'

Dressing for the third time that day in the white paper suits that made Morgan's skin sticky and hot, they were like walking around in a personal sauna, and she was thankful it wasn't summer, or she'd end up a melted pool of human fat and hair in the bottom of her boots.

Will passed them both a Maglite torch. 'Joe, our duty CSI, has gone in search of floodlights and a tent, seeing as how the area is too dark to see much, but to be honest with you I'm thinking of sealing it off and keeping it guarded overnight. There's literally too much ground to cover and too much crap on the floor to be thorough.'

Ben shone his torch around and nodded. 'I'd agree with you, Will, it's risky. There's too much chance something could get missed; although I hate to be the one to break this to you, but the guy from this morning left nothing of forensic value that we could find, apart from the flower crown and garland. Wendy didn't manage to retrieve any prints. Where are those, did you remove them before she got airlifted?'

'We did, they're bagged up in the back of the van.'

'It still might be worth checking the garland for prints; and is there any chance he could be watching all of this from somewhere? Is there a good vantage point of the stone circle where he could keep hidden yet observe?'

Will turned to Morgan. 'What makes you say that? I mean

there are probably plenty, but we think he left the area in a black car.'

'Maybe the black car is a false lead. I got the distinct feeling this morning we were being watched as we worked the scene. It was creepy as hell.'

'I'll keep that in mind, thanks. That is really creepy if he is and very brazen.'

She turned to the path behind her. It was wide enough for them to walk side by side, bordered either side by gorse bushes and huge swathes of bracken. The ground was uneven and hard to walk along. She wouldn't want to run down it in the dark, as it would be too easy to trip and break an ankle. She'd done that and worn the T-shirt, not that long ago.

The beam illuminated the stones not too far in the distance and they were tiny compared to Castlerigg. Although here there was an inner circle and an outer one, the outer stones much flatter than the inner stones. There was evidence of the paramedics and air ambulance team by the flattest of the inner stones. Discarded packets lay on the floor, soon to be blown all over if the wind picked up. She shone the beam onto the stone and saw it was coated with a thick, dark liquid that she knew was blood.

'What do you think?' Ben's voice was just behind her.

'Has to be the same guy, similar scene, flat stones, throat cut, flower crown and garland. Why though, what is he doing or trying to prove, what's his motivation, Ben? Does he not like women in general, does he not like women who like to have their photographs taken? Is he against pagan traditions? because I'm pretty sure Ostara dates back to pagan times. Does he have a thing about witchy women; and if he does then the world is in trouble because there is some kind of witchy awakening going on at the moment, and almost every woman is in touch with her ancestors who died because they were wrongly accused of witchcraft and betrayed in the most horrific of ways.'

'Whoa, that's deep, Morgan. Too deep for me, but you could have a point.'

She wished she could speak to her aunt Ettie and get her perspective on it, she was the true epitome of a real life witch and the only one she knew.

'We need to pinpoint his motive, Ben, because we don't have long before he kills again.'

'But it's not Ostara after tonight, is it? So what reason would he have to keep on killing?'

She shrugged. 'I don't know, but he bought three flower crowns, so it has to mean something, right? Is he mocking the Holy Trinity, by choosing three victims?'

'You lost me at the witchy awakening, I'm not even going to pretend I know what you're saying now. Can you help a guy out?'

'I'm just thinking out loud, I don't know if any of it makes sense. How many stone circles are there in Cumbria, I know they're all over the country, but the killer chose one in our part of the world so I'm assuming this means something to him or her? There have been no reports or bulletins to suggest this has happened elsewhere before. Therefore, I think he knows the area well enough to avoid the times it would be full of tourists, so he had his privacy to do what he needed to. I think we need to have them staked out, have undercover cops in place so if he turns up with another victim, they can stop him before he tries to kill again.'

She took out her phone and typed the question into the search engine, and when it finally loaded she blew out a long breath.

'It says there were some fifty stone circles in Cumbria at one point.'

'No, there can't be.'

She turned her phone towards him, and he squinted at the writing on the screen.

'We can't put cops on forty-eight of them, there aren't enough of us to go around.'

'Then we're going to have to go back to the office and figure out which ones to narrow it down to. He's going to try again, Ben; he won't stop until he's done all three.'

'What if he does? Maybe he got scared – this was a close call, he could have got caught. He almost got caught, it might make him lie low for a little while.'

'Let's tell Will and see what he thinks. I've seen enough here; this place is creepy in the dark.'

Morgan began to pick her way across the path to get back to where Will was waiting for them, leaving Ben looking around at the circle.

When she reached him, she asked, 'Do you want the good news or bad?'

'All of it.'

'It's the same guy, has to be. The chances of two different killers with the same MO are zero, unless they're working together. He bought three of those flower crowns, so I think he's intending to take his third victim to another stone circle and do exactly the same. The only problem is, did you know there used to be fifty stone circles in Cumbria alone? We only have another forty-eight to narrow down the search.'

Will let out a sigh. 'Bollocks.'

She shrugged. 'It's exactly that.'

'Should we go back to the office and discuss this where we can keep warm?'

Ben joined them. 'I'd say that's a decent idea.'

'Morgan, you two head off, you know where our office is, get yourselves a brew and make yourselves at home. I'll just wait for Joe to get back and tell him the plan, then I'll join you.'

'Thanks, Will, what are you going to do about the black car? Is there a patrol that can check the petrol stations to see if one has been through since the call came in, or if there is one parked up nearby? Are there any police CCTV cameras on the coast road?'

Will shook his head. 'I've got PCSOs checking the petrol stations and supermarket car parks to see if there is one parked up with someone inside. I'm afraid we don't have CCTV along the coast road, but we do have ANPR cameras which would pick it up if it passed through.'

She smiled at him, knowing what a huge task this all was, then turned and headed back to the car where they stripped off the suits, gloves and shoe covers, dropping everything into brown paper sacks, then headed back towards Ben's car.

NINETEEN

Barrow was a much bigger police station than Rydal Falls, which was a smaller version, similar in design but there were far more staff working in this one. Despite the size of it, apart from a duty sergeant on the phone in the office, the place was empty. Everyone was out either looking for the small black car or on scene guard. Morgan had worked here for a couple of weeks when Marc had tried to split her up from the team, but it hadn't lasted, and he'd been forced to admit he'd made a mistake. She led Ben up to the first-floor open-plan CID office and they took a seat at a desk that had no personal things on it. Ben dragged another chair over so they could share.

'What's your plan for searching the stone circles, Morgan, and don't say you haven't got one because you always do, even if you don't always tell me what it is.'

She logged on to the computer and brought up Google, where she began to search Cumbrian stone circles. 'My plan is to get a map of all of the stone circles and begin to tick them off, or to at least try to narrow it down to a manageable list. There should be some we can cross off because of the location. Some of them aren't easily accessible, so I think we can rule those out;

it needs to be within walking distance with parking close by, so he can make a swift escape after he's committed the murder. I can't see him walking a couple of miles to do it, especially if he's carrying a body, because we don't know if he's drugged them first; the results aren't going to be back for a while yet.'

She sent the image and list of them to print, then went to retrieve them while Ben updated Marc on what they had so far. There were little plastic drawers with stocks of stationery supplies by the printer, so she took out four highlighters, a notepad and Post-it notes. When she got back to the desk she stared at the list. Realising if she put them into north, south and west Cumbria she could group them together and look at how accessible they were with regards to using them as a killing field. It sounded awful, but technically that's what they were, killing fields, all of the stone circles were in fields. Some of them, judging by the locations, were easier to reach than others, and who knew one county would contain so many of them? What was that about?

She could see Ben; he was pacing up and down, something he also did when he was super stressed, and her heart skipped a beat. He looked so handsome, but he also had deep creases on his forehead, indicating the level of stress he was under, and she worried about him especially after his heart scare. She didn't ever want to think of her life without him in it.

Placing her supplies on the borrowed desk, Ben looked at her and grinned.

'Good one, stealing the office supplies from another station. You never fail to impress me, Morgan.'

She laughed. 'It's for work purposes, so not stealing at all. Are you okay? You look so stressed.'

He looked around then leaned towards her and pulled her close.

'As long as I have you, I'm always okay.'

'That's not what I mean.'

'I'm worried, I can't stop thinking about what's driving him to do this and who he is going after next and, by the way, just in case he has his sights set on you, please don't go anywhere on your own.'

They were standing so still the automatic lights blinked off, and his lips kissed hers; she kissed him back with a lot more passion than she should considering the circumstances and moved slightly at the same time, and the sensor kicked in and bathed them in harsh, white light. They both jumped apart like a couple of school kids caught kissing behind the bike shed, but she didn't care. They were professional almost all of the time, so they were allowed to be human occasionally.

She winked at him and sat back down; head bent she began to use a different colour highlighter to underline the stone circles still standing for each part of the county. South Cumbria, which they covered, had four; the west, which included Keswick, Workington, Whitehaven and surrounding areas, had nine; the north, which covered Penrith, Carlisle and Kirby Stephen, was the ultimate winner though: it had fifteen.

'This is going to take some time, unless we know an expert on stone circles, because I need to research each of them, look at the surrounding area and see if they are accessible by foot and not too far away from a road. Even then it's not to say that it's going to work, I might be grasping at straws.'

'No, that's good. It's better than the nothing we have to work on at the moment. It would be great if they could trace the car. I'm praying that it went through an ANPR camera or patrols have found it.'

She didn't think any of that was happening because there wasn't much activity over the airwaves, but they had to keep optimistic and hope that it was all going on behind the scenes. Voices filtered up from the atrium below and she recognised them as Will's and Adele's. A few moments later she heard the sound of the lift doors opening, and they greeted them both with big smiles.

'Not found our guy yet, but patrols are still looking. There's a lot of ground to cover, lots of places he could have parked up until the heat dies down along the coast road and the multiple little villages that lead off from the main road. I'm not going to lie, it's like looking for a needle in a haystack.'

She nodded, and Ben answered, 'It always is when it comes to something of this magnitude.'

'What about a briefing?' Morgan asked.

'I don't know about you, but I have every available officer out either on scene guard or searching for that car. I know you have your own case to get back to, so if we discuss what we have now you can both head back to Rydal Falls. Thankfully our victim seems to be holding up, and has gone into surgery. The surgeon thinks she's got a decent chance of survival thanks to the woman who found her; she's an off-duty paramedic, she saved her life. Talk about being in the wrong place at the right time.'

'That is so brilliant. He's either going to be scared and go into hiding or he's going to be furious and escalate.'

Morgan looked at Ben. 'I'm not sure he can escalate any further, one dead, one almost dead in the space of a day.'

Will was nodding. 'What's your plan, Morgan, I'd appreciate your take on what's happening up to now?'

'Firstly, we need to check that Jay Keegan, our victim Cora Dalton's partner, doesn't have a small black car, then there's Lewis, Jim and Elliot, her business neighbours who knew her well: we could get Amy to check that out just to make sure we've ruled them out. Also, there was a photographer, Oliver Parker, he was supposed to be photographing Cora, so we need to find out how our suspect managed to intercept her on the way to her photoshoot. Did he pretend to be Oliver and change the location? It's possible that the killer knows Oliver well enough to know who his clients are, so we need to ask him about this.

'We need to get the tech unit to check Cora's phone for any messages regarding this morning,' added Ben.

'He plainly has a thing for these stone circles, and he bought three of those Darling rose flower crowns, so he has another victim lined up. You can't just find three women on the spur of the moment who want to have an Ostara photo session. If we can figure out how they found him: did he put adverts in the local paper, Facebook, Instagram, is he known to the witchy community as someone who does photoshoots.' She turned to Ben. 'Ettie.'

'What about her? Do you think he'd go after her?'

She shook her head. 'I can't see her wanting a photoshoot, but she knows the local witchy shops and the women who run them, most of them stock her herbal teas. She might be able to give us something. We need to go speak to her.'

'Who's Ettie?' Will asked.

'My aunt, who is a kitchen witch; she lives in the middle of the woods and makes the most amazing herbal teas. She's got a pet raven called Max and she's pretty cool.'

'I love her already; I want to meet her one day. Tabitha King is also part of the witchy community, or so I was told.'

She laughed. 'I'll introduce you, Will.'

Will went across to a flip chart in the corner of the room.

'Give me what you have.'

Ben nodded at Morgan to continue. 'Flower crowns were bought from Rustic Rose in Ulverston, ordered on Monday, collected first thing yesterday morning. They keep fresh in a fridge for up to five days the florist said. No details given, cash sale, description vague, he did a good job of disguising himself. CCTV enquiries ongoing, and I think the florist was coming here to try and do a photofit of the suspect. Cora Dalton – found at Castlerigg Stone Circle by her group of yoga friends who found her body. She was supposed to meet them there for an Ostara session. She owns a witchy shop called Black Moon in Keswick.'

Will was bullet-pointing everything she was telling him.

He continued. 'Our vic is Tabitha King, she has a small shop in Ulverston called Past Lives; it's off a side street, and she does tarot readings, is a psychic from what I've been told and quite a good one.'

Ben stared at him. 'Maybe not that good if she didn't see this happening.'

Morgan turned to him. 'He said psychic not fortune teller, big difference.'

Ben gave her the look that said he didn't have a clue, but he shut up anyway.

Will said, 'Do you think the victims knew each other?'

Morgan nodded. 'Maybe. Cora and Tabitha might have been in contact with each other. There aren't that many businesses like these in the area, so it would make sense if they knew each other. If we can figure out a connection to them it might lead us to our guy.'

'We'll know more when we can interview Tabitha. She should be able to give us his contact details, how she found him.'

Morgan looked from Ben to Will. 'What are we going to do about the potential third victim? How many witchy shops are there? Maybe we need to find out and warn any that are owned or run by women. Go speak to them and see if they have a photoshoot arranged. Will, what about Annie's shop? Do you want to speak to her about it?'

Will grinned at her and nodded. 'Yes, I will talk to her, but it's shut for two weeks for a refurb, the kitchen is getting replaced so I'm not too worried about her, but I'll double check she hasn't been speaking to any photographers just to be on the safe side. Also, that's brilliant, we can do that. There can't be that many, I'll get my team to look into all the ones in South up to Bowness; you take the ones from Ambleside onwards.'

Ben agreed. 'We'll do that and in the meantime we'll see if we can narrow down his next kill site, or at least Morgan will.'

They stood up, Will reached out and shook first Morgan's and then Ben's hands.

Morgan liked him, he was a good detective and despite his years of experience he still put everything into the cases that came his way. In some ways he was very much like Ben, down to earth, hardworking, cared about the victims and his staff, which made him even nicer.

They bid goodnight to both Adele and Will, then left the station to drive back to Rydal Falls.

TWENTY

There was no disputing the fact that both of them were exhausted, it had been a long day, but Morgan was still buzzing with the need to keep working, to keep going until she fell asleep at her desk. Ben drove them home, which surprised her; she had been deep in thought and hadn't realised he wasn't at the station until she looked up and saw his house.

'Why are we home?'

'Because neither you nor I are machines, Morgan. Will's team is out searching for our guy, and there's a huge possibility he's still in that area or even lives in that area, if he bought the flower crowns and picked a victim from Ulverston; he might have chosen Castlerigg as his first kill site because it's very grand.

'We can grab a bite to eat, and a few hours' sleep before we go at it again.'

He got out of the car and before she could argue with him had opened her door for her. He held his hand out to her, and she took it, letting him pull her up.

'Thank you.'

He lifted her hand to his lips and brushed them across it. 'My lady.'

This made her laugh. 'Sometimes I think you're a little too old-fashioned and delusional, but it's cute in a way.'

She followed him up the steps and into the house. 'You go shower, I'll make something to eat.'

'You sure?'

'I'm not tired yet.'

He left her in the kitchen, where she began to make toasted cheese sandwiches, comfort food and to hell with the bad dreams that cheese was supposed to cause. She had enough of them without blaming it on some mature cheddar before bed. The truth was she was tired, but she wasn't ready to give in and call it a night. She was itching to look at the stone circles and see which ones could lead to potential sites for their killer; she also wanted to research the witchy shops that were in the area. If they could speak to all of the owners, they might find someone who knew the killer. Good old-fashioned police work could solve these crimes.

Ben came downstairs to a plate full of hot melted cheese sandwiches and sighed. 'Are you trying to give me nightmares or a heart attack?'

'Both, don't be so dramatic. Are you telling me you don't want them?'

He took the plate from her. 'Absolutely, in no way, shape or form am I saying that. It's just an observation.'

'Well, go observe from the sofa and put your feet up.'

He did as he was told, and she opened her laptop. Sitting at the kitchen table she began to look for the shops they might be able to at least go and warn the owners. She really wanted to go and visit her aunt Ettie, but wasn't sure if she could spare the time to make the trip. She decided she would phone her first thing; even though she didn't own a shop she was well connected in the community. Morgan didn't think Ettie fit the profile because both their victims had been much younger than her aunt, but she still wanted to warn her, and pick her brain on witches. She knew there was the gorgeous shop, Lady of the Swan and Stars, owned by the lovely Harriet, who made the most amazing candles, because she bought them herself. She would contact Harriet on Messenger and warn her in case she had a photo session booked; but this was an online shop and Morgan was going to concentrate on physical shops that the killer may have been inside and looked around.

She nibbled on her toastie as she listed the shops. There weren't that many so they should be able to speak to all of them tomorrow. Hopefully, they weren't too late, because he may have already set his next crime in motion and arranged to meet his victim. She stopped, she needed to focus on the stone circles; Ben could ask Amy and Cain to contact the shops and go speak to them in the morning. She was getting sidetracked.

She didn't see Ben was watching her from the doorway.

'You need to put that away, Morgan, and come to bed. We have Cora's post-mortem in the morning.'

She looked up from her laptop; he was right, she did and as if to prove it she let out the hugest yawn ever. 'I'm okay, but not yet. I'm too worked up to sleep.'

He shrugged. 'Half an hour, even if you can't sleep you can lie down and keep me warm.'

'Okay, night.'

'Night, I love you.'

She looked up at him. Even though it was March, and he was in his M&S Christmas pyjamas covered in wild animals wearing Christmas hats that she'd bought him, he still looked too damn good. 'I love you more.'

He turned and went up the stairs, leaving her sitting in the dark in the kitchen, her mind racing over so many different things it would be impossible to switch off. Unless she had a cup of her aunt's Sleep Well tea. She'd made her a fresh batch not that long ago. Her insomnia had cleared thanks to Ettie's concoction and the crystals she kept by her bedside table, but some nights she still found it hard to drift off because of the horrific crimes she'd worked on over the past couple of years. The faces of the victims she'd never been able to save played on some loop that only really kicked in once she lay down.

Morgan messaged Harriet, who replied instantly to say she had no plans to go for a photoshoot and would let her know immediately if someone asked her if she was interested. That one ticked off her ever-growing list, and she stood up to make herself a cup of Ettie's tea. She could sip it while looking at the stone circles of Cumbria until she was tired enough to sleep.

The three biggest were Castlerigg in Keswick; Swinside in between Millom and Broughton in Furness – though the latter was on private land so she didn't think this was an option – the third was Long Meg in Penrith – this was a possibility – it was a six-minute walk from the place where you could park to the stone circle, not too far to have to engage in conversation with a potential victim and, if he was strong enough, he would be able to carry an unconscious woman for that distance. Birkrigg and Castlerigg were only a minute away from the road, though. She sat back, the tea had cooled; she'd been sipping it while staring at the pictures. The circles were fascinating and she'd quite like to visit them without the imprinted memory of seeing a muti-lated body draped across them.

She let out a sigh, *what is the point to all of this? Are you seeking revenge on witchy women? Having the audacity to blatantly sell their wares and live their lives on their own terms? Who would care in this day about any of that?* She let out a long yawn, the tea was working.

Closing the laptop, she went upstairs to bed, where she

could already hear the gentle snores from Ben. At least he hadn't had any trouble drifting off. As she lay down next to him, she thought over possible motive and the reason for the murder and attempted murder: something was there, at the edge of her mind, but she couldn't grasp what it was. Maybe tomorrow she would figure it all out; hopefully, before anyone else got killed.

TWENTY-ONE

Morgan had expected to wake up to a phone call to say another body had been found, so when the alarm on Ben's phone went off it took her a moment to realise what was happening. They arrived at the office before anyone else, desperate to carry on looking for the next potential stone circle and catch up with the team who were on nightshift for an update. She walked over to the board to see if anything had been added and saw a note left by the nightshift duty sergeant:

> *Keegan, Boothe, Heywood, Jim Edwards and Parker all spoken to and alibied. King is stable in ITU, full notes on file for reference.*

Morgan sighed, she'd been hoping that they'd fail to speak to one of them, to give them the lead that they so desperately needed. She looked at the clock. It wasn't too early, and she knew Ettie was always up at the crack of dawn. Ettie's phone went to voicemail without so much as a single ring and suddenly Morgan couldn't help but worry that something had happened to her.

She went into Ben's office. 'Ettie isn't answering, can I go check on her?'

He looked up from his computer. 'She isn't? Does she always?'

'Pretty much, I won't be long.'

She turned to leave, and he called after her. 'Wait a minute, Morgan. I have a briefing, so I can't go with you. Can you at least wait for Cain or Amy?'

'No, sorry. If I think there's anything wrong, I'll call in for backup and wait outside.'

Ben was shaking his head and she knew he thought she was a pain in the backside, but this was her aunt, her only living relative and while she knew that the likelihood was that she was out in her garden or on her way to a market somewhere, she still had to check.

'Be careful, you know the drill, Morgan. Any funny business and you wait for officers to go inside first.'

'Yes, boss.'

She grabbed a set of keys off the board and was out of there before he could change his mind. Driving out of the car park as Cain drove in, she waved at him, and he mouthed, 'coffee', to her. She nodded; she would bring some back... they were going to need it.

Morgan loved the short walk through the woods to get to Ettie's cottage, but she couldn't shift the feeling of unease that had settled in her stomach, although her aunt's little white van was in the car park, relieving a little of the trepidation she felt, so hopefully she was at home. The first time she'd stumbled upon the cottage she'd had no idea the quirky, beautiful, amazing woman who lived there was her aunt. It had taken several visits to remember the right path through the trees, but now she could do it with her eyes shut. A loud caw from above her as Ettie's raven Max flew above her, made her look up.

She waved. 'Hi, Max.'

He led the way, as he'd done in the past, and she couldn't help but feel as if she had entered a different world, one in which all of the fairy tales she'd loved as a child were alive. It was such a shame that life-sized gingerbread houses weren't real or that the Magic Faraway Tree wasn't located next to Ettie's cottage, because it wouldn't surprise her one little bit if it was. The dense trees cleared enough that she could see the white walls in the distance, and she caught a flash of the purple door. She had read somewhere that a purple door was a sign a witch lived in the house. She would have to ask Ettie if this was true, or if it was one of those things they made up on the internet. As she got closer the door opened and there was Ettie, standing with her arms full of blooms of wild white flowers. She beamed at Morgan and a wave of relief washed over her that Ettie was safe.

'Well, what a pleasant surprise, you're almost as early as this cow parsley. It's not supposed to flower until April and there is a clump of it growing out the back and almost taking over.'

Morgan walked up to her, and leaning forwards she kissed her aunt's cheek.

'I love cow parsley, it's so pretty. It reminds me of lace. How are you, Ettie?'

'I'm good, not too sure if I should be worried about you calling so early though, should I be?'

'Maybe, I don't know but it's always wise to take precautions.'

Ettie shook her head. 'I knew it was going to be one of those days this morning, when I woke up on the wrong side of the bed. I never sleep on the left side and yet there I was. I didn't even realise until I put one foot out of the bed, and everything was back to front.'

Morgan smiled. 'I'm sorry, I always seem to bring bad news.'

'Well get yourself inside and after we've had some tea and cake you can tell me just how bad your news is.'

She followed her aunt inside the quaint, cosy cottage that smelled of lavender and lemons, every shelf and surface stuffed with books, plants, jars of herbs and baskets of crystals. Ettie picked up a large empty jam jar, and filling it with lukewarm water she cut some of the cow parsley and arranged it. She turned around and placed it on the antique pine chest that served as a coffee table.

'There you go, take that with you to put on your desk at work and brighten that office up. I imagine it's a drab old dreary space with very few good vibes flowing through it.'

'Thank you, I will.'

Ettie smiled at her.

As she sank down into the wide, overstuffed, dark green velvet armchair, Morgan couldn't believe how simple yet pretty the delicate white flowers looked. 'You know I would quite like to stay here all day and do nothing.'

Her aunt laughed as she turned the stove on and put the kettle onto the gas ring to boil.

'You're welcome to, my love, but I get the feeling you, as per usual, are up to your neck in work, and it doesn't take any special powers to work that one out, dear. You work far too hard, as does your good man and, talking about him, where is Ben?'

'He's at the station. We have a terrible case, have you heard anything?'

Ettie shook her head. 'I haven't left the house since Monday; I'm supposed to be at the market in Kendal today, but I just couldn't be bothered. It threw me for six waking up on the wrong side of the bed, so I decided to give it a miss.'

'The body of a young woman was found at Castlerigg Stone Circle yesterday, she was murdered.'

Ettie's hand flew to the smoky quartz pendant around her neck. 'Oh dear, on Ostara?'

Morgan nodded. 'It was terrible. She looked so beautiful; she had a flower crown on her head and a garland of oak leaves around her neck.'

Ettie busied herself pouring the boiling water into the teapot, leaving the tea to steep. Then she took two cups and saucers out of the cupboard, placing tiny silver teaspoons on each saucer. When she'd finished, she turned around and placed the tray on the pine chest and sat opposite Morgan.

'Do I know the woman? I have this feeling inside of my heart, a fluttery, jittery feeling that I'm going to know when you tell me her name.'

Morgan shrugged. 'I don't know, Ettie, you might know her. Cora Dalton.'

Ettie's eyes began to shine as they filled with tears, and she bowed her head. Pulling a handkerchief out of her sleeve she began to dab at them. 'Cora, of Black Moon, in Keswick?'

Morgan felt terrible, it was clearly obvious that Ettie did know her. 'Yes, I'm sorry for your loss. Can I ask how you know her?'

'She used to come to me for advice and tea, such a lovely soul. She'd come twice a month, she loved being here, loved everything about the cottage and my little herbal teas. I taught her about the crystals and then I told her she should think about opening her own shop because she was a natural at reading cards. We worked on her card reading for a little while, but she only needed a few pointers. I'm so sad to think she's not here anymore, she truly was a beacon of light in this world.'

Ettie began to pour the tea, adding a splash of milk then passing a plate of biscuits towards Morgan. She smiled at her. 'Eat some of these, you look as if you've lost weight and you know that's always a worry to me.'

Morgan ate some biscuits; in fact she ate most of them while giving her aunt time to process the bad news. As they sipped the tea in silence there was a pecking sound at the window as Max tapped his beak on the glass. Ettie stood up and unlatched it, opening it wide enough so that he could get in. He sat there watching the pair of them, and Ettie took a biscuit, and crumbling it up she put it on the window ledge.

'He loves these shortbread thins, they're his favourite, aren't they, Max? Although I'm pretty sure he's not supposed to have a passion for M&S biscuits.'

He ignored her and began to peck at the biscuit crumbs.

Ettie released a long, drawn-out sigh. 'So, why was the beautiful Cora murdered so brutally, do you know?'

'Not yet, but she wasn't the only victim. Another woman called Tabitha King from Ulverston was found at Birkrigg Stone Circle, near Ulverston, under exactly the same circumstances. She was lucky; a paramedic out walking their dog found her and managed to save her life.'

Ettie's eyes widened in shock, and she was nodding. 'That was lucky, I don't know Tabitha, but I know of her. I've heard such good things about her. She's a psychic and a good one too; so your man is after women who would be classed as witches or at least modern day witches. Do you know why?'

'I don't know, I was hoping you might be able to help me figure that out.'

Ettie sipped her tea. 'He might be a modern day witch hunter. Is he on some kind of mission to take out the women who are blatantly advertising their magic, open about being a witch?'

Morgan nodded; she'd wondered if it was connected to their witchy ways, it had to be. Both Cora and Tabitha owned mystical shops, they celebrated Ostara, he'd known they would be tempted by a photoshoot, he must have done his research.

'Is he on a mission, seeking them out to kill them?' Ettie continued. 'I'm not one for Instagram, but I do know how popular it is in the community, how everyone is a hashtag witchy woman. You should check them out. I think Tabitha has one, though I don't know what it's called. I love it, I love that after all these centuries of being persecuted for being nothing other than wise, loving, nurturing and at one with nature that we're finally out there, comfortable in public. You have to ask yourself, though: why he is choosing these types of women? Was his mother a witch? Did she abandon him, abuse him or is he just a sick guy with a fantasy?'

'Wow. Do you fancy joining the team?'

Ettie threw back her head and laughed. 'Absolutely not, but I have a brilliant detective for a niece, so I guess hanging around with you is rubbing off on me more than I realised.'

'Why the flower crowns and garlands of leaves? What do you think of them?'

Ettie shrugged. 'Why not, they're pretty popular, well flower crowns are. What kind of flowers were in them? You know there's a whole lot of books about the language of flowers, I'm not so sure about the garlands of leaves. The druids were big on oak leaves, so you could find out if there is some connection especially with his choice of stone circles.'

'You think he might be a druid? Are they still a thing?'

'I don't know about that; I think they probably are, but the ancient druids were barbaric and often used human and animal sacrifices as offerings. So that would seem to connect, as the stone circles were their churches. Am I helping?'

Morgan laughed. 'Totally, my head is spinning. The roses were beautiful pink ones, called Darling roses.'

'Roses are well known to be the flower of love, but there are different meanings for each colour. For instance a pale pink rose could be used to convey the message of grace and femininity, darker pink, gratitude, admiration or he could have chosen them not because of the colour but because of the name.'

Morgan sighed. 'Or it might mean nothing at all, but thank

you. I said from the beginning it looked as if she was a sacrifice.
Do you know of any stone circles near to a road? We think that's
significant.'

'I only really know Castlerigg, and Long Meg in Penrith;
there's one at Ambleside or what's left of one.'

Morgan felt a chill blanket her shoulders. 'There is, where?'

'It's called Hird Wood, but compared to Castlerigg and
probably Birkrigg it's not as dramatic, or accessible. There are
only a few stones, though. I would have thought he would go for
something that looks the part if you're right about why he's
using the stone circles.'

Morgan's phone and watch began to vibrate, and she knew
without looking it would be Ben. She should have let him know
all was good. 'Excuse me, I better answer this.'

She told Ben she was fine and, relieved, he ended the call.
'Ben sends his love and asked that you don't go with any strange
men to have a photoshoot.'

Ettie laughed. 'Oh Lord, God help the man. Who would
want to photograph me? Don't either of you worry about me, I
have no intention of doing any such thing.'

Morgan stood up. 'I best get back, thank you so much.
You've given me lots to think about.'

'I hope you find him, Morgan, before anyone else gets hurt.'

She hugged her aunt and whispered, 'So do I.'

Morgan stopped off at The Coffee Pot for five coffees – no idea
if the DI was in but figured she better take him one in case.
He'd been a bit peeved last time when she hadn't brought him a
drink; she also bought five assorted brownies to share, to ease
the burden a little of the mounting pressure they were under.

The only thing of any consolation in the investigation was
that up to now no other bodies had been found. Maybe his close
call last night had scared him enough to go to ground until the

heat died off, which might just buy them a little time. Although she didn't think it would stop him entirely. Who knew how he was going to play this? He might want to be caught, be hoping to get caught.

She carried the coffees, managing to only spill a little before she reached the lift. There was no way she was risking stairs carrying this much coffee and her jar of cow parsley. As she pressed the call button with her elbow, she saw Brenda and smiled.

'Book club is on if you're still interested. I can pick you up.'

She nodded. 'I most certainly am, thanks. I'm working until six so it will be easier to just grab me from here if you want, save me walking home. I'll bring my best perfume with me.'

She winked at Morgan, who laughed before stepping into the lift and using her elbow again to press the button for the floor number. She didn't tell Brenda she had an ulterior motive for attending, hoping to speak to the other members about Cora and see if they could provide her with further information, or maybe even a suspect which would be the best result she could hope for.

She pushed her way into the office to find it was empty and sighed, placing the flowers on her desk along with the drinks. Grabbing her coffee, she went to the blue room to see if there was a briefing on. She was kind of praying there was, and she hadn't missed a shout come in on the radio to send them to another body. Voices filtered through the closed door, and she opened it to see the whole gang sitting around the oval table. Marc was at the front talking. He looked at her and nodded.

'Nice of you to join us, Morgan, but we've finished. Ben will update you.'

He glanced down at the coffee cup in her hands; Cain was also staring and mouthing the words 'traitor' at her. She turned around walking straight back to the office, wondering what developments there had been.

'Brookes, where's my coffee?'

Cain's deep voice called behind her, but she ignored him and went to sit at her desk. He came in behind her, took a look at the coffee cups and smiled.

'Phew, that was close. I'd have cried if you hadn't brought me something decent to drink.'

'Yeah, I guess I'm not a traitor after all.'

'Nope, definitely not.'

'What was that about?'

'Barrow think they found the car, but it was burned out down the docks area around the old paper mills. A patrol came across it once it was really burning. No idea where that is but sounds the kind of place to dump and burn a car; false plates on it and the VIN number was removed.'

'So if it's his, he's from that area. How else would he know where to go and burn a car? And how did he get away from there? She took a sip of her coffee and continued. 'Any news on Tabitha?'

'In intensive care but holding her own and unconscious.'

Morgan smiled. 'Glad to hear she's fighting.'

Cain went on. 'As to how he got away: foot, bike, another car, motorbike, possibly. They think he could have had a bike in the boot of his car and cycled away after torching it.'

'Are they checking the train station to see if anyone is captured coming through there on a bike in that time frame? And what about tyre tracks if it was a bike, or footprints?'

'Apparently it's all gravel and road so no evidence to suggest how he escaped.'

Ben appeared and stared at the coffee cups lovingly before picking one up and nodding. 'They're on it and checking if anyone on a bike passed any CCTV cameras, or even on foot walking away from that area.'

Morgan was trying to take it all in, what did this mean? Was he trying to lie low and get rid of his evidence?

Ben was staring into the paper bag full of brownies; he chose a mint chocolate one and began to eat it perched on the corner of a desk.

'Ettie came up with some good points. She asked if he was on a mission to kill modern day witches, and I think that he is. If so, what is driving him?'

Ben pointed to the board on the wall, and she added Ettie's idea to the list she'd already started.

- *Why stone circles – druid sacrifice, connection to druids?*
- *Which stone circle is he going to use next? Needs to be accessible by car or near a road both the others were a very short walk from the road.*
- *Mission Killer?*
- *Why witches – was his mum a witch, is he seeking revenge?*

'Hey,' she said, turning from the board, 'we need to figure out if Cora and Tabitha knew each other. That might give us a lead, if they socialised out of work or were part of any groups that he could have found them through.'

Ben was licking the tips of his fingers. 'That was good. Cain, you can't eat yours if you're in training, so I can take that burden away from you.'

Cain opened the bag and grabbed a gooey caramel brownie out of it. 'Appreciate that, boss, but I'm good, thanks.' He shoved the entire cake into his mouth and began to chew.

'Urgh, that's disgusting. You absolute pig, Cain.' Amy was shaking her head at him, and he shrugged.

Marc walked in and Morgan pointed to the drinks. 'Got you a latte and a brownie, boss.'

He looked taken aback. 'You did?'

'Yes, I can confirm that.'

'Thanks, Morgan, that's very kind of you and appreciated.'

She shrugged and smiled. 'You're welcome.'

He picked up the last cup and peered inside the paper bag, taking a chocolate orange brownie. The smile on his face was so natural it made her feel bad. He was getting better and not as much of a pain in everyone's backside now. She guessed he was becoming one of them and that made her happy. She liked a happy team and not one full of ups and downs.

Ben waved a hand in front of her.

'Morgan, we need to set off to go to the post-mortem in the next five minutes. Amy, do you want to take a look at the stone circles and see if there are any that fit as a possible kill site? Cain, can you try to find Cora's partner, Jay, and ask him if she knew Tabitha King; and also, when you're both done with those enquiries, let's get on with making sure the owners of any witchy shops have been spoken to and warned there's a killer out there who could be targeting them as his next victim.'

'Yes, boss,' came the reply from all three of them in unison, their voices filling the office.

TWENTY-TWO

Susie greeted them at the mortuary with her usual cheery smile. Today her hair was a mixture of violet, purple and turquoise; she had it shaved on one side with little diamonds cut into it, each one a different colour. The rest of her hair had been cut short too, with a long fringe that was clipped back. Morgan thought that it was her most outstanding hairstyle yet.

'Wow, I mean wow, your hair is amazing.'

'Aww, thanks, doll. I love it, although it's a nightmare to keep up with the colours, but now there's only me and my dog, I have to spend some money on myself.'

Ben was, as usual, speechless and it amused Morgan how he could never quite process the colour of Susie's hair.

'Oh, I'm sorry did you split up?' She couldn't remember her partner's name.

Susie shrugged. 'Yeah.'

'Hey, I might be going to a book club tonight in Keswick, if I can get away. I know it's a bit far from you, but you're welcome to come if you have nothing better to do.'

'I am? Wow, thanks, Morgan, that's kind of you. I'll let you know.'

Morgan wouldn't feel as bad for Brenda if Susie came with them, the pair of them could chat books while she sussed the other members out.

Declan came out of his office in a pair of green scrubs, and she had never seen him look more like Ryan Reynolds, which tickled her. He'd grown his shaved hair and had it cut in a similar style to the actor, with a matching beard thing going on.

'Susie, stop gassing and get these gowned up, will you? Morning both, I trust you're well?'

'I like your hair and beard, has anyone ever told you that Ryan Reynolds could be your brother?'

Susie let out a groan and rolled her eyes. 'You did not just say that, Morgan, his head will explode. One of the assistant funeral directors told him that last week and I've never heard the last of it. He went out on a Tuesday looking a mess, came in on the Wednesday looking like this.'

Declan looked at her. 'Away with you, I'm hardly to blame if I could double as a movie star now, am I? At least he can play me when they make a film of young Morgan here's disastrous life.' He clapped his hands. 'Shoo, people, I'm in a mad rush to get started.'

Ben, who still hadn't spoken a word, put his head down and headed towards the men's changing room.

'Hey, Ben, what have you been reading this month?'

Morgan felt for him, it was Susie's go to question to ask everyone and it made Ben physically squirm because he didn't read.

He didn't look back but replied, '*Mindhunter.*'

'Wowsers, great choice. Have you watched the Netflix series? It's amazing.'

He disappeared through the door without answering.

'He's stressed, but no, he hasn't but he definitely will be when we get the chance.'

Morgan followed Susie into the changing room, deciding

she was going to make him watch it to make up for covering for him. Susie disappeared out of another door, and Morgan tugged a disposable plastic gown off the roll on the wall, tying it around herself, and slipped some shoe covers and gloves on, although she wouldn't be getting close enough to touch anything. There was a box of masks next to the gloves, but she didn't bother with one. Cora wasn't decomposed; she had been found minutes after her murder and she could cope with the usual smells without too much fuss.

As she walked into the cold mortuary, for a moment, she could have mistaken the room for a spa with the relaxing music that was playing. She felt like she should be about to have a full body massage and not watch Cora Dalton's post-mortem. She looked around for the source of the music and spied an Alexa next to the Roberts radio. The music was coming from her. Ben was already there, looking uncomfortable as he tried to fix his gaze on anything other than the body bag on the table.

Declan breezed into the room and smiled at them both. 'What do you think? We've gone all high-tech thanks to Susie's girlfriend leaving her Alexa behind when she did a runner. No idea why we never thought of this before; it's so much easier to tailor the perfect music for each patient.'

Susie was busy setting the X-ray machine up and turned to him and frowned.

'She did not do a runner; she decided to move to Edinburgh.'

'Near enough, or maybe I should say far enough away from you.' He began to laugh, and Morgan was horrified for Susie, but she needn't have worried because she burst out laughing too.

'It's a good job I like working with you, Doctor Death, and you can talk, you go through men like—' she stopped mid-sentence as Claire and Wendy shuffled into the room, fully dressed in full PPE, suits crinkling as they walked. Their entrance had brought everyone's attention back to the body on the steel table, and the seriousness of the task that lay in front of them all to find Cora's killer.

Declan waited for the two CSIs to get organised then asked, 'Good to go?'

Everyone nodded, then watched as he began his examination, while chatting to Cora, telling her what he was doing and why as if she was a living, breathing patient; and Morgan couldn't love him any more than she did. He would have made a wonderful surgeon and no doubt save many lives, yet here he was and in his own words 'doing his very best for the patients who may have suffered terribly before they arrived in his care'.

'The body is that of a well-developed, well-nourished Caucasian female stated to be twenty-eight years old. The body weighs one hundred and thirty-five pounds and measures sixty-three inches from crown to sole of foot. The hair on the scalp underneath the blood is blonde; the irides are blue and pupils are fixed and dilated.'

Morgan found herself zoning out – she had heard this so many times. All she could think about was the stone circles and which one the killer might be going to use next. How had the victims come into contact with him? That was the question she needed to answer.

Declan, Susie, Claire and Wendy worked diligently, processing and documenting every little detail. Declan pointed to the long white gown.

'The clothes show horizontal distribution of blood.'

Ben was watching carefully. 'Meaning?'

'Meaning that her throat was cut while she was lying down, not standing upright. So, your guy managed to convince her all was good before slitting her throat.'

Morgan tried to imagine how Cora must have felt; she must have trusted whoever it was enough to lie down and close her eyes, only to have him come so up close that he was able to take a sharp knife and slice her throat open.

'Rigor mortis is fixed, and there are no defensive wounds on her hands so no signs of a struggle. Poor, poor girl I can't even begin to imagine the pain and terror she must have felt. One minute she was lying there happy and the next...'

Ben asked. 'Was she killed at the stone circle or somewhere else?'

He looked up at him. 'Although there was a lot of blood at the scene and she definitely bled out there, I think she was dead before she was taken there because I can see what look like finger shaped bruises above the cut. It was hard to notice them before because of the nature of the open wound and the dried blood, but it's likely she was strangled manually. Where, I can't say, but if she was already dead that would explain the lack of arterial spray.'

Declan went back to studying Cora's right hand, turning it from side to side. 'Her natural nails are clean.'

He continued, and with Susie's help removed Cora's clothes, taking samples, fingernail clippings, hair combings – all to send off for forensic testing. Declan didn't speak much except to Cora and the occasional instruction to Susie; he was unusually quiet, and Morgan thought that the sheer brutality of the crime had shocked him a little more than usual.

'The neck shows sharp force injury, so deep the larynx is visible through the wound. There are no hesitation marks. He didn't pause. He went for it, drawing the knife from left to right and deep too, but as I said there are some bruises on there. Wendy, can you get a close up for me of the wound and those bruises?'

Wendy stepped forward snapping what Declan needed, whilst he measured the marks.

'I wonder if the wound is as deep on Tabitha King?'

Declan looked up at Morgan. 'Who is Tabitha King?'

'Another victim, attacked last night, found in similar circumstances, with her throat cut, at Birkrigg Stone Circle – only she was saved by a passing paramedic.'

'Well, thank God she was. I don't think I could cope with two of these in one day. Did they catch the guy?'

'Not yet.'

'Mother Mary, it gets worse. Where is she now?'

'Preston.'

Declan looked from Ben to her. 'Guys, I don't ask a lot of you, but can you please find him like today? I can't bear to have to keep looking at cut throats. Out of all the ways to die, this one really makes me squeamish. It's the stuff of nightmares, just the thought of it. If you send me pictures of the wound I can see if they're similar, but I imagine she's been to theatre so it might be difficult.' He shuddered, took a deep breath then turned his attention back to Cora.

TWENTY-THREE

Cain found himself with his hands cupped around his eyes, staring through the window of Black Moon. He was there to see if he could find Jay, who hadn't answered his door when he'd knocked on the flat. There was movement at the back, but he couldn't tell who it was or even if it was Jay, because although he'd seen his photo that someone had stuck next to his name on the board and had his description, he hadn't dealt with him yesterday and couldn't tell from this distance. He knocked on the glass and a shadowy figure came into view. Whoever it was stood inside the shop, not moving, staring through the glass at Cain, who thought how awkward this was going to be. He moved to the door and waited for it to be unlocked. There was no sound of approaching footsteps and he knew that the boyfriend had been a bit of an asshole yesterday, until Ben had rugby tackled him to the ground. Raising his hand, he closed his knuckles and hammered on the wooden door so hard that it vibrated in its frame. He pressed his face to the glass again, but didn't see anyone this time. From this angle he could see the back of the shop and it looked as if it had been ransacked.

'Control from 1613, I'm going to need patrols to Black

Moon in Keswick; there's a burglary in process. I'm forcing entry, crime in progress.'

He didn't wait for a reply; instead he took a step back and ran at the wooden door with his shoulder. The door didn't stand a chance under Cain's bulk, and it gave, splintering open with a sound as if a gun had gone off.

'Police.'

Cain looked around the messed-up shop; there was no sound from anywhere. He pulled a pair of gloves out of his pocket and snapped them on then went further inside. The mess was by the narrow desk at the rear, where there was a small pink filing cabinet, next to a cash register.

He ignored the mess, instead looking for the person who had been inside rifling around. A cool breeze blew in from the open back door and he rushed towards it, out into the yard, and looked around frantically. He couldn't see anyone or hear footsteps. The back gate was ajar, and he tugged it open wide enough so he could get into the back alley that he'd not long exited after knocking on the door to the first-floor flat Cora and Jay shared above the shop. He went into the alley looking for anywhere his suspect could be hiding, scanning it as he went but keeping an eye on the shop, too, which was his responsibility now he'd put the front door in. He had no idea where his burglar had gone, but they were some runner to get to the top of the alley and out of sight, unless they were hiding.

'Control, is there a dog handler on duty?'

Cain would not bet any amount of money on their being one when he needed one.

'*I believe Cassie is on at seven. Do you want me to try and get hold of her now?*'

'Yes, please. I'm at the shop belonging to the murder victim from yesterday and it's clearly been broken into. The suspect is in the area or at least I believe they are. I think he was male and wearing all black. If patrols pass anyone matching that description on the way in, please stop them and check them out.'

'*Patrols attending the burglary, did you hear that? Description is male dressed in black heading in the opposite direction of Black Moon. Anyone matching is to be stop searched and PNC'd.*'

Cain also wouldn't bet on patrols coming across the suspect with such a scant description, but if they were anything like him and as diligent, they would hopefully speak to anyone dressed from head to toe in black. It wasn't lost on him that it could be the killer. If it was, he was looking for something.

'Control, one last thing. He could be armed and dangerous so proceed with caution.'

'*All patrols on route, approach with caution.*'

He was torn what to do: he wanted to search the alley, but he also couldn't leave the shop wide open. A guy came out of the gate next door, and he stared at Cain with a look of fear on his face.

'Is everything okay?'

'Police, did you see anyone running out of here or up the alley?'

His eyes wide, he looked up the alley, but the other end was a dead end.

'No, I'm from the bookshop next door. I've just come out to see if anyone needed help.'

Cain eyed the man; he was wearing a pair of brown cords and a beige jumper – he was definitely not the person he saw moving around in the shadows, unless he could change super quick and not break a sweat.

'Someone broke into Black Moon.'

For a second he thought the guy was going to burst into tears; his eyes began to water.

'Oh, no. What on earth is going on? It's bad enough we've

lost Cora and now her shop has been broken into. Some people have no respect. Does Jay know about it?'

'I'm trying to find Jay, that's how I discovered the break-in. Have you seen him today? Do you know where he could be?'

'He's not answering the door?'

Cain shook his head. 'Can I get your name, fella?'

'Lewis Heywood, from the bookshop next door. Jay could be at Cora's parents' house maybe. I don't know, he might be avoiding people and holed up in the flat.'

'How well did you know, Cora?' He'd been about to say the deceased and realised it sounded awful.

'Well enough that my heart is broken, and I couldn't sleep a wink last night thinking about her.'

'I'm sorry for your loss, Lewis, it's tough losing someone you care about.'

Cain looked at the guy again. He was around five ten, skinny, and didn't look as if he could fight his way out of a paper bag.

'Could you maybe keep an eye on the front of the shop from your shop for me, to make sure no one goes inside before my colleagues get here, while I search the alley?'

He nodded. 'Sure, no problem.'

He went back through the doorway and into the rear of the bookshop. Cain figured that his intruder wouldn't have run down towards the dead end unless he had somewhere he could duck into to hide, so he began to check the doors and open yards to see if there was anywhere, he could be hiding. His phone began to ring, and he saw Morgan's name and smiled.

'Hey, what's up?'

'I came to speak to the boyfriend and saw an intruder in the shop. I'm sure it was a he and he did a runner out of the back; I'm just searching the alley now the guy from the bookshop is watching the front of the shop till patrols arrive.'

'You dragged poor Lewis into this?'

'Lewis?'

'The guy from the bookshop.'

'Yeah, sorry, do you know him? In my defence he came out being nosey, so it's kind of what you get for being too inquisitive for your own good. Is he a suspect at all, Morgan?'

She laughed.

'Not even on the radar. Why do you say that?'

'I don't know, I'm just thinking that, he works next door. If he broke into the shop it wouldn't have been hard for him to escape. He'd have been back inside of his within seconds and he could have changed out of the clothes he was wearing, couldn't he?'

'I suppose so, but what's his reason?'

'Have we even nailed down a reason yet?'

She went quiet on the other end of the phone then whispered, '*Nope.*'

'Are you coming here?'

'Yes, Ben said we won't be long. Have you found Jay? because he also lives above the shop and if he's trying to make it look like a break-in, it wouldn't be that hard either.'

'Not yet, he's not answering the door.'

She hung up, and he turned around to stare at the steps leading up to Cora's flat. What if it had been Jay and he'd purposely not answered the door, so Cain thought he wasn't in and he was trying to mislead them and draw attention away from him by pretending to break into the shop?

TWENTY-FOUR

It was chaos outside Black Moon. Two police vans were parked outside next to Cain's car and the street was crowded with market stalls. Not to mention people. There were people everywhere. Morgan glanced across at Ben, and he looked as if he was in some kind of physical pain.

'Are you okay?'

He shook his head. 'Not really, this whole case is one big circus, there's so many tourists and people everywhere we turn. Look at this, whoever was inside of the shop could easily have slipped into the crowd.'

Cain came out of the bookshop. 'I forgot to say it was market day, sorry, boss.'

Ben shrugged. 'It's like disorganised chaos. Do you think whoever it is planned this?'

Morgan looked at the stalls that began a little further down from where they were congregated. 'Hard to say, but it's a good place to lose yourself if you needed to.'

Ben turned to look at the shop, the front door open and an officer standing outside of it while they waited for CSI to arrive.

'How did you get in?'

Cain pointed to the busted lock on the door. 'Had no choice, boss, had to put the door through but then the guy at the bookshop, Lewis, told me he has a spare key. Cora has one to the bookshop in case they needed to get in for emergencies. I checked: they are both listed as keyholders for each other's property.' Cain shifted from one foot to the other, unable to stand still he continued. 'I'm still not convinced he's not involved.'

Morgan was usually a good judge of people's characters, and she didn't get anything from Lewis except that he was maybe a little lonely.

Ben was nodding. 'Shame you didn't catch whoever it was in the act then we could have put this to bed.'

'Sorry, how was I to know there was going to be someone ransacking the shop while I was trying to get access to the flat above?' He shrugged and looked a little put out.

Morgan smiled at him. 'You weren't. We need to search the shop and figure out what he was looking for.'

'Crack on, Morgan, I'll hang around with Lewis. He makes a decent cup of coffee by the way – have you had one?'

She shook her head. 'If you think he's a suspect, how do you not know he hasn't poisoned it?'

Smiling at Cain, she turned and walked towards the flower shop, to speak to Elliot, the owner. As she reached the buckets of sweetly scented flowers on the pavement outside, she inhaled and sighed. This was much better than the depressing corridors of the hospital. Being outside in the watery March sunlight, even dark clouds and rain were better than the antiseptic smell of Declan's domain. They had left in a sombre mood. There was no denying that and things didn't seem to be improving, although this was an unexpected twist to the whole confusing case. Why would someone break into Black Moon? Unless Cora had something that could tie them to her. Elliot was standing in the window to the florist, arms folded across his chest as he watched the activity next door. He nodded at her when she walked in.

'Blimey, this part of Main Street has never been so popular. What the hell is going on now?'

'Break-in next door.'

He stared at her, his mouth open wide. 'No way, someone broke into Cora's shop? That's awful, my God some people have no respect.'

'They really don't. Did you see anything?'

'Not from in here. As you can see, I have to strain my neck to get a good view and that's with my face pressed against the glass. I've been busy all morning getting orders ready for delivery. I haven't paid much attention to anything. Well I hadn't until that police van screeched to a halt, mounting the pavement with flashing lights and sirens.'

Morgan had to stop herself from letting out a huge sigh. She felt as if they were going around in circles. 'Okay, thanks, I don't suppose you've seen Jay or spoken to him lately?'

'I haven't, poor sod. I popped a sympathy card through the flat letter box this morning, but he's not been around that I know of. Maybe he's gone to stop somewhere for a few days.'

'Do you have an idea where he might have gone?'

'He was very friendly with the yoga teacher who spent a lot of time at Cora's shop.'

Morgan felt her senses prick at this new information. 'He is?'

'Oh, I don't want to drop him in it. I mean the poor guy is grieving and all that.'

'But?'

'I saw them a couple of times and they were a little too close for someone whose mutual friend was his partner and her best friend.'

'You think they could be having an affair?'

He shrugged. 'I'm not trying to gossip and get him in trouble, or her, they're all very nice people, but I did feel a bit bad for Cora. Then again maybe she knew or turned a blind eye to it. She could have been secretly hoping he'd leave her for the super bendy woman.'

Morgan took out her notebook to write down what he'd just told her. 'Would you be willing to give a statement about Jay and Freya?'

He shook his head. 'Absolutely not, sorry but I'm not getting involved, please don't write any of this down, this is between you and me.'

'Cora was brutally murdered; you knew her, don't you care about us catching the person responsible for it?'

'I care, of course I do. I just don't like the police or getting mixed up in things way out of my depth.'

Morgan stared at him, turned and left. She was furious that he didn't care enough to give them something to work with, and she was also secretly gutted that Freya hadn't told her the truth. She'd really liked her, she seemed like such a warm, friendly woman and now she knew that she wasn't the good friend to Cora that she'd pretended to be, had probably been sleeping with Jay behind her back. It was low and mean, not to mention the ultimate betrayal there could be between friends. They had to find Jay and she wanted to speak to Freya again, to ask her if she'd been cheating with Jay. It made her question everything and if he was telling the truth, she felt angry for Cora who was the innocent victim in all of this and didn't deserve how she'd been treated.

As she approached Ben he asked, 'What's the matter?'

'According to Elliot, Jay might be having an affair with Cora's best friend – the yoga teacher.'

'The one who found her yesterday morning?'

'One of them, yes.'

'Interesting, what are you thinking?'

'That the pair of them could be involved and he could be hiding out at hers.'

Ben nodded. 'That's a possibility.'

'We need to go back and check, I'm so mad.'

'Why are you mad about that?'

'Because I really liked Freya, she seemed nice – she didn't come across as the devious, murderous type.'

'And you think she's betrayed your trust?'

'I don't know, I mean I hardly know her, it's just I don't like to think I would miss something of this magnitude. If they are having an affair we have a motive, don't we? And Cora would trust Jay implicitly if he told her to lie down while he photographed her. There is no way she would think he was going to do what he did.'

'We should check if the florist in Ulverston Photofit matches Jay's description. Do you think this Freya could be involved or is she blissfully unaware?'

'I don't know, but we have to find him and question him, and her too.'

Cain was listening and he sauntered closer to them. 'Why break into Cora's shop, though? He would have a key and he is the only person with a legitimate reason to be in there. Why risk all of this?'

'You have a very good point there, Cain. Why would he not just go in and search for what he was looking for?'

Morgan felt a surge of heat rise from her throat up to her cheeks, which pretty much matched the angry churning inside of her stomach. She felt it was all too much. It was all wrong, they were missing something, and she couldn't figure out what.

TWENTY-FIVE

Ben stood behind Morgan as she hammered on Freya's front door with her knuckles. The door opened and the woman stared at them, her eyes wide.

'Is everything okay, Morgan?'

She shook her head. 'Not really, is Jay here?'

'No, why would he be here?'

'Because the pair of you have been having an affair.'

Freya threw her head back and laughed, then stepped to one side and waved them in. For the second time, Morgan entered her house only this time she was angry.

She and Ben followed Freya into a lounge with two huge old sofas. Freya pointed to one of them as she sat on the other, tucking both her legs underneath her in what looked like the most uncomfortable position ever.

'Why did you laugh when I asked about Jay?'

'Because someone has been feeding you lies about me, and I can guess who. I am not and would not have an affair with Jay. I told you earlier he's got his problems and I am too jaded and sick of men to put up with his for a quick fling. Not to mention he's my friend's partner... was... I wouldn't do that to Cora.'

'Have you ever kissed him?'

'Yes, many times – on the cheek. It's how I greet my friends, a quick peck on the cheek. Tell me: did Elliot tell you that we were having an affair?'

'I'm not at liberty to disclose my source.'

Freya waved a hand in the air. 'He's a jealous idiot. He asked me out and I said no, actually I said no several times because he wouldn't let it drop.'

'Why would he want to make something up like that, if the information did come from him?'

'Oh, it came from him, trust me, I know it did. Have you checked his alibi out? He also asked Cora out many times, but she wasn't interested either. I bet he never told you that.'

Ben glanced at Morgan, and she realised her mistake: she had taken Elliot's word at face value. What if he was sending them on a wild goose chase to draw attention away from himself?

'Look, Freya, there is no judgement here, we just want to know if Jay was unfaithful to Cora or if he had a reason to not have her around, like a hefty life insurance payout.'

She turned her gaze from Morgan to Ben. 'I know he was sometimes angry with her; he was loud and would pick fights, but as far as I know they were never physical. Cora never had any suspicion he might be having an affair, neither did I. If anything he resented me because of how close we were. If I was you, I'd be looking into Elliot Boothe, because he's not the nice guy he wants everyone to think he is. He's got stalker tendencies; the way he would watch Cora's every move was downright weird. She would go out and he'd be out, it didn't matter which way she went, somehow, he'd know and bump into her. She even told me she was getting a bit freaked out by him. She didn't think he was dangerous but just odd.'

'Thank you, we will take a closer look at him. Is there a reason you didn't mention this before?'

'I think it was the shock about finding Cora that kind of messed me up. I'm sorry, I should have mentioned Elliot.'

'And one last question: is Jay here? We need to speak to him.'

'No, he's not here, but I can phone him for you and try to find out where he is. Have you checked Cora's parents' house? He might be there. He gets on well with her dad, they sometimes go fishing together. It might be worth calling there.'

They all stood up. 'Thank you for your time.' Ben nodded at her, and Morgan, who was feeling a little calmer, smiled.

Freya walked them to the door and waved them off.

As they drove away, Ben said, 'We need to conduct background checks into Elliot Boothe and also find Jay; but I'll get Amy and Cain to go chasing after Jay. We'll take this Elliot guy and see what more we can find out about him.'

'He knows how to make flower crowns; he also knew which florist to direct me to in Ulverston. Do you really think he would send me somewhere that would link back to him?'

'He sent you back to Freya though. We need to figure out who is lying and who is telling the truth, because right now, I'm not convinced either of them is completely innocent.'

Amy had printed out a list of the stone circles she thought had potential to be the killer's next site and stuck it on the whiteboard. Morgan walked straight over to it.

'Kemp Howe and Long Meg are both near to Penrith, right? I don't think he's going to go that far away; I think it needs to be more local to us. Ettie mentioned Hird Wood. Did that come up? Which is the easiest to reach on foot?'

Amy sighed.

'Hird Wood isn't very accessible; it's on the side of a steep hill and quite hard to find. According to a post I read it's a ten-minute walk from where you can park and that's if you know where you're going. This is a right royal pain. It's taken me longer trying to figure this out than anything I've ever done before. I'd rather be out on endless house-to-house enquiries.'

Ben grinned at her. 'Well then, your wish is my command. Cain is coming to pick you up and I want you two out searching for Jay Keegan. Try Cora Dalton's parents' house first, he could be there.'

'Why do you want him again?'

'Let's just say we need to question him properly; he may be involved, or he may not but either way we need to rule him out for definite.'

Amy didn't say anything, but the look on her face was a picture. 'Is this a pointless exercise, boss, or is there a legitimate reason? Is he to be arrested or asked to come in voluntarily?'

'Whatever you think when you find him. If he won't come in of his own free will I'm happy for you to arrest him.'

'So, we're totally not thinking that creepy photographer is involved?'

'He's involved in something, but not these murders unless he's working with someone else. He was with us during the second attempt, which makes it hard to try and pin that on him. He's not into grown women, so I don't see a motive for him.'

Morgan wasn't so sure.

'I don't know, what if he's working with the killer? Of if the killer overheard. We need to find out if he has any friends or acquaintances who knew about the photo session Cora booked; otherwise, how was she intercepted if she didn't turn up to his session?'

It was Ben who answered. 'Maybe she wasn't. She could have told anyone about it and they could have messaged, pretending to be him to get her to meet them at a different location.'

Amy shrugged and walked out, leaving them looking at each other.

Morgan picked up the printout of stone circles, and started to read.

'I'm going to try and work out which one might be on his radar; also, what's the significance of the Darling roses; there has to be some personal meaning to him, because the florist said he was pretty specific in his choice of flower for those crowns. Darling roses aren't commonly used. Maybe he has mummy issues, and they were her favourite flowers.'

Ben laughed. 'I love that you always think outside the box. Who knows, maybe he did?'

Marc appeared and waved at Ben.

'Meeting now, got Will and his DI on conference call about the attempted murder.'

Morgan said, 'I'll take a look at Elliot Boothe's records.'

Ben nodded and followed the boss out, leaving Morgan in an empty office, breathing a sigh of relief at the thought of having a little space to herself and time to do her own research.

TWENTY-SIX

Morgan read the printed list of stone circles and noticed that none of them were as accessible as Castlerigg. Would he use the same one twice? It was anyone's guess. Setting aside the stone circles, she then began to search for information on Darling roses, and found that she could order them from an assortment of rose growers; the tea rose with its candy pink petals tinged with streaks of magenta were strikingly beautiful. There were also roses called Darling daughter, husband, wife, Jenny and Edith – but the flower crowns definitely looked as if they were the candy pink flowers. How on earth had the killer come across them? Did he think of the victims as his darlings?

Pushing herself back from her desk she lifted her feet up and balanced her Docs on the edge, stretching her arms behind her head. As she did so she knocked the stack of books that Lewis had brought in for her onto the floor. Morgan stared down at them, thinking she'd pick them up in a minute. She was exhausted. It had been nonstop since the phone call at the crack of dawn yesterday morning. She had to tilt her head to read the titles: *Pure Evil, Convicting the Moors Murderers, The Ultimate Serial Killer Factfile*. She smiled, definitely her kind of bedtime reading; but she could understand why the lovely people of Keswick weren't interested in them. Who wants to read about true crime when they lived in such a beautiful insular place or at least it was on the surface? She wondered if she would make it to book club later; if nothing pressing came in, she might, even if it was for an hour. It would be nice to get some recommendations for books that might lift her spirit and take her completely out of her comfort zone.

She picked up the desk phone and dialled the front desk.

'*Front office.*'

'Brenda, it's Morgan, are you coming to book club?'

'*Are you getting time off for good behaviour?*'

Morgan laughed. 'I'm hoping to.'

'*I can't go tonight, lovey; I forgot I said I'd visit my dad and take him some supper, but I will next time. You can let me know what book they choose so I can read it in preparation.*'

'Of course, I might not get there either.'

There was some shouting in the background.

'*Got to go, Kath's banging on the glass and shouting at the nice members of the public in the waiting room.*'

Morgan smiled, everyone knew Kath, she was a local legend, zooming around on her mobility scooter and shouting at tourists for no particular reason.

It was time to do the background checks on Elliot. She kind of hoped he was just a hopeless gossip and not some psychopath hiding behind his pretty flower shop. There was only one incident on file for Elliot: a broken shop window two years ago, and he was on record as the victim. She tried spelling his name several different ways in case it had been input wrongly, but nothing came up. Maybe he had been telling the truth. The only way they were going to know if Freya and Jay were having an affair, was if one of them owned up to it or they seized their phones. But while they probably had enough reason to seize Jay's they didn't for Freya's.

Ben came rushing through the door. 'Good news. We can go and speak to Tabitha King – she's awake.'

Morgan glanced at the clock on the wall and realised that she would not make it to book club and felt a wave of sadness for her lack of living a normal life, where she didn't work almost forty-eight-hour shifts, and the missed opportunity to speak to the other members about Cora. She felt a connection to her and wanted to know more about her life. Then she looked at the close-up of Cora Dalton's body that someone had Blu-Tacked to the board and felt that familiar spark of excitement take over that an eye witness or potential lead could bring about.

Tabitha must have seen the person who tried to kill her.

'What about Will's team? Do they not want to speak to her first?'

'He said he'd let us go first in case she can offer something up to help identify and catch our killer.'

Morgan bent down to retrieve the books, which she put back on the desk, then grabbed her laptop bag and jacket.

She followed Ben out to the car park and to his car.

'Are you not using a div car?'

He shook his head. 'We can go straight home if we take mine. Besides those white Corsas hurt my back, the seats aren't comfy.' He had a point, although nothing would be comfortable compared to the worn leather seats in his BMW that were moulded to his shape.

The car park at Royal Preston Hospital was carnage and it took Ben one whole circuit of the one-way system before he managed to turn into the right car park. His cheeks were red, and she knew he was stressed before he began to swear under his breath. They walked down the long corridors to reach the Critical Care Unit, where they then had to explain why they were here and wanting to speak to Tabitha King. The sister had looked them both up and down, then requested to see their warrant cards which they handed over obligingly.

'What's the password?'

Morgan looked to Ben hoping he knew because she certainly didn't.

'Baby Jane.'

'Hmph, right give me a minute.'

She turned and left them standing by the seating area.

'Baby Jane?'

He shrugged. 'Nothing to do with me, blame that on Barrow. I'm just following orders.'

She smiled at him, and he grinned back. 'Might as well take a seat, she might be phoning headquarters to confirm our identities.'

'Actually, I was making sure the patient was ready to see you.'

The sister, who had appeared again, smiled sweetly at Ben whose already burning cheeks took on a super high-powered glow.

'Thank you, we appreciate that. Is she ready to see us?'

'She's ready, one of my nurses will stay with you, if that's okay, to make sure she doesn't get too upset or worked up.'

He nodded. 'As long as they know this is highly confidential and anything we discuss must not be talked about to anyone.'

'My staff are all consummate professionals, Mr Matthews – they are aware of the confidentiality surrounding Tabitha.'

They followed her into a large, noisy ward, where she took them to a side room. Tabitha was sitting up in bed surrounded by machines and monitors that were beeping away in the background, buzzing as they monitored her blood pressure, heart rate and oxygen levels. There was a huge dressing across her throat, the skin around it stained orange off the iodine they must have used to swab it with, and there were also traces of dried blood on the gown she was wearing. Morgan realised that she may not be able to speak.

She stepped into the room first and smiled at the woman, who looked scared. The clinical smell reminded her a little of the mortuary only much milder.

'I'm very pleased to meet you, Tabitha. I'm Detective Morgan Brookes and this is my boss, Ben Matthews. Can we speak to you for a couple of minutes?'

Tabitha lifted her arm slowly and waved them in. Ben hovered behind Morgan, letting her take the lead. Tabitha was staring at Morgan who was dressed in her usual attire of all black, her Docs, her black coat and chipped black nail varnish. Then her gaze turned to Ben who was dressed far more like a conventional copper than she ever would, in his suit trousers, shirt and tie. There was a nurse checking the machines, pretending not to be paying much attention to either of them. Tabitha's eyes were glassy from the pain meds, and Morgan wondered if they should even be here, bothering her when she hadn't long woken up from what must feel like a living nightmare.

'We're very sorry about what happened to you and hope you can forgive our intrusion, but we are trying to find the man who did this to you. Would you be able to answer some questions? You don't have to speak if it's painful. Can you nod your head?'

Tabitha gave the slightest nod, then grimaced; she didn't attempt to speak. Morgan looked to Ben to see if he wanted her to lead, and he too nodded at her.

'Did you know the person who did this to you, before it happened?'

A tiny shake of her head.

'Can you describe them, or give us a name?'

Tabitha shrugged, then made a squiggle sign in the air. Morgan patted her pocket for a pen, pulled one out and realised she had no paper, other than her official notebook. She caught the nurse's attention.

'Would you have some paper Tabitha could write on, please?'

She stuck a hand inside her pocket and pulled out a folded piece of paper, and taking a clipboard from the end of the bed, she clipped the paper onto it and passed it to her.

'Thanks.'

Morgan stood up and passed the clipboard to Tabitha. She watched as the woman tried to write with trembling hands.

Stranger, leaflet through door with details on offering Ostara photoshoot, tall, hat, shaved head, friendly on telephone, blue eyes, scar on left hand, wore all black like you.

Morgan watched as she was writing, and realised that was why Tabitha had looked so fearful when she'd walked in – she must have triggered some bad memories for her – and she felt awful.

'Name?'

Mikey Black. Not from here, from Keswick or Ambleside.

'Phone number? Email?'

Leaflet at shop.

Morgan turned to Ben, he nodded and smiled at Tabitha. 'You're doing great, thank you.'

She bent her head and scribbled.

Caught him?

Morgan wished she could say yes, he was in custody, but shook her head. 'Not yet, but we will.'

Tabitha's eyes filled with tears.

'Can we search your shop for the leaflet?'

Yes, noticeboard in kitchen.

'Did he ever go into your shop?'

A slight shake.

'How did you get the leaflet?'

Letterbox.

'Would you recognise him again?'

She nodded twice then lifted a hand to her neck and grimaced.

Morgan took out her phone where she'd took some screenshots from Jay, Elliot and Lewis's social media profiles, along with some of Cain, Mads and Declan. Not something that was police protocol, but they were desperate. She turned her phone to Tabitha and scrolled through them, watching her for a spark of recognition but there wasn't anything, she looked at each picture with a blank expression.

The nurse turned to Morgan.

'I know this is important, but I think that's enough for now, don't you?'

'Of course, you've been a huge help, Tabitha. Where can we get a key for your shop?'

She made a patting motion on her legs.

'Do the police have your clothes?'

A slight nod followed by another grimace.

'Thank you so much.' Morgan reached out and took hold of Tabitha's hand. Gently squeezing it, she was surprised when

Tabitha placed her other hand on top and squeezed hers back in a tight grip.

Tabitha whispered, 'Thank you,' her voice barely audible, and Morgan felt her eyes prick with tears as she tried to imagine how scared and in pain she must be.

'You're amazing, Tabitha, so brave and you're doing brilliant, we will keep you updated.'

Tabitha made a slight nod again then she pressed her head back against the pillow and closed her eyes.

Morgan and Ben left her to rest and walked out of the unit. There was no sign of the sister and Morgan was glad; she already felt bad that they'd had to disturb Tabitha this way, and she didn't need it rubbing in how mean they were.

There was one thing, though, she thought as she walked out into the long hospital corridor, her jaw set with a steely determination. She was going to find Mikey Black and enjoy slapping a pair of handcuffs on him as she read him his rights and put an end to his reign of terror.

TWENTY-SEVEN

'We need to get into that shop.'

Ben was already on the phone. 'Will, can you meet me at Tabitha King's shop? Have you got the door key? Actually, did anyone seize a leaflet off the noticeboard for a Mikey Black, photographer?'

Morgan couldn't hear Will's response, but she assumed it was a no by the roll of Ben's eyes. She tugged at his sleeve and whispered, 'We're in Preston, Ben, they're going to have to go check and report back.'

'Sorry, mate, forgot where I was. Could you send someone to go and retrieve it? It needs sending off for prints and potential DNA; but also, can you get it photographed and a picture emailed to me ASAP? She was very good considering her ordeal, very helpful. Thanks.'

He pushed his phone in his pocket. 'What do you think? Mikey Black is his real name or some made-up bullshit?'

'You never know, he might not be as clever as we think he is.'

'I doubt it, he's probably called Aaron Smith with a full head of ginger hair.'

'What is it with you and gingers? I'm feeling victimised.'

He looked mortified and she laughed, elbowing him in the side. 'I'm not, it's a joke. What are we doing now?'

'Right now, we are walking down the longest corridor known to man to get to the worst car park ever known to retrieve my car and go back to the station.'

She looked down at her watch. If they drove straight back, she could make it to book club for the last thirty minutes. She knew it wasn't going to happen, but the thought had been nice for the second that it had entered her head.

'Why the long face?'

'I was hoping to go to book club, but it doesn't matter this is far more important. I can go next time.'

'Sorry, Morgan, I totally forgot. I really wanted you to go too, it would do you some good to have something else to think about.'

She smiled. 'It's okay, this takes precedence, I can always pop in the bookshop and ask Lewis what the book is for next time. Hey, do you think Cora had a leaflet too? We didn't find one, did we? I wonder if that's what he was doing when he broke in, looking for the leaflet and, if he was, he must be panicking for some reason about it. Maybe he overlooked something vitally important that is going to lead us straight to him.'

'God, I hope so. I really do, we could do with a break.'

She wasn't going to argue with him there, they desperately needed something, divine intervention would be good, and she didn't say what she was thinking: that if he'd broken into Cora's looking for a leaflet then maybe he'd also broken into Tabitha's shop. That was for the Ulverston patrols or whoever went there from CID.

Wendy came rushing out of the CSI office when she saw Morgan and Ben climbing the stairs, and yelled, 'I got something you might want to take a look at.'

Ben rushed up the remaining stairs that led to the first floor where the CSI was. Morgan close behind him.

'What?'

She grinned at him. 'I got me some prints from the shop.'

'You did not?' Morgan grinned back at her.

'You bet I did, well one excellent latent impression and a partial thumbprint.'

Ben was smiling too. 'Have you run them?'

'That's the bad news, whoever they belong to is not on the system.'

'Could they be Cora Dalton's? Or her partner Jay's.'

Wendy shook her head. 'They're definitely not Cora's, as she was printed before the PM, and they were put on file; her partner Jay's prints are on the system too, for an OPL when he was seventeen and just crashed his moped. They don't match his either.'

'Wendy, I thought you were going to tell me you had a match.'

'No, sorry. I have some to compare to the suspect, when you find them though, and prove that they were at the break-in; it's better than nothing.'

Morgan realised he'd inadvertently offended Wendy. 'That's great, this is really useful. When we bring him in, he can't deny being at the shop, thank you. Where did you lift the print from?'

'A shard of broken glass that was smashed in the rear door so he could put his hand through and unlock it.'

'Why do you think he didn't he wear gloves?'

'Maybe because he knows his prints are not on file, he's not scared, or he could have been panicked and was careless.'

Morgan sighed. 'He will be on record when we catch up with him though. Did you come across any leaflets for photographers while you were there?'

'No, sorry.'

'Don't worry, you were not to know. We just found out that he might have posted leaflets through and that's how he made contact with them.'

'What about other shops in the street? Have you checked with them?'

'No, good idea. I'll do that first thing.'

They carried on up to the next floor and the office, where laughter greeted them. Amy and Cain stopped whatever they were laughing at when they saw Ben's face.

'Are you two so happy because you found Jay Keegan and he's downstairs in custody waiting for me to interview him?'

Amy shook her head. 'No, boss, just one of his stupid jokes. We haven't found him yet. We tried Cora's parents, and the flat a few times, we even parked up outside the yoga teacher's address, but nothing.'

Ben walked into his office, and Amy whispered, 'What's up with him?'

'Same as everyone else, tired, stressed, it's not personal. I wonder where Jay is hiding out? Why does he not want to be found?'

Cain shrugged. 'The guy's partner was murdered, maybe it's all been too much for him and he needs a bit of time to process it all.'

'He's in the clear though. Wendy found a couple of prints from the break-in at the shop and they're not his. What if he's tried to harm himself? Do you think we should be treating him as a missing person?'

Amy peered over Morgan's shoulder to look at what Ben was doing in his office and pointed in that direction. 'Up to the boss, but I think so, yes, because numerous people have tried to locate him with no luck.'

Cain was at the board with a pen. 'So, where are we up to? I can't keep up.'

'We managed to speak to Tabitha King, bless her, what a brave woman. She could barely talk yet managed to answer questions. She got a leaflet through her door from someone called Mikey Black offering Ostara photoshoots. We need to focus on any witchy, new age kind of business tomorrow and see if they've had similar.'

Cain wrote the name down, then stopped and turned to look at them both. 'Mikey Black, that's an interesting surname, don't you think? I've only ever known one other person called Black.'

Morgan gasped. 'Des, Des Black. Do you think he's related to him?'

Amy's fingers were flying across the keyboard as she entered the name into the system.

'There's a Blackley, a couple of Blacks but both females, and definitely no Mikey Black on here and, before you ask, Des was an only child. He has an aunt who may have had a son, but who knows? I don't think this is anything to do with our Des.'

The mention of Des's name made them all share the same sad expression, his murder had affected them all.

'It's a pseudonym, it has to be, and maybe he's playing with us by using that name or it might be totally coincidental.' Morgan was staring at the board. 'Suspects – write these down, Cain: Mikey Black, Jay Keegan, Elliot Boothe – according to Freya, the yoga teacher, he is a bit weird and won't take no for an answer; he also is a florist, which is a big help, and he lives next door to Cora so would know her every move.'

Amy looked at Morgan. 'This Freya, she was Cora's best friend right, so she would also know what she was up to. How come she didn't know about the photoshoot? Wouldn't she have told her?'

'Not necessarily, she may have wanted to keep it a secret.'

'Hm, I'm not convinced she would. I'd tell my best friend.'

'Do you even have a best friend?' Cain was grinning at Amy, who picked up a ruler and threw it in his direction.

'Of course, I do. She's called Steph, but we don't see each other very much now she's got twin girls, though we used to tell each other everything.'

Cain nodded. 'What about you, Morgan, who is your best friend? And don't say Benno because I'll puke into my own hands.'

Morgan paused, she had to think because she hadn't seen any of her friends since she'd joined the police. Ben really was her best friend, along with Cain, Amy and Wendy.

'Declan, actually.'

They both looked at her. 'Declan aka Doctor Death that Declan?' asked Cain.

'He is, we talk all the time, and he always gives me great advice.'

Cain was shaking his head. 'You always surprise me, Morgan, just when I think you couldn't get any weirder, you pull that out of the hat. Good effort I say.'

'What about you, Cain, who's your best friend? Are you still seeing Bella? I won't puke in my hands if you say yes.'

A sad smile crossed his lips, and he shook his head. 'We still talk, we get on so great, but it's impossible having a long-term relationship when she lives so far away. I was going to say that you two are my best friends, so there you go.'

Amy laughed, and Morgan wanted to hug him she felt so bad for him. 'Thank you, that's sweet of you to say, but is this just bribery?'

'Nope, it's not, because I'm still going to whip your arse in the Keswick half marathon.'

She let out a loud groan. 'Christ, I'd forgot all about that for forty-eight hours.'

'Don't think you're getting off that easily, Brookes, you challenged me so technically it's your own fault.'

'I know.'

The phone on her desk rang, making all three of them jump a little. She picked it up.

'It's me, Brenda, there's a guy here a bit worse for wear wants to speak to you, lovey, doesn't want anyone but that goth copper who doesn't wear a uniform. I surmised he was referring to you. Can I get a job with you lot yet?'

Morgan laughed. 'I'll let you know when there's an opening, be right down.'

She stood up. 'Someone at the front desk for me, won't be long.'

She left them arguing amongst themselves over who was going to brew up.

TWENTY-EIGHT

Morgan poked her head in the front office to speak to Brenda and take a look at the CCTV monitor to see who was asking for her.

'He's gone into the toilet, looks familiar though.'

'Cheers, did he give you his name?'

She shook her head. 'Said you'd know who he was.'

This left her feeling more than a little perplexed. How would she know? She went into the waiting room and leaned against the wall, relieved to hear the tap turn on and the hand dryer in the toilets in case she had to shake this mystery guy's hand. There was some fumbling from the lock and then the door opened, and she stood up straight.

'I've been told you all keep looking for me. Can't you all piss off and leave me be, I'm grieving.'

Jay Keegan stumbled out of the toilet, almost falling into the row of seats and doing a somersault over them. His unkempt clothes, unwashed hair and face full of stubble making him almost unrecognisable.

'We have, why don't you come take a seat and I'll get you a coffee then we can chat.'

'About what? My dead girlfriend, the break-in at her shop or the fact that you all think I killed her?'

Brenda was watching them, ready to hit the red panic button on the wall in case Morgan needed backup.

'About the truth, that's all, we want to help. I want to help; I want to catch whoever did this to Cora and Tabitha. Who told you about the break-in, Jay?'

Jay's face paled. 'Tabitha, who is she? Oh God, don't tell me there has been another, please not that.'

He stumbled towards Morgan, who knew then that he wasn't their guy, and they were wasting time; but seeing as how he was here, she better make sure he got home somewhere safe, because he was drunker than Ben got when they lost the quiz and, now he'd come looking for her, she felt responsible.

She turned to Brenda and mouthed, 'Ben.' Then led Jay into one of the side rooms. He sat down on a hard blue plastic chair, looking around the confined space with not much room to move in. Someone had drawn a row of smiley faces on one of the magnolia walls in red ink, which he pointed to and shook his head in disgust before placing his elbows on the cheap plastic-coated wooden table then leaned his head on top of them.

'Can I get you a coffee, tea, water?'

He looked up at her not moving his head off his arms.

'Can you wake me up from this fucking nightmare?'

'I'm sorry, I wish I could.'

'It was Freya, she messaged to say something was going on at the shop. I loved her, I don't know what people have told you, but I did, and I was a prick to her at times. She didn't deserve that, I realise that now, but it's too late and I wasn't there to protect her when she needed me the most. Do you have any idea how that feels?'

The door opened and Ben stepped inside, and closing it softly behind him he spoke, 'I do, I have been in a similar situation many times. I let my wife down so badly when she needed me that she died, and I've let my current partner down more times than you could count when she did too.'

Jay stared at Ben. 'You have?'

'Yes, and it weighs heavy on my mind, but not as heavy as it feels inside of here.' He patted his heart.

Jay sat up and looked at Morgan. 'Can I have a glass of water, please?'

She nodded, unable to speak. She slipped out to go to the water cooler, Ben's words making her own heart hurt. She came back into the room with a paper cup of cold water and placed it on the table in front of Jay.

'Thanks.'

'In answer to your questions – I have not been having an affair with Freya.' Morgan raised her eyebrows. 'Freya messages me, she told me you suspect something. I tried to at one point, but she wasn't interested in me and told me to back off or she would tell Cora. I was an argumentative arse towards Cora. I didn't like the shop because it's weird and I don't get why women are so into this reading cards and lying on a mat covered in shiny rocks, but it did well financially – in fact it did far better than I could ever have imagined. She made twice what I make a year teaching, possibly more...' He took a breath. 'I've been staying with my boss, you met her at the school. She is a lovely woman who will help anyone in their time of need.'

'Beth Brown?' Morgan asked.

He nodded. 'You can confirm it with her, but please don't drag her into this and, before you ask, I'm not screwing her either. I couldn't stay in the flat. It's too Cora, it hurts my heart being in there and it's so empty without her. She had the radio on constantly. I miss her singing along and dancing. I phoned Beth from the pub, and she came to pick me up, after I got out of here yesterday. She made me eat, then told me to go to bed in her spare room.'

Ben nodded. 'Which pub? We need to confirm your alibi,

Jay, because this is serious. We've had another attempted murder, and I want to rule you out more than anything.'

Morgan wondered why Ben hadn't mentioned the finger-prints, but she guessed he was keeping those to himself for the time being.

'The Oddfellows Arms, it's our local; it's across the road from the shop. What happened?'

Ben sat down. 'A young woman was attacked and left in similar circumstances to Cora.'

Jay looked up at him. 'She survived?'

He nodded.

'Wow, good for her. I mean that's great, but I wish Cora had survived too. It's so unfair. She never got a second chance.'

Morgan reached out and squeezed his shoulder. 'Tabitha was extremely fortunate. There was an off-duty paramedic walking her dog nearby, and she found her and called for an ambulance. I wish that Cora had survived, too, I would have liked to have met her. I think we would have got on well.'

Jay turned to her and smiled. 'Yeah, she would have loved you.' He sipped at his water. The air inside the small room reeked of stale booze, lager and something stronger, not whisky, but gin maybe.

'Have you checked out that weirdo Elliot from next door?'

Morgan purposely didn't look in Ben's direction.

'Should we?'

Jay moved his head up and down. 'He's all sweet and inno-cent with those flowers and stuff, but he's weird. I heard him asking Freya out and he wouldn't take no for an answer, then Cora told me he'd started hanging around the shop and bugging her to go out for a drink.'

Morgan wondered if she should believe him – he'd said he'd spoken to Freya and his story was so similar – had they agreed on these lines?

'What did she do?'

'Said no, but he's always watching people out of the window.'

'Do you know why anyone would want to break into the shop?'

He shrugged. 'Not really, sick bastards. There's very little money in the till, everyone uses contactless these days. There's nothing of any real value in there either, I mean there are the books and boxes of tarot cards that seem to fly off the shelves.'

'What are you going to do now, Jay?'

'I'm going back to the flat. I guess I should in case whoever it is comes back to break into it. I'm not having someone rifling through Cora's personal stuff for whatever reason. I'm telling you now though, if I catch who did this, I won't be held responsible for my actions. I have nothing to lose now, it's all gone, my future isn't worth thinking about.'

Ben nodded and Morgan knew he empathised with Jay far more than he could ever know because he'd been there himself.

'How about you don't give up, Jay; instead of that you fight for Cora, you continue to live your life as hard as it is, because I'm pretty sure she wouldn't want you to stop living because she wasn't. She would want to see you succeed, to carry on for her sake.'

Tears began to pour from his eyes, and he buried his head back into his arms as he quietly sobbed into them.

TWENTY-NINE

Morgan had to do something to get rid of the pent-up energy charging around her body. She was so frustrated with everything that she changed into her Nike leggings, trainers and a long-sleeved running top. Ben had offered to cook, and she hadn't complained; she didn't like it or didn't enjoy it, not like he did. It didn't matter to her that he used every pot in the kitchen and made more mess than was humanly possible, she would happily clean it up if it meant that he could switch off from work for a while. She didn't feel like running, but she didn't mind a brisk walk and if she broke into a jog then she'd take that. It still irked her how easily she'd told herself she would beat Cain. As she set off with her new all singing, all dancing watch, she had promised Ben to keep to well-lit streets and not go off the beaten track.

She didn't think that whoever had killed Cora would have any reason to come after her, but she wasn't a fool: she knew that some people were driven by the strangest of reasons. She'd told Ben that she didn't live in Keswick, and she was convinced their killer did or had connections to it because the probability was that most killers committed their first murders in a geographical area they were familiar with or comfortable with, but she wanted time to think and clear her head. They were no nearer to finding Mikey Black than they had been this morning, but at least they had a name even though the description sounded nothing like Elliot Boothe. A couple of task force officers who were the elitist of the search team had been sent back to Cora's shop to look for a leaflet or anything that mentioned Mikey Black, and the high-tech unit had been told to fast-track Cora's phone to see if there was a connection to Tabitha or whoever this Mikey Black guy was.

She walked down the main street until she could see the steeple of St Martha's come into view. The church, despite all of its hidden horrors that had taken place there, was a beautiful place and she felt drawn to it.

When she reached the old, rusted cast-iron gates, she slipped through them feeling the need to go inside and sit on one of the worn wooden pews, even just for a few moments. There was a circular ring pull on the door that you turned to open it, and Morgan didn't expect for it to open, but it did. The musty smell of old books and an even older building filled her nostrils. There were some lights on inside and, as she walked in, there were a couple of tea lights flickering on the metal stand, where parishioners could light a candle and say a prayer for a loved one or themselves. She picked up a small candle for Cora and Tabitha, then tried to light it off one of the others, singeing the tiny hairs on her fingers and almost burning her arm in the process. She let out a small yelp.

'For the love of God, don't you drop that and set my beautiful church on fire.'

She turned to see Father Theo smiling at her from the vestry doorway.

'Theo.'

'Morgan. What brings you here? The service finished an hour ago if you were looking for that.'

She shrugged, trying not to see the horrific image of Des's body posed on the altar steps; even though it had been twelve months since his brutal murder it was still as fresh as the day it happened. She had to blink to clear it from her mind and, for a second, she wondered why she was here.

'I don't actually know, I just felt as if I needed some inner peace.'

'Well then, this would be the place. The whole reason for all of these churches is to give some solitude and inner peace to whoever might need it. Forgive me being so forward, but you look tired.'

She laughed. 'I'm knackered.'

'Then why are you dressed as if you're about to enter the London Marathon? Have you taken up running?'

'Not exactly, it's a long story, but I have a stupid bet with Cain I could beat him in a half marathon.'

'Pride is painful, can you be bothered? I mean if you can that's all well and good for you, but if you can't tell him that.'

'The whole station is running a sweepstake on it.'

Theo laughed. 'Oh, dear then you're screwed.'

He sat down on the pew closest to her.

'How are you?'

'Good, I'm waiting on a phone call from Declan, to let me know if he can get here tonight for a late supper.'

This made her smile, and her heart began to warm a little. 'That makes me so happy, are you both still getting along?'

He nodded. 'Like a house on fire. Who knew a guy who cuts up dead bodies for a living could be so much fun and passionate about life.'

'To be fair he probably thinks the same about a guy who works for God.'

Theo's laughter echoed around the church, and it sounded so good that Morgan joined in. When she'd composed herself, she turned to him.

'Thank you, I needed that and feel a little better for it.'

'That's what I'm here for, I keep telling you that. I worry about you and Ben. I heard about the terrible murder in Keswick, and I knew that the pair of you would be working it, then Declan said he'd seen you both earlier and I felt bad for you. It must be so tiring seeing this level of violence close up and so frequently.'

'It is, that's why I needed to clear my head.'

'I'm here anytime you need to talk. That's the one thing working for God has taught me: how to be a good listener.'

'Thanks, I appreciate it.'

'The paper called it the Ostara Killings, those poor women.'

'I can't figure out what his motive is. Why did he feel the need to kill and to attempt to kill them on that specific day?'

'Forgive me if I'm speaking out of turn – Declan didn't say anything about what had happened, but I've been thinking about it. Putting everything together and doing a terrible job of it. There's this whole movement of women who are calling themselves witches and, trust me, I think it's a brilliant thing, after the centuries of horrific crimes carried out against them, but maybe he has something against them, some reason why he hates them so much. I think of all the things I watch and read about, and a lot of these killers have a reason why they snap and take action after years of thinking about it. If you can figure out what that is, you might have a better idea of who he is.'

She knew this, but hearing Theo say it out loud brought everything back into perspective. What had happened to this guy to make him act out these fantasies? Something about Ostara must be very personal to him. What could that be? Did he get married, was it his birthday, did his wife leave him, did someone die on that day?

She stood up and smiled at Theo.

'It was good to see you, Theo, maybe when this is over you and Declan can come for supper.'

'I'd like that a lot, I enjoy your company.'

She turned to walk towards the door.

'Oh and, Morgan.'

She stopped, looking over her shoulder at him.

'We've come on leaps and bounds; you didn't try to accuse me of the murders. Thank you, it means a lot to me.'

Morgan laughed. 'Hey, there's time yet if we don't find a viable suspect.'

Theo's mouth dropped open.

'Gotcha.'

She walked out to the sound of his deep laughter echoing around the church and felt a little better. He was right: what was the link between the meaning of Ostara to the killer, and why had the killer chosen that particular day? But then, what did it mean for the potential third victim? Ostara was past now. Was there only ever going to be two? Had he only bought a third flower crown as a spare? Maybe it was over. There had only been the break-in at the shop today, no bodies had been found. She hoped so, for everyone's sake.

Her watch began to ring, and she answered it, telling Ben she was on her way back.

Morgan didn't want to be out on her own. She began to pick up the pace and broke into a gentle jog to get back home where, hopefully, Ben would have finished cooking and they could sit together and eat like a normal couple who worked a nine to five and didn't have to piece together cryptic clues to save lives and catch the bad guys.

THIRTY

Morgan had been busy; she had a selection of prints spread across her desk, all articles about Ostara. She already knew some bits, about day and night being equal, but she had no idea that modern day pagans and wiccans believed it was the time the goddess Eostre, who is the goddess of dawn, meets up with her reborn consort in the form of Pan or the Horned God. She was staring at pictures of a guy with the scariest horns, and it was freaking her out. So engrossed she didn't hear Cain get up from his desk and cross the room until he was staring over her shoulder and muttering, 'What the hell?'

She jumped. 'Jesus, you scared me.'

'Not as much as him I bet, what's this about?' He was pointing to the printouts.

'Research into Ostara.'

'Oh, well have fun while the rest of us go out on enquiries, won't you.'

'Where are you going?'

'Our very own god of CID, Marc, wants the shops canvassed all along Main Street in Keswick, again.'

Morgan gave him a pity grimace. 'Do you need a hand?'

'He was quite specific that it had to be me and Amy. Lucky you, he probably has something even better planned for you.'

'I hope not, I'm busy.'

He laughed. 'Yeah, maybe, don't tell him that if he pops in to speak to you and, whatever you do, don't let him see those, Morgan, he'll think you need time off.'

He tapped the side of his head with a finger, and she rolled her eyes at him, but gathered all the sheets of paper together in case he did come in and question her. It made perfect sense to her that there could be some weird connection between the victims and Ostara, or the killer and Ostara, she just had to figure it out before anything else happened. There was an itch at the back of her mind; she knew there was a personal connection. As she stared at the picture of the horned god she wondered if the killer thought he was the horned god and he was collecting sacrifices.

She glanced across at Ben's empty office. He'd gone to meet Will in Ulverston.

The phone on her desk rang and she knew it would be Brenda or Marc; they were the only two people who still rang: everyone else either instant messaged or emailed.

'Morning.'

'Morning, lovey, that nice young man from the bookshop is here asking to see you. He seems a little bit agitated. Are you free?'

'Yes, I'll be right down.'

She wondered what Lewis could want. Going downstairs, she waved at Brenda and walked straight out into the front office, to see him pacing up and down. He looked at Morgan and rushed towards her, grabbing onto both of her arms a little too tight for her liking.

'You have to help me; I don't know what to do.'

She looked down at his fingers that were gripping her elbows, his eyes darting from left to right. She pulled away from his grip. Brenda was watching them both to make sure she was okay, and she nodded at her. Brenda picked up the phone and Morgan knew she was calling for someone to come and help should she need it. The irony wasn't lost on Morgan that this was the second man who knew Cora to have come see her in a terrible state.

'Lewis, I need you to take a deep breath. We'll go into this room where you can tell me what's upsetting you. Is that okay, do you understand?'

He was nodding frantically. 'I don't know what to do. I don't know if she's okay.'

Morgan took hold of his arm and led him to the room where she'd sat and talked to Jay Keegan, what seemed like an hour ago. Lewis didn't take a seat, but he continued pacing up and down the small space, making her feel claustrophobic.

Morgan pulled out a chair and smiled at him. 'Why don't you tell me what's wrong?'

'My nan, I can't get hold of her. I've tried ringing, I've texted, messaged, sent her a WhatsApp and rang the shop. There is no answer. I drove there and it was all in darkness, so I went to her flat and there was no reply there either. She never not answers her phone.'

'Could she have gone away and forgot to tell you?'

He stopped pacing while he considered it, then shook his head. 'Nah, she would tell me. She wouldn't go somewhere and not say where she was going. She's responsible, she's older not reckless.'

'Have you ever not been able to get hold of her before?'

He paused. 'Yes, but only twice.'

'And what was the reason that time?'

'She was busy.'

'Lewis, have you considered that she might just be busy this time?'

'She owns a shop that sells witchy stuff in Kendal; she reads people's tarot cards for a living, Morgan, just like Cora.'

She felt a chill press against the back of her shoulders.

'What's it called?'

'Spellbound.'

'Wait there, I'll get patrols to go check.'

Morgan could feel the pounding of her heart as it pumped the blood around her body. She rushed towards the duty sergeant's office, where Mads was eating a sandwich.

'Who's Kendal cover?'

'Amber and Scotty, why?'

'I need them to go check out an address for me, it's called Spellbound. There might be a potential victim missing from that shop.'

He was nodding. 'Shop address, name of misper?'

She realised she hadn't asked. 'Hang on.'

She practically broke into a run the short distance to the room she'd left Lewis inside.

'What's your nan's name and address for both properties?'

'Violet Darling, the shop is on Finkle Street, and she lives at 13a Quarry Lane.'

'How old is she?'

'Sixty-eight.'

Morgan wanted to offer him some form of comfort but also not insult his nan at the same time. 'She's quite a bit older than the other two victims, so hopefully this is a huge mix up and she's fine. She could be in a meeting or at a spa day, there are plenty of places she could be. I wouldn't worry too much.'

He glared at her with an expression of anger, causing his blue eyes to look much darker than they had last time she'd spoken with him and, for a fleeting second, she could see a look of pure evil that made her senses scream – and then it was gone. Back was the worried face of the man she'd met for the first time two days ago and had been so friendly.

'I'm sorry, I'm really panicking about her. She is so independent but very close to me, and she wouldn't ignore my calls and messages like this. Something is wrong and I'm scared to think of what it could be.'

Morgan rushed back to Mads and relayed the information to him.

'They're en route to the shop. Amber said she knows where it is.'

'Thank you.' As she turned to leave, he asked, 'Her grandson, have you checked him out? It's just a thought but you know.'

'We did initial checks on him the day of the murders and he's clean.'

'It still might be worth keeping an eye on him. He knew Cora Dalton, and now his gran is missing. Does he have any connection to Tabitha King?'

'Not that I know about, but thanks, I'll bear it in mind.'

She didn't tell him that she was already going to be doing what she could to find out more about Lewis.

He was still pacing when she went back to him.

'Lewis, do you know Tabitha King?'

His face wore a blank expression as he shook his head. 'No, why?'

'Just wondered, it's okay. Would you rather go home and wait there? I'll update you as soon as we know anything?'

He stared at her. 'I don't know: what would you do if it was your nan?'

Morgan didn't know, she'd never been lucky enough to know her grandparents, as they had died before she was old enough to remember them.

'I would be worried sick, but I'd also bear in mind that there could be a reason she's not answering. I think I'd rather be at home than stuck in this stuffy, poky room. Could she be with another family member?'

He shook his head. 'I've asked around and no one has seen her.'

'Have you got a list of friends, family we can check with? And do you have a photo of her on your phone I can print off?'

He tugged his phone out of his pocket and with a few taps had a picture of a beautiful, elegant woman who Morgan, if asked, would have said was in her early fifties. She was dressed from head to toe in black, and her steel grey hair was in a low bun with wisps hanging loose around her face. She had a pair of large gold hoops in her ears, and a tattoo on her arm of a witch riding a broomstick across a new moon, surrounded by delicate roses.

'Oh wow, I love her already. She is beautiful.'

He nodded. 'Yeah, hard to call her nan at times. She is younger in her ways than me and very, very spiritual.' His voice cracked and a river of tears began to flow down his cheeks that he couldn't stem despite furiously rubbing at his eyes.

Morgan couldn't stop herself, she leaned forward and hugged him briefly.

'Go home, Lewis, we'll find her and, as soon as we do, I'll let you know myself.'

He nodded. 'Thank you, Morgan, I knew you'd understand.'

She smiled at him, her heart breaking a little in case they were already too late to save this beautiful woman. She took a quick snap of the photo on his phone and walked him to the exit.

'I'll be in touch as soon as we've found her.'

He nodded, and she watched him walk to his beat-up old Mazda. He opened the door then stopped and turned to look at her.

'Hey, we chose *Strange Sally Diamond* as next month's book club read if you want to read along.'

She nodded her head. 'Thanks, I will do.'

'Yeah, it's on a Kindle Daily Deal today so it's only 99p. Or we have a couple of copies in the shop if you prefer a hardback.'

He got inside the car, and she lifted a hand to wave at him then turned to walk back inside. She would buy the e-book and if she loved it, would buy a hardback copy as well, because she adored reading in any format.

She paused and turned to look at the small black car Lewis had got in to. He had gone from super worried to talking about book club in an instant. And she had expected his nan to look like, what? she asked herself. She thought she would be old, with short white hair, wearing a twinset. She had not been expecting the elegant, beautiful, much younger-looking woman in the photograph. She changed her mind: Violet Darling fit the killer's profile. What if that killer was Lewis?

THIRTY-ONE

Amber parked on the double yellow lines as near to Spellbound as she could get, and it was still a minute's walk. Scotty jumped out of the van and with a few of his large strides was at the door before she'd even got out of the van. He was hammering on it, and she wondered if he was about to break the glass without even trying. She pulled on her hat after getting told off by Mads for getting her photo snapped at the last crime scene she'd attended without wearing one. Scotty hadn't bothered, as usual, and she sometimes wondered if he should have been called scruffy instead, with his too long hair and straggly beard that would drive her insane if he was her boyfriend.

As she caught up to him, she nodded. 'Maybe if you hammer a bit harder you might put the door through and save us a job.'

He snorted. 'Mads said this was urgent.'

She tucked her hands inside her body armour and watched as he moved to the large plate glass window to hammer on that. She bent down, lifted the letter box and shouted, 'Violet, are you in there?' Then turned to Scotty and shushed him. 'How am I supposed to hear anything with that racket? She might be ill or injured.'

A man of few words, he shrugged but stopped the hammering on the window.

A guy came out of the coffee shop next door.

'Problem?'

'Have you seen Violet lately?'

He nodded. 'Last night when she was locking up. I gave her a couple of cakes to take home with her, lemon drizzle and some Biscoff flapjack.'

Amber wished she had a neighbour who would give her free cake, she could just eat some flapjack. 'Was she okay?'

'She was fine, going home for a glass or two of wine and to catch up on the *Steeltown Murders*; she said she once lived in a village not too far from where it happened and remembered it like yesterday.'

Amber nodded; she had no idea what he was talking about. 'Did she mention if she was meeting anyone?'

'Sweetie, we chatted about the TV shows we'd missed with working every hour God sends, and she went home, it was a polite, neighbourly conversation. What's wrong? Is she okay?'

Scottie, bored of the conversation, joined in. 'She's missing.'

The guy opened his mouth so wide she could see the fillings in his back teeth.

'Oh my God, she's not.'

Scotty continued. 'Well, her grandson is worried she is, but she's probably not.'

Amber was usually the one to put her foot in it, and was shocked by his blasé attitude. She had learned the hard way how to be a little more tactful, after plenty of run-ins with Cain who had tutored her, and the neighbour who had slapped her across the face at the scene of a murder. Now she tried to think before she spoke, though it wasn't always easy, but she thought she'd improved slightly. She missed working with Cain;

compared to Scotty he was a gentleman and a damn good copper.

'Thank you, I don't suppose you have a spare key for the shop?'

He shook his head. 'Sorry, it's one of those things we talk about, yet never get around to going to get the keys cut. I'm worried now, she's so lovely. I hope she's okay.'

Scotty, who was now picking at a hangnail nodded, and Amber had a sudden urge to kick him in the shin.

'I'm sure she's fine and it's been a big misunderstanding.'

She walked off and Scotty called after her, 'Where are you going?'

'To check the back of the shop, basic policing 101, check all entrances and exits to see if they are secure.'

'I'll wait here in case she turns up.'

Amber bit her tongue; he was lazy too.

She turned the corner and walked along the backstreet until she found a wooden gate that had a small hand-painted sign on it that read 'Spellbound'. Pulling on a pair of blue nitrile gloves from the pocket of her body armour she tugged them on, hoping to find something that would impress both her boss, Mads, and Cain. She quite fancied working in CID one day, they got to wear their own clothes and not these awful, sweaty uniforms that stuck to her like a second skin. Plus, they seemed to actually enjoy coming to work. She often heard laughter filtering down from their office, when the report writing room had as much atmosphere as a viewing room at the undertakers.

The back gate wasn't locked. She pushed it open and stepped into the tiniest yard she had ever seen. There was enough room for a recycling box and a small rubbish bin; both of them had been spray-painted with glitter. The back door to the shop was painted black with a coat of the glitter as a topcoat. She knocked on this door too, but there was nothing but silence from the other side. Pressing down the handle, she let out a sigh of frustration that they couldn't gain access without having to get permission to put the door in.

'Control from 2623, the shop is in darkness and secure, we'll go check out the home address and take it from there.'

'Received, we'll await your update.'

She typed Mads's collar number into her keypad. 'Did you get that? Shop's inaccessible unless we put the door through.'

'Yeah, go check out her home address. I'd rather we put that door in first if we have to. There might be keys for the shop in there.'

He cut her off and she shook her head. He wasn't one for small talk, at least not with her.

Scotty was leaning against the small portion of wall in between the café and the shop, holding a small, brown bag by the handles. He was grinning at her.

'Been shopping while some of us are busy working?'

'Naha, that guy came out with a bag of cakes to take back to the station, but I reckon we should get first dibs, because if we hadn't come here, he wouldn't have felt the need.'

Amber's stomach let out a small groan of pure pleasure; she had badly wanted a cake and now there was a bagful, this manifesting stuff actually worked. She'd been listening to an audio book and a couple of podcasts all about changing her mindset, to try and help her have a more positive attitude at work.

'Come on, we need to go check out the flat.'

He followed her to the van, where he put the bag on the back seat and, despite the fact that she wanted to rip it open and stuff her face with cake, she didn't because it wouldn't have looked very professional at the scene of a possible crime.

'What do you think then? Think she's been taken by a homicidal maniac and sacrificed at some weird stone circle?'

'I don't know, I hope not, Scotty, I wouldn't wish that on anyone.'

He thought about this for a moment then nodded. 'Except for my ex maybe, she was a complete psycho.'

She stared at him. 'You can't wish that kind of thing on anyone. It's not good karma and, to be fair, you probably did drive her insane, because you get right on my tits most of the time.'

He began to laugh. 'Cheers, don't hold back, will you, just say it like it is.'

Amber began to drive towards Quarry Lane, which wasn't too far in a vehicle, and she cursed herself for not asking the guy from the café if Violet had a car or was on foot. At least it was an excuse to go back and next time grab a coffee.

Quarry Lane was a newer development, full of modern semi-detached houses and a larger building full of flats that were only leased to people over the age of fifty-five. Amber pressed the services buzzer, hoping it would still allow them access to the communal entrance. The door clicked, and she grinned at Scotty, who muttered, 'Open sesame,' then followed her inside.

It smelled like a combination of school dinners and a sickly sweet floral scent that turned her stomach. Scotty, oblivious, didn't notice and began to walk up the stairs to the first floor. She followed him, hoping that Violet was at home, and this had all been some big mix up, because it didn't seem right that there was a chance she could be lying on a cold stone circle some-where, dead. As tactful as ever, Scotty hammered so hard on the door that neighbours all along the corridor opened theirs and stared at them.

Amber smiled. 'Has anyone seen Violet today?'

Their heads shook in unison, making them look like a group of those bobble head toys.

She tried again. 'When was the last time anyone saw her?'

One woman next door but one stepped out. 'Yesterday, before she went to work.'

'You didn't see her come home? Was she okay?'

'She was fine, we chatted about next door, who has a new girlfriend and been keeping us both awake at night. Honestly, you'd think he was too old for that carry on, but apparently not.'

Scotty let out a snigger, then cupped a hand over his mouth and coughed.

'Do you have a spare key for her flat, or do you know anyone who does?'

'What's going on, is she okay?'

'Her grandson is worried, as he can't get hold of her. We're just checking to make sure.'

'He's a good boy is Lewis, such a sweetheart. I don't have a key, but doesn't he have one? I'm pretty sure he does. I've seen him go in when she wasn't here on several occasions.'

Amber nodded. 'I'll go ask him.'

'If he hasn't, there's a number on the noticeboard downstairs with the duty manager's phone number, they should be able to let you in.'

'Thanks, we'll do that. When was the last time you saw Lewis?'

'Couple of days ago, I think.'

She smiled at the woman then turned to go downstairs and phone the duty manager to come open the door. If not, they'd have to go check with Lewis; but why hadn't he told Morgan he had a key when he'd reported her missing?

THIRTY-TWO

Morgan's radio began to ring, and she saw Amber's number on the screen.

'Any luck?'

'*The neighbour hasn't seen her since yesterday morning, but she said the grandson has a key. Maybe you could go get that from him, because I've just rung the duty manager for the flats where she lives and there's been a sudden death at the other complex she runs, so she can't get here for a few hours. Unless you want me to put the door in, happy to do that.*'

Alarm bells were ringing inside Morgan's head. Why hadn't Lewis offered her the spare key? In fact, why hadn't he used it himself to go in and check? 'Ask Mads but I'd like you to put the door in.'

Amber laughed.

'*I thought you'd say that. I haven't got a whammer in the van, but I bet Scotty's thick head could do it.*'

'Haha, actually, I'll go speak to Mads then I'll let you know.'

She tucked the bulky radio back into her pocket and went downstairs, to see if Mads was still in the office. He was and he didn't look particularly happy to see her.

'Problem?'

'Yes, Amber can't get hold of a keyholder for the home address. Can she put the door in?'

'Are you convinced this is life or death?'

'Yes, are you not?'

He shrugged.

'Maybe I should ring the grandson and see if he can get here with a key.'

'How long will it take?'

'An hour, maybe?'

Mads shook his head and said, 'Your call, but the van with the whammer is sitting out in the back yard because it needed a tyre changing.'

'I'll take it to them.'

'I knew you were going to say that. I'll come with you.'

'No, it's fine. I don't mind.'

'It's not fine. If you get sidetracked and some maniac gets hold of you though, is it? Ben will kill me; and where is your boss, shouldn't he be keeping you under some sort of control?'

He was laughing but she knew that he meant it.

'On his way back from Ulverston.'

Mads was pulling on his body armour. 'On a jolly is more like it. Come on, let's go and get this over with.'

She smiled at him. 'I don't need a babysitter, I'm capable of driving a van to drop off a whammer.'

'I know you're capable, Morgan, I'm just covering my own arse should you get yourself in trouble. Do you know how many sleepless nights I've had worrying over what almost happened to you last time?'

She looked at him to see if he was being sarcastic and realised he wasn't.

'Why?'

'Because I let you go on your own and I felt responsible that you were run off the road by a violent killer, and then he kept you hostage until he could kill you.'

'You shouldn't, I'm a grown woman I make my own decisions and, granted, sometimes they're not the best, but it wasn't your fault; it wasn't anyone's fault.'

He began to laugh, a deep belly laugh, and she grinned at him.

'Not the best, that's the understatement of the year, Brookes. I worry about you because you are a damn fine copper, even if you're a liability; and officers like you are hard to find. Get smacked in the head with a hammer and knocked unconscious, most of my unit would have taken six months off on the sick to recover. Not Morgan, she's back at work the next day ready to dive straight back in. I think they broke the mould when they made you, kid.'

She realised he was being kind and not sarcastic. 'Aww, I didn't know you cared – that means a lot.'

'Yeah, it would mean more to me if you kept yourself alive when you drag me into a job.'

Sarcasm was his best defence and she laughed. 'I'll try, but I'm not making any promises.'

He walked out of the office. 'I guess that will do.'

Scotty was waiting for them at the entrance to the flats, and Mads said, 'Would you look at that, prime example of someone who would take six months off after a hammer attack. He's so idle he makes me pull my hair out. I had to put him with Amber because I know she won't take any crap and will make him work.'

Morgan laughed. 'That bad, I suppose he must be if he's having to work with Amber.'

Mads nodded. 'She's getting better, I think she misses Cain.

It wouldn't surprise me if she applied to do a secondment with you lot.'

She didn't reply, not sure how she'd cope working with Amber for a full shift.

They got out of the van, and Mads waved Scotty over. 'Whammer is in the back.'

He sauntered over and Mads whispered to Morgan, 'Tell me: if your life was in danger do you think he might break into a run?'

She shook her head. 'I won't count on it.'

'What's this? Pick up the pace, this is urgent, Scotty, or you out for an amble with the over sixty ramblers?'

Scotty slid the van door open and grabbed the heavy iron battering ram aka the universal key, as they called it. He gripped it in two hands and carried it towards the door. Mads slammed the van door shut and they followed him inside.

As they got up to the first floor, Morgan was relieved to see the doors were made from wood: if they had been composite doors there was no chance they'd have been able to get in without taking down the whole wall and wrecking the spot.

Amber smiled at her, and she nodded. 'Amber.'

Scotty, who had broken into a cold sweat, put the whammer down and wiped his hands on his trousers. 'Ready?'

Mads said, 'Smash it down, Scotty, with the least amount of damage if you can.'

Scotty picked up the bar and swung it back then hit the brass lock with an almighty crack. The lock splintered, and the door swung inwards.

Morgan had already pulled on a pair of gloves, and she motioned to the others to hang fire while she went inside.

As she stepped into the small entrance there was no awful smell, which was a good sign; although if Violet had been taken by the same killer there wouldn't be because he was never going to make a mess here and leave them with evidence they could forensically tie to him.

She walked into the lounge-small dining area and looked around. The entire flat was painted an off-white, with matching sofas. There were vintage oil paintings in gold frames hung on the walls, and it was not at all what she'd expected. It was stunning. The kitchen was all white and in pristine condition, there was a Nespresso machine on the side and a toaster – nothing else. The two bedrooms were also painted the same shade of white; the master bedroom had lots of plants on the windowsill, some beautiful statement pieces of clear quartz and smoky quartz crystals, and there was a bookcase crammed with books. The bed was made and there wasn't a thing out of place. She could quite happily live here herself. She'd been expecting black walls, and lots of sumptuous velvet cushions and throws, but not this.

It was clean, there was nothing to suggest anything had happened here. No sign of a struggle. Which could suggest that Violet had either gone away for a few days, without telling Lewis, or she had gone to meet someone of her own accord.

Morgan began to open the kitchen drawers, looking for a leaflet from Mikey Black, but she couldn't find anything like that. There were a couple of framed photos on the fireplace. She picked them up. In one Violet was with a much younger Lewis, and there was a photo of a younger Violet with a pug, standing in front of a huge stone. Morgan smiled. That dog was certainly a character, she loved it. Turning to walk away, she stopped dead and spun around, picking up the photograph again. It looked like part of a stone circle – it was just the one stone, but it was as tall as Violet. Morgan didn't have an evidence bag to put it in, but she took it anyway, she needed to try and find where the photograph had been taken.

'Anything?'

'Nothing at all, it's clean. Except this picture might be useful, I'll get it bagged up.'

She heard Mads muttering under his breath, and she went out in the hallway to join them.

'You two are going to have to wait for the joiner unless I can find a PCSO to take over. Actually, Scotty, you can wait here; Amber you take the van and, when he gets relieved, you can pick him up. I can't have the pair of you here doing nothing, I need someone out on patrol.'

Amber was grinning at Scotty. 'Yes, boss, see you later.' She turned and left them before Mads could change his mind.

Scotty was glowering at Amber's back; he then turned his attention to Mads. 'She's got the cakes in the van.'

'I'm sure she'll not eat them all and save you one.'

Both Morgan and Mads left him to it.

Mads asked her, 'What's your big plan now?'

'I better go back and meet Ben, see what he wants to do. Thanks though, I appreciate this. I want to check this photograph out. I think we're going to need Scotty to speak to everyone in those flats before he leaves, and to check the last time anyone saw Violet, so we can nail down a time.'

Amber, who was about to get into her van, turned to her. 'Her neighbour next door but one spoke with her yesterday morning, before Violet left for work, but didn't see her after that.'

'Thanks, Amber.'

Morgan didn't speak to Mads on the way back – there was too much going on in her mind.

She wanted to know why Lewis hadn't checked the flat himself. If he had a key, why would he not tell her that? She was also going to try and identify the location of the stone Violet was standing in front of in that photograph; and she wondered who the photographer was.

THIRTY-THREE

Ben was waiting for her in the office, a look of concern on his face.

'I'm glad you went with Mads, thank you for that.'

'I think we need to show Tabitha King a picture of Violet, and maybe of her grandson Lewis, too, to see if she knows either of them.'

She wanted to tell him she was quite capable of going out on jobs alone but stopped herself, knowing she was tired and frustrated and none of it was Ben's fault.

'I've already phoned the hospital and she's gone down for another surgery, so she's out of reach for hours.'

Morgan blew out a long breath. She felt deflated, there were obstacles in every direction. She held out the plastic evidence bag towards him and he took it, staring at the photograph.

'This is the missing woman, Violet Darling.'

'I thought she was older than that?'

'Look closer, where is she standing?'

He peered at it, trying to smooth out the plastic bag to get a better look, then he looked up at Morgan. 'It looks like a stone from a stone circle. Does it say which one on the back? Back in the days where we took actual photographs with a camera, and then got the prints developed, people would write the time, date and location on the back.'

Morgan nodded, took a pair of gloves from a box on the shelves and Ben passed the photo frame back towards her. 'Should I open it?'

'Is this evidence? Any possible forensics on it?'

'The flat was spotless, not a thing out of place and it was sitting above the fireplace.'

'Then open it and take a look.'

She cut along the sealed bag and removed it. Turning it over she used the tip of the scissors to open the small black metal clips holding the back of it in place, then removed it. The photograph fell onto her desk, face up. Turning it around she held her breath as she saw the tiny, neat handwriting on the back of it.

Our second meeting, sunrise March 20th 1998, at the stone circle. Love at first sight!

Morgan sighed. 'It doesn't say which stone circle it is, but what if we have this all wrong? What if he's using Ostara as a cover for what he's really doing? I think it's Violet who is his third and final victim, her surname is Darling it could be the link to the flower crowns. It all leads from this, whatever it is. I need to speak to Lewis and find out about Violet's past lovers, if she was married, and if he knows who she was dating in 1998. And what he knows about this photograph.'

'Or is this a coincidence and it has nothing to do with a past lover from nearly thirty years ago? Has Violet been targeted because of her shop and not her past?'

'Hmm, maybe. We need to ping her phone, Ben, if she has it on her. We don't know where she is, and I think there is a very real possibility that whoever is killing these women might have her.'

'But he didn't abduct any of the others, why take Violet? Unless she's already dead and we haven't been alerted to where her body is yet.'

'Then we need to send patrols to the stone circles, starting with the nearest two and working their way out from Castlerigg.'

He picked up the phone off her desk and rang the control centre.

'I need an authorisation for a cell site analysis of a mobile phone. Hang on, I'll get you the number.' He looked at Morgan and she let out a small 'oh' and shook her head.

'Scrap that for now, we don't know the number. I'll ring back when I do.' He hung up, arching an eyebrow at her. 'I think we need to talk to this Lewis and find out as many details about Violet as possible. I'll get patrols to check the stone circles like you suggested, but we're working this on too little information. Where does he live? We need to go visit him.'

'Above the bookshop next door to Cora Dalton's shop. Sorry, I've made a mess of things,' Morgan replied.

'No, you haven't. You were acting in Violet's best interests; I can't fault that.'

Morgan felt stupid. Why had she not taken down every last detail before putting Violet on the system as a missing person? She wouldn't normally do it with so little detail because it made it impossible to chase up basic leads without it.

She didn't speak but followed Ben out to his car.

He drove to Keswick and parked as near to the back alley as possible, so they could walk down it to the entrance to the flat at the rear of Lewis's shop.

'Morgan, how sure are you that Lewis isn't the guy we're looking for? He might be the killer. Have you seriously considered it?'

'I can't say either way. He seems like a nice guy, friendly, runs a book club, kind.'

'That's what they all said about Dennis Radar, BTK – he was a nice bloke, he ran the Scouts, was a church leader and the perfect family man. Then he went and horrifically killed so many innocent victims.'

'How do you know that?'

'I was reading that book about him you had in the bathroom.'

'You better tell Susie you actually read a book next time you see her.'

He smiled at her. 'I only read a couple of pages, but I'm being serious just because he seems nice...'

The bookshop gate was ajar, and Ben mouthed, 'Do we need backup?'

Morgan was torn. She wanted to say no, but what had that look been this afternoon when for a fleeting second the darkness in Lewis's eyes had scared her? He had a small black car. What if the one found burned out in Barrow had nothing to do with this case. She nodded.

Ben called Cain on his radio. 'Where are you?'

Cain's voice boomed over the handset. *'Keswick.'*

Ben frantically turned the volume dial down. 'I need you to come to the back of Black Moon ASAP, and hang around while me and Morgan go and speak to the guy from the bookshop.'

'On our way, boss.'

Morgan looked at Ben. 'Let me go see if he's in. If we go in heavy-handed, he might not open the door. I told him I'd give him an update. You're only a few feet away if I need help.'

'Absolutely not.'

'Ben, I don't think he's the guy. Why would he go to all this bother to kill his gran? It doesn't make sense. Please, let me see if he's there and then you can come join me when he opens the door.'

She knew he was thinking about the odds on it being

dangerous, but what could go wrong when he was literally twenty seconds away?

'Don't go inside and close the door, keep him talking but on the doorstep where I can see you and, Morgan, if he tries anything, you kick him in the nuts as hard as you can and scream.'

She nodded. She had to put right the colossal mistake she'd made by not taking a proper missing person's report, and now they were wasting valuable time here when they should be out searching for Violet. She walked up the steep metal steps to the flat door and used her knuckles to rap on it as hard as she could. She waited, listening to see if there were any signs of life coming from inside, but there weren't. Leaning over the railing at the top to reach the window, she knocked on that too, then back on the door even harder. Bending down she lifted the flap on the letter box and shouted, 'Lewis, it's me, Morgan, open the door.'

The flat was devoid of any sounds or movement, and she felt deflated. Where was he? She turned around and looked at Ben. 'Not in.'

She began to walk down the steps; it was hard, and she was glad she didn't have to navigate these on those late nights and early morning wake-up calls she got from the control room to attend crime scenes.

Ben's face was a picture of relief, and she smiled. 'Sorry, I guess you could say I've royally messed up.'

'Is there anywhere else he could be? Where does he hold the book club? or he might be in the shop still.'

She walked to the shop door and peered through the glass; it was in darkness with no sign of movement. She felt her heart do a double beat when she saw the stand nearest had a display of books with Castlerigg Stone Circle on the cover. She was pretty sure that hadn't been there when she was last inside. Was he blatantly gloating or trying to cash in on Cora's murder?

'We could try The Oddfellows Arms across the road, he might have gone for a drink.'

They met Cain and Amy at the end of the alley. 'It's okay we didn't need you but thanks, we're trying to find Lewis from the bookshop. His gran is missing.'

Cain looked surprised. 'She is? Isn't it a small world. Why is she missing?'

'We think it might be connected to the murder because she owns a shop called Spellbound in Kendal.'

Amy tutted. 'Who knew there were so many witchy shops around here? What are they like, sitting ducks for this maniac?'

Morgan looked at her. 'It appears so.'

'But how old is his gran? I mean Cora and Tabitha are what, in their late twenties? Why would he want to kill someone that old? She doesn't fit the victim profile we've built.'

Morgan agreed. That was why she was in this mess in the first place: she hadn't taken Violet's disappearance too seriously because Violet was much older than the others, not until she'd seen the photograph of her. Unless they needed to widen the victim profile because he was targeting anyone who sold witchy stuff, which made her stomach drop to the bottom of her boots.

She could feel her face going pale as she took out her phone and dialled her aunt Ettie's number. There was no one more openly witchy than her aunt; she even wore a velvet cloak to go to the farmers market in Kendal, where she had a stall selling her teas, crystals and potions.

'Morgan, what's wrong?'

She looked at Ben, fear imprinted in her gaze. 'Ettie.'

He shook his head. 'No, he wouldn't go after her. She doesn't have a shop for starters.'

'But she openly calls herself a witch, Ben, and she looks more like a witch than Cora or Tabitha. I can't say about Violet because I've only seen photographs, but...'

The phone went to voicemail, and she felt as if she was

struggling to suck enough air into her lungs. 'I want to go check on her.'

Ben looked torn and for the first time she wondered if he was going to tell her to behave herself and stop panicking. He didn't; he lifted a hand and scrubbed at the stubble on his chin instead. 'Let's see if Lewis is in the pub, then we'll split up. Cain and Amy can go door to door looking for him, we'll go check Ettie.'

'I can go on my own. I know I'm being ridiculous, but I have a bad feeling in the pit of my stomach I can't ignore.'

'You're not going alone and besides we only have two cars. I'll go with you after you take a look around the pub.'

She nodded, then broke into a jog towards the door of the pub.

Cain looked at Ben and shook his head. 'Is she okay, boss? She's a bit all over the place.'

Ben shrugged. 'I don't know what's going on with her, but I can't not take her to check on Ettie.'

Amy smiled at him. 'I guess not, she does have a point. Her aunt is the only woman I've ever seen who can wear the shit out of a velvet cloak and look amazing.'

They followed her into the pub which only had a handful of customers sitting around drinking.

Morgan was already at the bar. 'Have you seen Lewis tonight, from the bookshop?'

The woman shook her head. 'Not tonight, flower; he was in last night for book club though. Have you tried the flat?'

Morgan nodded. 'Does he have any friends he might go visit that you're aware of, anyone from book club?'

'Have you talked to Jim who owns the bookshop? Lewis could be at his house. Considering they work together they still see each other out of work. He's a bit housebound at the moment with his knees, so Lewis goes to see him; and he's taken the news about Cora pretty bad.'

Morgan could have shaken herself. Why had she not thought about Jim? He only lived a few doors away from Cora's parents. She thanked the woman and turned around to see Ben, Cain and Amy waiting for her at the door.

'Did you hear that?'

'Where does Jim live? Why don't me and Amy go visit him, to see if this Lewis is there, while you go check on your aunt?'

'Is that okay?'

'Absolutely, where does he live?'

'I think it's 26 The Headlands, Cora's parents live at 32.'

'Leave it with us. What are we doing with this dude when we locate him?'

Ben answered, 'I want a full missing person's report filing, and I need a phone number for Violet so we can get a trace on her phone started. I've already got patrols attending the stone circles.'

Morgan looked at Ben. 'Should we do Castlerigg? We're not that far away.'

'Makes sense, if that's okay with you.'

She nodded. 'Of course.'

Morgan felt as if she was overreacting about her aunt, but she had to satisfy the niggle of fear that had lodged itself into a corner of her mind. She knew Ettie was a strong, fiery woman and they'd warned her to be careful, but still, until she'd made sure she was okay she could never settle, even though it meant wasting precious time away from the investigation. If the killer had taken Violet, then what was to stop him going after Ettie? She was the only family Morgan had left in the world.

THIRTY-FOUR

He took the shoebox out of the hall cupboard, where he had several shoeboxes stacked neatly on the shelf that he kept covered with a white cotton dustsheet. He liked to keep the pictures pristine and protected from sunlight, because they were the most precious things he owned. Each box contained the memories of his life through the years, the good and the bad. He had so many beautiful and not so beautiful photographs of the women in his life, and it had been a long time since he'd taken this particular box out to look at them. She had been so bewitching to him, a mysterious woman with a mind of her own. There had been something about her, she was an enigma, and he should never have let her go. He should have stopped her when he had the chance instead of watching her walk out of his life and into the arms of another man. All these years he'd harboured the desire to hurt her like she'd hurt him, and he hadn't done anything about it, until he could bear it no longer and he knew that time was running out.

He lifted the lid from the box and stared down at the pictures. He had been shocked to find that Tabitha had survived. That had not been a part of his plan: there weren't supposed to be survivors. He stared at her picture, the glazed look of shock in her eyes he'd mistaken for death; he had made a huge error, so panicked when he heard a low whistle somewhere in the distance he'd taken off when he should have made sure he'd finished the job. Dead women can't tell tales and, according to the news last night, she was alive and fighting to survive.

He'd underestimated Tabitha King and been too damn flippant about it after Cora. There had been minutes in that too – cutting it fine had added to the thrill though.

He picked up a photograph of Cora. She had come into his shop when he called her without hesitation and hadn't understood what he was doing until it was too late. He placed her picture back into the shoebox and put the lid back on. Taking another box he stared down at the pictures of his mother. She was as beautiful as the rest of the girls. Back in the day she had trailblazed her own path very much like his darlings, his stolen darlings. She was a hard woman to please. He had never been able to make her proud, and she had made it quite clear she had wanted a daughter to teach her witchy ways to and not a son who wasn't interested. He smiled to himself, it had hurt him deeply when he was a child; her constant rejection. The day he'd met *her* had been the day he'd ended the complicated relationship he'd had to endure, and he hadn't felt bad about it at all. The look of fear in his mother's eyes had been almost hypnotic as he watched the light dim from them. He hadn't been able to look away, and she knew that he'd poisoned her with one of her own concoctions as he'd taken her tea to her in bed. How lucky that she'd seen the doctor the previous evening. It had gone down as natural causes when he came back from his walk where he'd met *her* – she had not only stirred something in his loins but had been a great alibi without even knowing it. By the time he'd got home his mother was cool to the touch, and he'd phoned for an ambulance, crying and begging for help. Not before he'd managed to take enough photographs to last him a lifetime though, and now it had come full circle. The woman who'd stolen his heart and then smashed it into a million pieces was about to die, and he couldn't be happier.

THIRTY-FIVE

The night had closed in around them, but Morgan hadn't even realised until Ben parked the car in the lay-by opposite the field for Castlerigg Stone Circle.

'Have you got a torch?' Morgan asked Ben.

'Might be one in the boot.'

He walked around and began searching. She didn't wait for him and crossed the road, turning on her phone torch so she could see where she was walking. From here the majestic stones were dark shadows against the night, and it was an eerie sight. Morgan's feet crunched on the grass, and she zipped her jacket up. So consumed with trying to find Violet she hadn't even noticed the change in temperature until now, when her entire body shivered.

She kept on walking towards the stones. For a moment her eyes sought out the large, flat stone where she had first set eyes on Cora Dalton's desecrated body, and she saw her lying there still, waiting for someone to come and rescue her. Morgan blinked and the image was gone. Was that Cora's ghost, or what it was like to see a ghost? She wrapped her arms around herself at the thought of being stuck out here for all of eternity. Could these stones do that and trap a person's soul? She didn't know, but they had been used for magical rituals and who knows what else for hundreds of years. She knew very little about them. How many other women had died here that they hadn't heard about, because back in the days of the druids a human sacrifice was acceptable.

'Morgan.'

Ben's voice shook her; she'd forgotten about him – she had properly zoned out. She turned around. 'Anything?'

She scanned the stones, her eyes searching the area behind them and shouted back, 'Nope.'

'Thank God for that.'

Her phone began to ring, and the relief when she saw Ettie's name flashing across the screen was almost too much to bear.

Morgan began to walk back down the grassy slope towards the gate where Ben was waiting for her as she answered.

'Ettie, I'm so glad.'

There was silence on the other end. All she could hear was someone breathing.

'Ettie.'

Her aunt's voice whispered, *'There's someone knocking at my front door. No one ever calls this late.'*

Morgan ran the last few feet towards Ben. 'Is it locked?'

'I don't know, I can't say.'

'Ettie, I'm on my way. Can you go out of the back door and hide? Pick up a rolling pin and if you have to use it then make sure you hit whoever it is good and hard across the head. Stay on the line too, you don't have to speak, just keep this phone line open so I can hear you.'

Ben saw the look of panic on her face.

'Someone is at Ettie's house; she's not expecting anyone. Backup now, please.'

She heard Ben calling for all available patrols to meet them at the car park to the woods that edged where Ettie's cottage was hidden away. It wasn't easy to find, so whoever was there this late must either know Ettie or followed her home.

They dashed into the car and Ben did a three-point turn before racing down the narrow lane. Patrols would no doubt beat them to it but wouldn't be able to find her cottage. Ben picked up his radio. 'Silent approach, please. I don't want whoever is there to be alerted we're on the way.'

Morgan had her phone on loudspeaker and could hear someone hammering on her aunt's front door. She glanced at Ben, who put his foot down on the accelerator. Lowering her voice, she whispered, 'Ettie, are you okay? We're on our way.'

Ettie's voice quivered as she whispered, *'I'm okay, I don't know who it is though.'*

The air in the car was fraught with so much tension it was hard to breathe, and neither she nor Ben spoke as they were listening to what was happening at the cottage. Sounds of Ettie opening a drawer, then closing it again filled the air, and Morgan hoped her aunt had one of those heavy duty, old-fashioned rolling pins that could knock someone for six if it was smashed across their head. There was the sound of Ettie moving around and the key turning in the back door. Morgan couldn't breathe. It was so hard to listen to it and she wished that she was in Ettie's cottage and not her wonderful aunt. The door creaked as it opened and then she heard Ettie screech, *'Oh my God.'* Then her phone went dead.

A wave of bile rushed up Morgan's throat and she thought she was going to vomit. She wasn't losing her aunt to some sick killer. She'd lost her dad, Stan, to a murderer; her mum had taken her own life when she was fifteen, and her entire family was either dead or in prison. She wouldn't lose the only person she had left.

'Please, Ben.'

But he was already driving way too fast for the steep,

winding roads, and she knew if he went any faster there was a chance he would lose control and then they'd end up in a ditch somewhere and be no good to anyone. The drive felt like forever, but it was the quickest she had ever travelled in an unmarked car with no sirens or lights to clear the way. They were lucky the roads were quiet.

Ben reached the car park with a police van close on his tail. She had no doubt had they not been travelling to the same destination he would have been pulled over and his licence removed. She was out of the car before he'd turned the ignition off, and took off running through the woods to the sound of his voice calling her name.

She heard the sound of boots on the path behind her and was glad that the officers in the van were hot on her tail. She rounded the bend as she reached the clearing in the trees where Ettie's cottage was standing as if stuck in time. There was no movement, no one was at the door, and her heart was pounding so fast she knew that anything could have happened in the time it took for them to get here. She went through the gate and around to the back of the cottage, where she took in the sight before her and almost screamed out loud.

Ettie was standing there clutching a rolling pin in one hand, and Lewis was sitting on the step clutching the side of his head, where a steady stream of blood was flowing from a deep gash.

Morgan reached her aunt and hugged her. 'Oh my, I was so scared.'

'I'm okay, but poor Lewis here isn't. I proper whacked him and knocked him for six. I had to sit him up. Now you're here I need to go get a cloth to stop the bleeding.'

Ettie disappeared into the kitchen and Morgan heard the sound of the tap running.

'Lewis, what are you doing here?'

He looked up at her, dazed. 'She hit me?'

Morgan nodded. 'Yeah, sorry about that. I told her to.'

'Why?'

'Why are you here so late, knocking on her door?'

'I'm looking for my nan. I wondered if she'd come to visit Ettie, as they've been friends a long time.' He let out a groan. 'I feel sick.'

Ettie came out and bent down to press the damp cloth to the wound. 'I'm sorry, Lewis, but you scared the shit out of me.'

He looked up at her and smiled. 'That's okay, I forgive you, Ettie. I'm sorry I scared you; I'm worried about my nan. I was hoping she'd come to see you. I can't find her, and you know what happened to Cora.'

Ettie was nodding. 'I do, son, and it breaks my heart. I wish Vi was here, but I haven't seen her since last month. I don't know where she could be.'

Ben reached the corner of the garden and stared at the carnage in front of him. 'Is everyone good?'

Morgan grimaced. 'Except for Lewis, yes.'

Ben's sigh was so loud it echoed around the trees.

'He's breathing, and Ettie is okay.'

He beckoned Morgan over and whispered, 'We can't charge her with assault, it was self-defence and you told her to hit whoever it was at her doorstep.'

'I know, what a mess.'

Ben crossed to where Lewis was holding his head.

'Sorry, Ettie, but I need to check if Lewis wants to press charges.'

Ettie stared at Ben. 'For what, scaring the crap out of me after Morgan phoned up panicking?'

Lewis was shaking his head. 'I'm good and no, this is my own fault.'

'Good, that's great. Should we get you checked out at the hospital, mate, and make sure there's no damage?'

He pushed himself to his feet. 'No, thanks. Sorry again, Ettie, I don't know what to do.'

Ettie hugged him. 'At least come inside and let me clean you up properly, give you a cup of tea and some paracetamol. You can't go looking for her with a concussion and blood running down your face.'

Ben turned to the patrols who were watching with their arms crossed.

'Thanks, guys, we'll take it from here. No, harm done.'

The officers glanced at each other with a look of disbelief at what they were witnessing on their faces that Morgan caught. They nodded and turned to walk away back to their van. Morgan wondered what the hell they were going to write this up as in their notebooks. A disaster would be the most appropriate entry. Ben leaned down and grabbed Lewis by the elbow, and pulling him to his feet he led him into Ettie's brightly lit kitchen and sat him down at the table.

Both Morgan and Ettie bent to look at the wound on his head, which didn't look as bad under the lights.

Morgan smiled at him. 'Oh, it's more of a deep graze; you're lucky. I got smashed over the head with a hammer a couple of months ago and that was a mess. I was unconscious and everything.'

Lewis looked up at her in awe. 'You did, wow, this still hurts though but I'm okay.'

Ettie stared at her, horrified. 'Morgan, darling, I think that you would be far more suited to a job that doesn't involve chasing killers and getting the living daylights beat out of you on a regular basis.'

Morgan shrugged. 'Someone has to do it, Ettie.'

'Yes, I agree, but why does it have to be you? Ben, can you not do something about this?'

Ben smiled. 'No, I can't, I wouldn't dare. Morgan is my best detective, and she has a head of steel. Plus, she wouldn't do what I told her to for love or money, she's far too independent and stubborn for that.'

'Thanks, boss.'

He nodded at her and sat down opposite Lewis. 'Can you answer some questions?'

'Yes.'

'Why do you think Violet has been taken? Because you can't get hold of her?'

'Yes.'

'Why didn't you tell us you had a key for her flat? Why didn't you go in and take a look?'

Lewis looked down at the table, a look of misery etched across his face. 'I lost the spare set of keys a few weeks ago and I meant to tell her but forgot.'

Ben glanced at Morgan. 'Where did you lose them?'

'I don't know. I keep them in the shop on a hook behind the till, so I know where they are. One day I noticed they weren't there. I searched everywhere but couldn't find them.'

'Who else knew about them?'

'Well Jim owns the shop, but he's never bothered about them. I don't even think he knows what they're for, as he's never asked.'

'How well does Jim know your nan?' asked Morgan; she was thinking about the photograph.

'He knows her well enough, but they're not friends or anything. I think they hung around when they were younger, but kind of fell out of touch with each other. Jim got married, and Nan had a long-term relationship with my grandad, who died six years ago.'

Morgan was thinking about Jim, but he was too old. The woman in the flower shop said the guy was in his thirties, maybe, and she never mentioned if he walked with a limp. Jim has bad knees, so he wasn't going to be able to hike up to the stone circles to kill these women. She wanted to pound her fists against the wooden table because this was hopeless.

THIRTY-SIX

Violet Darling had never felt so much fear combined with a deep burning anger in all of her life – to be physically restrained was most unladylike and uncomfortable. He could wear a mask all he wanted, but she knew who it was underneath it – the coward. She might be in her late sixties, but it didn't mean she was an idiot. She was on a single bed in a spare room she hadn't seen in since God knows when. As she lay on her back contemplating her predicament, she wondered how it had come to this: how many years had he harboured this grudge, letting it simmer away inside of himself, until it reached boiling point, making him explode? A creeping feeling of unease made her realise just what he was capable of. He was a far more violent man than she'd ever suspected, and this thought scared her on a deeper level than she would ever admit. She didn't want to die like this. She felt tears begin to pool in the corner of her eyes and blinked furiously to chase them away, because she wouldn't let him kill her. More to the point why had he waited so long to exact his revenge on her? Why kill darling Cora and almost kill Tabitha? It broke her knowing that she was the reason for Cora's horrific death and

Tabitha's life-changing injuries, when it never had to be this way.

Scared of what he might do to her, she made up her mind: it was unfortunate for him that she wouldn't go without a fight; in fact she would fight him to the death, because one of them was going to die and she was damn sure it wasn't going to be her.

He had been the sweetest back then, or he had at first, but as time had gone on, she had seen through him, deep down into his soul, and it had terrified her. She had always been good at reading people, but she'd got him all wrong and it had been a sharp wake-up call when she realised that he wasn't who he pretended to be and never had been.

Footsteps outside the room made her heart race faster, and she had to try and breathe as deeply as she could with this revolting gag in her mouth. It was hard trying to regulate her breathing when her heart was racing with stone-cold fear, and she could only breathe through her nose.

She looked around the sparsely decorated spare room that had once been full of books and his study papers. Now it was an empty shell, and she wondered why she was here when the others had been led to their deaths and died – or almost died – instantaneously. There was so much she wanted to say to him, so many questions, but she wouldn't ask and give him the chance to make up excuses; she'd rather die trying to escape than to plead with him for her life. If she knew he would stop after her, she would let him kill her and hope he'd be done with it, but she had this sneaking suspicion that now he'd started to kill that he'd never be able to stop until someone put a stop to it, and right now that someone was her.

The whole time she was thinking things through she was twisting her wrists to loosen the ropes he'd used to bind her hands and feet together. The tender skin was red raw, but she continued through gritted teeth. The only thing of any use she could see to use as a weapon was an ancient glass ashtray with

Tetley's written on it that they'd stolen from the beer garden of a pub one hot July evening. It was heavy enough to do some serious damage if she swung it just right and she would make sure that she did.

Violet closed her eyes and took herself deep into her mind, going back in time to the first time they'd met. They had been so perfect for each other in the beginning. They still had the same interests only she no longer saw him as her best friend, her lover, her confidant. Once upon a time they had promised to spend all their life together. Now she saw him with nothing but distaste, and in those moments when he'd let the darkness shine through, she would sigh or tut at him, would tell him to quit complaining and live life to the full. On the days his dark mood consumed him she'd stay away from him for hours and some-times days.

They had met early one morning up at Castlerigg Stone Circle. He'd told her he'd been unable to sleep. She was chasing her small pug that had slipped its collar and was trying to round up the sheep as if it was a border collie and not some ugly little pug crossbreed. He had come to help her, managing to dive at the dog and grabbing it in a rugby tackle. He'd also managed to wind himself in the process, and had lain on the floor, the mutt held tight to his chest as he gasped for air. It hadn't been the most romantic of introductions, but the look of joy in his eyes and the smirk on his lips after his successful capture of Captain had set off something inside of her chest that felt like small sparks of electricity.

He'd jumped up and introduced himself after she'd put the collar and leash back onto that damn dog. Their fingers had brushed, and his touch had left her fingers tingling. When she'd told him her name was Violet Darling, he'd laughed and asked if she was for real because he'd never heard of anyone called Darling. She'd been insulted by this and had turned and marched away with the dog dragging behind her. He had to chase after her and apologise for being so ignorant. She had given him a lecture on his rudeness.

'Actually, there is a very famous Darling who is one of my ancestors.'

He realised she had a faint Geordie lilt when she spoke and asked her where she was originally from.

'Northumberland, and you should look her up; she was a brave, brave woman who saved nine people who were ship-wrecked in the middle of a storm back in 1838, and when you are not feeling so ignorant you can tell me what you've learned, and I'll take you out for drink as a thank you for catching my dog.'

He'd stared at her, mouth open in shock at how rude she was to him; but still he'd come back for more.

'How will I know where to find you?'

'Same place, same time every day.'

She'd walked away and he'd watched her go, and she knew fine well that he would be back here because there had been something so intense and passionate about him that she could not exist without ever speaking to him again.

He told her the next time they met he had gone home and looked up Grace Darling, whose pictures Violet shared an uncanny resemblance to. As he'd searched the internet for her surname, an advertisement for Darling roses had popped up and, on impulse, he ordered a rose bush to give to her the next time he saw her. He told her he'd purposely not gone to the stone circle until the rose arrived five days later, and then he'd got there even earlier, around six, and had sat on a stone to wait for her, his rose bush by his feet. He waited for what seemed like forever until her figure appeared at the gate in the distance.

This time there had been no sheep around and she had let her dog off. It had gone racing towards him; the damn dog had been a traitor and a terrible judge of character, though she hadn't been much better herself.

It was only twenty-five years ago but it felt like forever.

'Good morning.'

She nodded at him, and he'd grinned at her.

'Good morning to you.'

She'd looked down at the rose bush by his feet and smiled.

'Taking your plant for a walk? I suppose it's less messy than my four-legged friend.'

'What? No, of course not, it's for you. Grace Darling was a very brave woman, she was strong-minded. I guess you get that from her.'

He picked it up to show her, and she'd bent her head to read the label.

'A Darling rose, why you have been doing your research. Grace was phenomenal. I guess I owe you that drink.'

'I guess you do.'

He'd told her that everything changed that day. He had come here five days ago to clear his head from the increasing dark thoughts he'd been having, and here he'd met a woman he thought he could fall in love with.

She hadn't known if he was in love or lust with her, but there had been one thing she had been sure of: that he'd never hurt her.

How wrong she'd been.

THIRTY-SEVEN

Cain was eating his sandwich, dropping bits of tuna and crumbs all over his shirt and the floor of the car. Amy was staring at him.

'Has anyone ever told you that you eat like a pig?'

He shoved the rest of it in his mouth and nodded, speaking through a mouthful of mashed-up bread and tuna. 'My ex-wife used to on a daily basis.'

She turned away. 'Is that why she left you, because you have no manners?'

Cain paused for a second then shook his head. 'You need to eat because you get all shitty and personal when you're hangry, Amy, do you realise this?'

She stuck her middle finger up at him, and he shook his head.

'So much anger radiating off you in waves. I've got a KitKat in my coat pocket. Do you want it?'

'No, I'm good thanks. I prefer my chocolate cold and hard, not all soft and melted.'

'Just like you.'

'Have you got a death wish, Cain, because I'm not in the mood.'

He shrugged. 'Not really, just trying to be helpful.'

She let out a groan. 'What the hell are we doing here outside the bookshop? This is pointless, I hate waiting around.'

'We're on a stakeout until the boss says we can come back to the station.'

'I don't know if you missed all that excitement ten minutes ago, but the boss is with that Lewis dude so there is no point in us being here. We might as well go back to the station.'

Cain smiled at her. 'You are a complete pleasure to work with, Amy, it's such fun.'

'Go back to Amber then, she's missing you from what I've heard. Apparently, Scotty is even lazier than she is and she's having to do all the work.'

He laughed. 'I am not going back on section to work with Amber. I'd rather put up with your miserable face than her attitude.'

'Cheers, I love you too.'

He got out of the car and shut the door; Amy rolled down the window.

'Where are you going?'

'To stretch my legs, I can't keep sitting cooped up, I need to move around a bit.'

She shrugged. 'Whatever Trevor.' Then put the window back up and lay her head back against the headrest, closing her eyes.

He walked along Main Street, peering in the shop windows. If Ben was with Lewis and he wasn't with his gran, where was she? He paused to look through Black Moon's window. Who the hell had broken in here and what for? This whole investigation was like being on a giant hamster wheel, they were going around in circles and getting nowhere fast. He carried on walking, wondering about that weird photographer they had first brought in and then let go.

Cain glanced back to see what Amy was doing and saw she had her eyes closed. He felt bad; she'd told him she was tired and had been struggling to sleep at night because all she kept seeing when she did get into bed was Des's dead body, and it was driving her insane. He'd told her she should refer herself for counselling, but she'd laughed and said it was a waste of time. He'd give her ten minutes to have a break, so he turned the corner and carried on walking towards the photography studio, thinking it wouldn't hurt to have a mooch around and see what the creep was getting up to. Apparently, he liked teenage girls, but who was to say his tastes hadn't changed or evolved? Whatever, he was still a weirdo who needed a good shake now and again to remind him he was being watched and wasn't getting away with any of that crap on Cain's watch.

He sauntered along the road, turning another corner until the small shop came into view. It wouldn't hurt to give him a knock on the door, would it? Just a friendly catch-up.

The shop was in darkness, but the flat above was lit up, so Cain leaned forward and pushed his finger against the doorbell so that it continually buzzed. It was the kind of thing that would drive him mad if someone did it to his door, but it was one of his tried and tested methods: nine times out of ten it worked, and the door would be opened by whoever had initially thought they could ignore him. If the bell didn't work, he knocked continuously too. He liked to think it was a productive way to get a reply.

Eventually a light came on in the stairwell, and he heard thunderous footsteps rushing towards the door. It was unlocked and thrown open. The guy looked as if he wanted to punch Cain; he could feel the anger rolling off him.

'What the hell are you playing at?'

'Now then, Mr Parker, don't be like that. I just thought I'd pay you a visit and see how you are.'

'Really, that's kind of you but who the hell are you?'

Cain lifted up his warrant card and smiled at him. 'Police.'

'Why are you here? I told you I know nothing about that woman.'

'So you did, or you told my colleague but I'm a bit thick and sometimes I don't understand what's going on. Do you want to let me in so we can have a chat?'

His eyes darted to the stairs, instantly putting Cain on edge. 'I can't, I have a guest over. Come back when you have a warrant.'

He pushed the door ready to slam it in Cain's face, but Cain was too fast and shoved his foot in the gap.

'It won't take a moment; you can introduce me to your guest.'

Parker began to stutter. 'I can't, they don't like the cops and it would be awkward.'

'I don't mind.' He pushed his way inside the small stairwell. 'You lead the way, I'm right behind you.'

Parker hesitated, looking unsure whether to do as Cain was telling him. In the end he gave in and began to climb the stairs, and when they got up to the spacious flat Cain looked around. There was a large, open-plan kitchen-dining room and a couple more doors that were closed.

'Where's your friend hiding? What did you do with them?'

Parker grunted. 'I lied, okay? I don't want you in here. I've not done anything wrong.'

Cain took a seat on the grey leather armchair. 'Did no one ever tell you that you shouldn't lie to a copper? Especially not when it's an investigation as serious as this one.'

'Fuck off, you're invading my privacy. I'm going to phone the cops and get you removed.'

Cain began to laugh, a real hearty chuckle. 'Good luck with

that one, they're all busy. You don't mind if I check out your flat, do you, Mr Parker? I'm pretty sure that it will say on the conditions of your licence that you are subject to checks by police to make sure everything is tickety-boo.'

'Get out, you have no reason to be here and I'm not on licence any more. I've kept my head down, I don't do anything I shouldn't so no, go get yourself a warrant if you want to search my flat.'

Cain stood up. 'You're very angry, why's that? Are you hiding something or someone?'

There was a muffled cry from behind one of the closed bedroom doors. Cain's eyes met his and there he realised his mistake. He'd left his radio in the car along with his phone that was plugged into Amy's charger.

Parker grabbed something off the kitchen side and ran at Cain, who lifted up his hands to protect himself while shooting out a fist that connected with Parker's nose.

A warm gush of blood exploded over Cain's knuckles as the cartilage crunched. Parker let out a loud grunt and swung his arm towards him. He tried to duck but he lost his footing. Cain felt something cold and hard stab deep into his side, setting off flashing lights behind his eyes, and then his legs started to crumple beneath him.

Parker was running at him, his head bent. He hit Cain in the midriff and with an almighty crash the pair of them fell backwards down the stairs in a jumble of arms and legs.

THIRTY-EIGHT

Morgan could not dispel the churning deep inside of her stomach at the thought of losing another lead. She had wanted Lewis to be their killer just so they could end it before anyone else got hurt. Frustrated they were no nearer to finding Violet, she watched Ettie who was busy filling an old ceramic mixing bowl with warm water. She began to cut strips off a white linen cloth she'd taken out of one of the cupboards. Carrying the bowl and cloths over to the table she expertly cleaned up Lewis's graze on his head, using strips of linen to soak up the warm water and dab at the blood that was beginning to dry. When she had finished, she folded up a square of linen and handed it to Lewis.

'Press that against the wound until it stops bleeding completely. It's almost dried up so won't be long.'

Ettie turned to look at Morgan, who was beckoning her to come outside. 'Ettie, please, to make me happy and stop me worrying about you, will you pack an overnight bag and stay with me and Ben? You'll have the house to yourself, but there is an alarm system, so I know you'll be safe. Hopefully, we'll have located Violet by tomorrow and you can come home.'

She expected her aunt to argue with her, but she didn't. She nodded. Morgan realised just how scared she had been when there had been the knock at her door, and she didn't know who it had been.

'I know you seem quite close to Lewis, but don't tell him either okay? This is between us; we'll say we have to take you to the station for a statement or something and drop him off at home.'

'This is a huge mess, isn't it?'

'More than you could ever imagine, but we'll sort it out and find Violet.'

Ettie reached out her hand and stroked the side of Morgan's cheek affectionately. 'I have no doubt that you will, I just hope it's not too late.'

'Did she ever mention any relationships or even friendships she had that broke up, leaving her feeling a little worried?'

Ettie shook her head. 'She is quite the dark horse when it comes to men, a very private person.'

'What is she like? Does she belong to any social groups, have lots of friends?'

'She is a lot more sociable than me. I like my little cottage hidden away from people in the woods, whereas Violet loves living in her retirement flat. It makes me shudder, the thought of all those other people living in such close proximity to me.'

Morgan smiled. She definitely took after her aunt far more than she'd realised; she'd never been a people person or one for crowded places.

'She is a lovely woman, Morgan, she never really found happiness with a man; her relationships never lasted long. I guess we're both very similar. We're far too headstrong and know what we want out of life, and sometimes you realise that you don't always need another person to make you whole; you can be everything you need for yourself. I wish more women knew this instead of thinking they have to spend their whole lives living to please other people. You have to find her. She doesn't deserve to die in such a horrific way, nobody does.'

'I will, I promise you I'll keep on searching until I find her. You go grab some bits and we'll go to the car.'

They walked back inside, where Ben was helping Lewis up. 'I'll get Lewis to the car, and we can get him dropped off at home.'

'We won't be long, we'll follow you.'

The men left, and Ettie went into her bedroom, returning immediately with an overnight bag.

'That was quick.'

'I always have one packed, just in case I have to go into hospital. You just never know when something is going to happen, do you?'

Morgan hugged her aunt, then watched as she made sure her cottage was secure and then they walked down the tiny garden path out into the woods. Max the raven who was Ettie's pet and best friend was watching from an upstairs window.

'I'll be back soon, keep an eye on the place and don't let the damn cat out, Max,' she called up to him. He let out a loud caw then took off into the air, soaring high above them.

'Does he understand you?'

'Every single word. He can speak, you know, but he only does it when he thinks no one is listening. I kept hearing voices and thought that it was time to book myself in to a nursing home and then I caught him telling the cat off. I honestly didn't know what to do, it was so surreal.'

Morgan laughed. 'Clever bird.'

'Oh, he's clever okay. I'm pretty sure he's a human being in bird form.'

Ben drove Lewis home and escorted him inside the flat, to make sure he was okay. When he came back to the car, he looked at

Morgan. 'I checked the entire flat, every room, wardrobe, there's nobody in there.'

'Good, because I'd hate to think he had anything to do with this.'

Next, they took Ettie to their house, and it was Morgan's turn to escort her inside, where she showed her how to arm the alarm and then gave her a huge kiss. Morgan waited on the doorstep to hear the numbers being keyed into the pad on the wall and breathed a sigh of relief that at least her aunt was safe for the time being. Now they just had to find Violet, and the person who was keeping hold of her.

Morgan's radio began to ring inside the car, and she saw Ben pick it up to answer it as she jogged back to get inside. Amy's voice sounded panicked.

'*Cain went for a stroll about fifteen minutes ago to stretch his legs and hasn't come back. Have you heard from him?*'

Morgan stared at Ben who was shaking his head. 'No, what do you mean he went for a stroll?'

'*I was moaning at him, and he got out. I can't get hold of him.*'

'Have you rung him?'

Morgan was already dialling his number, and they heard his ringtone echo in the background when Amy pressed the speaker button.

'*He left it charging in the car, along with his radio.*'

'Well, where is he?' Ben's voice was high-pitched with the rising panic.

'*I don't know.*'

Morgan interjected. 'Has he walked back to the station?'

Ben cut Amy off.

'Control, this is Sergeant Matthews, have you heard from Cain lately?'

'*That's a negative, Ben.*'

Morgan was trying not to imagine that something terrible

could have happened to him. There was no reason it should have but there was a nagging sensation deep inside her stomach that she couldn't disperse.

'All patrols, has anyone seen Cain in the last fifteen minutes? Is there anyone in the station who can go check CID, the gents and the locker room?'

Mads replied. '*On it.*'

'Control, I want all units to Keswick to search for Cain. He's out on foot with no radio or phone. I want the entire area flooded, every available officer and PCSOs out on foot walking around and door knocking. Amy, get yourself to the stone circle just to check he hasn't gone up there for any reason.'

'*Yes, boss.*'

Morgan could see the tremor in Ben's hands as he put the radio down and gripped the steering wheel. 'Christ, where is he and what's he playing at?'

He began his third trip back to Keswick, driving just as fast as he had when they had rushed to check on Ettie.

Amy was waiting for them to arrive; she was parked outside of Black Moon where she had been when Cain had got out of the car. She'd already driven to Castlerigg and hadn't spotted Cain wandering around, so had come back to wait for Ben. She was pacing up and down the street, and Morgan felt bad for her. There was no colour in her normally rosy cheeks. She jumped out of the car.

'Where could he have gone? We were only here twenty minutes ago; we must have just missed him.'

Ben was out of the car too. 'Who are our suspects? Is there anyone he would have gone to pay a visit to? Did he not say anything?'

A police van raced into the street, its sirens and lights all singing and dancing. Amber was out of the passenger door before Scotty had put the handbrake on.

'What's happening? Where should we go?'

Morgan closed her eyes. Black Moon was in darkness, but there was a light on in the flat above it, so Jay was home. There was also that weird photographer guy, nearby, and it wouldn't hurt to check Jim out either, even though he was the bottom of their list; in fact he hadn't ever really made it onto it.

'Amber, go check out the flat and speak to Jay Keegan. Ben and Amy, do you want to go check on Parker, and I'll go check the old guy from the bookshop, Jim; he doesn't live that far away.'

Ben nodded. 'Sounds like a plan. Morgan, take Scotty with you?'

Morgan looked at Scotty. 'I'm good, thanks. I don't see any reason why Cain would have headed there, but at least it can be ticked off the list. I'll take the van.'

She held out her hand for the keys, and Scotty reluctantly passed them over to her. Amy got in the car with Ben, leaving the plain car behind should Amber need it. Morgan began to drive to The Headlands and Jim's bungalow.

The street was full of parked cars, and she had to abandon the van in the middle, blocking traffic, but it was only a quick check. She hammered on his door and wasn't surprised to see the hallway light turn on and hear the shuffling of his feet as he walked towards it. Her stomach was a mess of knots, first the panic about Ettie – which, thank God, had been unfounded – hopefully Cain was just sulking and making Amy feel bad for being mean to him. But he would have heard the sirens, surely, and gone back to the car to see what was going on.

The door opened and Jim stood there, leaning on a walking stick.

'Hey, Jim. Sorry to bother you, it's Morgan from the police.'

'It's no bother, love. Sorry, I'm a bit slow. Come in and tell me how I can help.'

He turned and hobbled down the narrow passageway that opened into a small lounge.

'Thanks, have you had a visit from any of my colleagues this evening?'

He shook his head. 'No, love. I haven't.'

'That's okay, I just wanted to check.'

'Can I get you a drink or something, you look tired?'

She smiled. 'No, thanks, I'm good. It's been a long day; I'm hoping it's going to be time to go home soon.'

He nodded. 'I bet you are.'

'Thanks, take care. I'll see myself out.'

Satisfied that Cain wasn't here, she turned to walk back to the front door, when she saw the photograph on the wall. It was in a black wooden frame, and it was the exact same picture as the one that she had picked up off Violet Darling's fireplace in her flat.

THIRTY-NINE

Ben had given his orders for the streets to be searched on foot, the officers that had arrived all sent in different directions. Leaving him and Amy staring at each other.

'Where could he have gone?'

Ben tried to think of all the people they'd spoken to. 'Let's check Parker's shop, like Morgan said; did he mention anything about that? It's not too far away, and he could have gone to pay him a visit.'

Amy nodded. 'True, but he never said anything other than he wanted to stretch his legs.'

'Let's go find out.'

He drove in the direction of the photographer's; as he turned into the street he could see the hall light was on. They could see it shining like a beacon into the darkness, and Ben got a feeling of absolute dread as he stopped the car. Some inner warning signal was pulsating inside his mind, and he knew something was terribly wrong. The door was ajar, and he could see what he knew from years of experience – even in the dark – that it was fresh blood on the doorframe.

Amy screamed so loud down his ear that his feet cleared the floor.

'Cain.'

The both of them took off running. Ben pushed the door open with his elbow and stared in horror at the slick of blood spreading across the floor. Cain was propped against the wall, clutching his side. The blood had soaked through his fingers, his face pale and clammy.

'What took you so long?'

Amy began to cry and whispered, 'You arsehole.' Then she tugged off the sweater she was wearing and rolled it up like a towel. Bending down she knelt next to him and pushed the sweater as hard as she could into the wound to stem the flow of blood. Cain squeezed his eyes shut and let out a sharp breath. Ben had already requested paramedics and patrols to seal off the street.

'Where is he?'

'Took off, boss, dirty bastard shanked me. There's someone in a room upstairs, no idea who it is as I never got that far.' He squeezed his eyes closed, talking was painful for him.

'You're not going to die, are you?' Amy whispered.

He smiled at her and whispered through clenched teeth, 'I'll do my best, you've already got a bad rep, no one will work with you ever again. You're like the black widow.'

She smiled. 'God, you're an even bigger arsehole when you're bleeding.'

He closed his eyes. 'Yeah, but you love me.'

She looked at Ben, who was frantically trying to take control of the scene, and smiled; they were a misfit bunch of coppers who worked hard. 'Yeah, I love all you freaks.'

Ben had pulled a pair of gloves on and was climbing the stairs to go see who was in the bedroom. He prayed it was Violet Darling, then they could all go home and go to bed to sleep for a week – or they could once Cain had been sewn back together.

Ben opened a closed door that led into a bathroom. He tried the next and felt sick when he saw who was on the bed. There was a girl in her late teens, her hands and feet bound to the bedposts. She looked terrified.

Ben held up his hands. 'It's okay, you're okay. Did he hurt you? I'm a police officer.'

The girl shook her head, a deep red flush rapidly rising up her neck. 'No, this is consensual, it's a business arrangement.'

Ben was shocked. 'It is? He isn't keeping you against your will?'

'No, he's not. Look, this is a bit embarrassing; we were just having a bit of fun that's it and he pays good money for it.'

Ben shook his head. 'I'm going to untie you. I don't know where he's gone, he's just stabbed my officer and run off, so he's not going to be coming back here for quite some time. I'm going to need your details and then I'm afraid I'm going to need you to come to the station to give me a statement, because the place is now a crime scene, and the suspect is at large. I don't know if you're in any danger so it's safer to get you out of here, okay?'

The girl groaned. 'This couldn't get any worse. Yes, please. Look, I don't know him at all, this is our first meeting.'

Ben crossed the room, trying to divert his eyes away from the restrained teenager's naked body.

'How old are you? I'm not interested in what you're doing as long as you're the legal age to do it. You're not in trouble for this, but I have to take your well-being into consideration, and I do need to find your friend, because he's just tried to kill my officer. I'll let you get dressed then one of my colleagues will drive you to the station to get your statement.'

Ben untied the knots then turned and left the girl to get dressed.

'I'm nineteen, I just look young; my driving licence is in my bag if you want proof. Am I in trouble?'

'Not as long as you were consenting, you're not.'

She was nodding emphatically. 'I absolutely was, thanks.'

He didn't have time to be arresting whoever the girl was; his concern was finding Parker and fast.

As he walked out of the room, he phoned Morgan to let her know about Cain, but her phone rang out and he assumed she was driving, so he left a voicemail.

'Cain's injured, been stabbed but he's okay. Paramedics are sorting him out, at Parker's shop. No sign of Violet Darling though, come back and we'll regroup.'

FORTY

Morgan felt as if time had slowed down significantly. Her heart was thumping so loud she could hear it inside of her head and she felt as if she was walking through a sea of treacle to reach the front door that was almost in touching distance. She could hear the sound of Jim's shallow breathing too close behind her, and her knees felt as if they wanted to give way, but she needed to stay strong, get out of this dim, confined hallway and call for backup, but she didn't want Jim to know that she was aware of him and knew who he was and what he was capable of, or how he had fooled them all.

'Morgan.'

His deep voice called out behind her, and she turned to him with a smile on her face.

'Yes?'

'Did you make it to book club last night?'

'I didn't, work was extremely busy, but I'll make sure I go next time.'

'Good, that's good. Young Lewis could do with some new members to breathe a bit of life into it. He's a good boy, you know. A bit soft-hearted and is obsessed with his books. He could do with toughening up a little but there are worse things he could be.'

She smiled at Jim thinking, *yes, a lot worse: he could be a stone-cold killer just like you.*

Her fingers reached the door and twisted the handle. The cool metal felt good against her skin. She could taste the freedom. She pulled the door open, and a wonderful cold rush of March air kissed her cheeks.

Jim's garden was full of thorny rose bushes, and she would bet any amount of money that when they bloomed, they would be Darling roses. She was going to do this, she was about to step out into the street where the police van was in reach and then she was going to grab a baton, a set of cuffs or whatever was available in there to use, and go back in and arrest Jim's sorry arse so he would never see the light of day again.

'Could you come back inside? I have some books that you might have some use for. Lewis said you were a book lover, and they're no use to me now I've had my use from them.'

Her phone was vibrating in her pocket, and she wanted to get out of this house but was terrified he would know that she knew about him. She turned and smiled.

'Thanks, that's kind of you.'

He led the way back down to his living room and she followed, knowing that she shouldn't, she was putting herself in an extremely dangerous situation.

He was standing there with three books in his hands which he offered to her. Her throat so dry it was hard to form any words and she wanted to retch, the thought that she had willingly followed him back into his lair making her hands shake. She glanced down at them, they were all true crime books.

'Thank you.'

He nodded. 'Books are such an integral part of life; you can keep your internet. There is nothing like researching the old-fashioned way.'

Morgan knew she had to get out of there.

'I have to go, Jim, but thanks for these.'

This time she forced herself to walk the short distance at a much faster pace, and as she stepped out into the cool night she felt her knees jolt then give way as something hard was jabbed into the back of her leg so violently making her lose her balance. Morgan stumbled forwards as a sharp pain in her other leg made it impossible to keep her balance, and she found herself falling towards the floor, the books landing with a heavy thwack on the path. She saw Jim standing behind her, the walking stick in one hand and a smile on his face.

'Come on, did you really think I didn't see the look you gave my photograph?'

Morgan frantically pulled out her phone and dialled 999. The call connected, but before she could speak it was knocked out of her fingers. Her skin was on fire. She heard the plastic casing bounce against the concrete path out of her reach. Opening her mouth to scream as loud as she could for help, and hoping someone heard her, a dark figure in the hallway caught her eye and she watched as Violet Darling, her wrists bleeding, smashed a heavy glass object into the side of Jim's head.

It was his turn to stumble forwards; Violet didn't give him a second chance and she brought it crashing down onto the back of his skull. There was a sickening crunch as he slumped to the floor in a heap, his metal stick hitting the ground with a clatter. Morgan reached out for it, ready to use it to defend herself and Violet should Jim try to get up.

Violet let out an anguished howl of pain and anger at him, then she was pushing past him to where Morgan was kneeling on the floor, her hand outstretched. Morgan took it and felt herself being pulled to her feet.

'Are you okay?'

'Fine, are you?'

Violet held out her hands to show her the bleeding mess of

her wrists. 'A small price to pay for our lives. I'll live.' She turned to look at Jim then shook her head.

'You bloody psychopath, what the hell were you thinking?'

Jim was unconscious.

Morgan was relieved; she ran to the van and called for immediate help, assistance and an ambulance. She found some cable ties in a box in the middle of the van. There were no cuffs, but she wasn't taking any chances with the man who was much stronger than he looked. He might wake up and fight the pair of them. Taking them back, she tightened the ties around his wrists as the sirens began to fill the night air. Violet was shivering so she took off her jacket and wrapped it around her shoulders.

'It's over now, you're good, and Lewis is fine. You stopped Jim before he could hurt anyone else. Thank you.'

She nodded. 'Good, but I feel so responsible.'

'This is not your fault, Violet; you didn't tell him what to do and nothing you could have done to him deserved this kind of reaction. He's a sick man, with sick ideals.'

Violet bent down to pick up Morgan's phone, which was at the corner of the path. She passed it to her, and she hung up her 999 call to ring Ben.

A car screeched to a halt in front of the van, and she heard Ben's phone ringing both in her ear and in the street. Then he was there, running towards her, and she knew it was over.

FORTY-ONE

Amy and Morgan waited in the family room until they could go in and see Cain, who was being prepped for surgery. Neither of them spoke. Ben had escorted Jim back to custody, where Marc was waiting for the pair of them to get him booked in. The paramedics had cleaned up Violet's wrists and wrapped them in bandages before putting her in the ambulance.

A nurse came in and smiled at them. 'You can pop in for five minutes. He's nil by mouth, don't let him eat; he's complaining he's hungry.'

Amy rolled her eyes, and Morgan smiled. 'That's a good sign, he's always hungry.'

They walked to the cubicle the nurse pointed them to and tugged back the curtain. Morgan was shocked to see just how frail he looked in the hospital bed. His usual ruddy cheeks were devoid of colour, and his eyes were wide and a little glassy with the pain meds.

He stared at the pair of them and then smiled. 'Brookes, you better had brought cake with you, you promised.'

She shrugged. 'Sorry, it's been a bit mad. I promise when

you wake up tomorrow there will be the biggest cake you've ever seen waiting for you.'

He nodded. 'Good, hope so. Did Amy tell you she cried over me?'

Amy gave him the finger. 'You're infuriating.'

'I know, but at least we know she has a heart now.'

Morgan crossed to sit on the side of his bed. She took hold of his hand and squeezed it; he squeezed back.

'I'd give you a hug, but it hurts when I try to move my side; he caught my kidney.'

'Well, if you need another, I have a spare.'

He looked at her and smiled. 'Hear that, Amy, she's offering a kidney and you didn't even bring cake.'

Amy laughed. 'I'm not giving you mine anyway. You'd do nothing but complain about it.'

Morgan whispered, 'I hear Amber was beside herself when she found out you were hurt. Apparently, she's missing you. I think she has a bit of a crush on you, Cain, maybe you and her could...'

The curtain opened and Amber was standing there with burning cheeks.

'I never said I had a crush on him, but I did bring you cake, so now who's your favourite?'

Cain laughed, then grimaced. He looked from Morgan to Amy, then to Amber.

'Amber, obviously, it has to be you. Sorry, girls, you had your chance, if only you'd brought me a slice of lemon drizzle, we'd have got serious.'

The nurse walked in, saw the paper bag in Amber's hands and removed it.

'Sorry, you are not having cake, you are having surgery. The porter is on his way to take you down.'

Morgan stood up, and leaning towards him, she kissed his

cheek. 'You are such a tart; we'll see you on the other side. Have a nice sleep and behave yourself.'

Amy kissed his forehead and stepped back; Amber smiled at him.

Cain closed his eyes.

'Never been so popular, I like it. Oh and, Morgan, don't think I'm letting you win the half marathon because I almost died, so you better get training.' The smile on his face was huge.

The curtain was pushed back, and the porter began to take the brakes off the bed. They watched as he was wheeled away along the corridor, and Amy shook her head.

'He's bloody loving this.'

Morgan nodded. 'I agree.'

Amber smiled at them both. 'I hope he'll be okay.'

And then he was out of sight as they wheeled the trolley around the corner, leaving all three of them staring into the empty space and contemplating how precious life was and how they would risk everything in an instant to make sure the people they loved and the strangers they didn't were safe and protected from the evil that walked among us.

EPILOGUE

Morgan saw Daisy standing next to the bed where Jim was still lying unconscious. He was handcuffed to the bed rail and looked much older in the hospital bed than he had seemed at home. Daisy nodded at Morgan and whispered, 'Well done.'

Morgan felt her cheeks begin to burn and shrugged. She turned away, needing to get out into the fresh air. She passed another ambulance, this one containing Violet who was being wheeled into the A&E department. Violet beckoned her over and smiled up at the two paramedics. 'Can you give us a minute, please?'

They nodded, wheeling her into a cubicle and pulling the curtain around.

'I want you to know that he has always had a dark side, so don't be fooled by his little old man persona. No matter what he tells you, he killed those women and would have killed me if you hadn't turned up. I think he would have killed you too, Morgan, given the chance. He is a pathological liar, always was and could spin tales that would make your mind go dizzy. He is also charming as hell, and I fell for his charms a long time ago. He likes photographs, he always did, he never went anywhere without his camera. Make sure you search his house for them, because I know he would have taken pictures of what he did to Cora and Tabitha; he would have wanted to be able to look at his crimes again and again.'

'Thank you, we will and don't worry, Violet. He is never getting out of prison. There is already too much evidence stacked against him. Kidnap and assaulting a police officer will keep him in custody while we work to make sure he's tied to both Cora and Tabitha. We have someone on route to Preston with a photograph of him to show to Tabitha King, and I'm pretty confident she will be able to identify him. Did he ever use the name Mikey Black that you know of?'

Morgan watched Violet's eyes brim with tears and her voice broke as she whispered, 'He didn't?'

She leaned down to hug Violet, feeling as if the woman needed a little comfort. 'He did.'

'The bastard. Mikey was the name we gave our baby who died at birth, and Black was the surname of the true love of my life, the man who I spent many happy years with after I left Jim.'

'Oh, I'm sorry, Violet, I really am.'

Violet sniffed and brushed the tears away with a piece of the gauze that had been pressed against her bleeding wrists.

'It doesn't matter, he couldn't hurt me any more than he already has, but he didn't win, did he? And winning was always so important to him. Make sure you tell him I said he lost badly to two women of all things. He won't like that, Morgan, but it will make me feel a little better.'

'I promise I will, you take care, Violet. I'll speak to you soon; Lewis is on his way. An officer went to pick him up and bring him here.'

'Poor Lewis, he's going to be devastated about Jim.'

'That's why it's better he hears all about it from you.'

Morgan straightened up, squeezed Violet's shoulder gently and turned away.

'Morgan.'

She looked over her shoulder.

'Thank you.'

Morgan smiled at her. 'You're welcome.'

She walked out of the hospital, determined to turn Jim's house upside down to find the photographic evidence that would get him a guilty conviction and a whole life sentence in a maximum security prison, where he couldn't hurt anyone else.

A LETTER FROM HELEN

I want to say a huge thank you for choosing to read *Stolen Darlings*. If you did enjoy it, and want to keep up-to-date with all my latest releases, just sign up at the following link. Your email address will never be shared, and you can unsubscribe at any time.

www.bookouture.com/helen-phifer

I hope you loved *Stolen Darlings* and if you did I would be very grateful if you could write a review. I'd love to hear what you think, and it makes such a difference helping new readers to discover one of my books for the first time.

I love hearing from my readers – you can get in touch on my Facebook page, through Twitter, Goodreads or my website.

Thanks,

Helen

www.helenphifer.com

facebook.com/Helenphifer1
twitter.com/helenphifer1

ACKNOWLEDGEMENTS

I'd like to say a massive thank you to my fabulous editor Jennifer Hunt for being so brilliant and for all her input to make this a much better book than what I sent to her, thank you, Jennifer. I'd also like to thank the rest of Team Bookouture for their amazing input and help with the copy edits, proofreads, cover design, marketing, audio, everything that makes the whole thing sparkle. You really are all brilliant and I love working with you all.

A huge thank you to Jenny Geras for being so lovely and funny as well as an absolutely amazing, very young-looking Managing Director. I'm still not over it, Jenny!

As always, a huge thank you to my wing gal Noelle Holten for the hard work on cover reveal and publication days. Thank you to Peta Nightingale for taking these stories to Bookouture Deutschland, I'm so excited about this fabulous opportunity.

A massive thank you to the extremely talented Alison Campbell for bringing Morgan and the team to life so brilliantly, with the rest of the wonderful team at Audio Factory.

These stories need some expert opinion and research, I'd like to thank the brilliantly funny Claire Benni Benson, my very own CSI who is always so kind to answer all my weird questions without getting me arrested.

It goes without saying that my biggest thank you goes to you, my readers who are just the most wonderful, beautiful souls there are. Your support for my stories and me makes my heart so full at times, you don't know how much your kind words and jokes mean to me. I'm so grateful to you all for being on this journey with me.

A heartfelt thank you to the wonderful, amazing blogging community, you guys are the rock stars of the writing world. You give your time to read these books when there are so many out there to choose from, it is so deeply appreciated, and I cannot thank you all enough.

As always, a huge thank you to my gorgeous family, Jessica, Tom, Gracie, Donny, Lolly, Matilda, Josh, Danielle, Sonny, Sienna, Jerusha, Roley, Jaimea, Jeorgia, Deji, and Bonnie, I love you all more than you could ever know and I'm so proud of every one of you.

A massive thank you to the wonderful, amazing, Selena Smith for taking care of Jaimea so well that he'd move in with you if you let him. I can't ever thank you enough for all that you do for Jaimea and us, giving me the much needed respite so I can work and have some time off in between the writing.

It goes without saying how much I love my coffee gals Sam Thomas and Tina Sykes, you two never fail to make me laugh and it means the world to me.

As always a huge thank you to Paul O'Neill for giving this book his surveyor's report when I'm so tired of looking at it I can't see the words anymore. You're amazing, Paul!

All my love,

Helen xx